The Puppeteer

The Puppeteer

Sedition and Devotion

Andrew A.

Copyright © 2010 by Andrew A.

Library of Congress Control Number: 2010912514
ISBN: Hardcover   978-1-4535-6276-5
               Softcover   978-1-4535-6275-8
               Ebook   978-1-4535-6277-2

All rights reserved. No part of this book may be reproduced or transmitted in any form or by any means, electronic or mechanical, including photocopying, recording, or by any information storage and retrieval system, without permission in writing from the copyright owner.

This is a work of fiction. Names, characters, places and incidents either are the product of the author's imagination or are used fictitiously, and any resemblance to any actual persons, living or dead, events, or locales is entirely coincidental.

This book was printed in the United States of America.

To order additional copies of this book, contact:
Xlibris Corporation
1-888-795-4274
www.Xlibris.com
Orders@Xlibris.com
85988

CONTENTS

Prologue:	The Seed	9
Chapter 1:	Soiled	13
Chapter 2:	Truths and Revelations	19
Chapter 3:	Sprouts and Bloom	26
Chapter 4:	Clipping of Leaves and Releasing of Seeds	32
Chapter 5:	Trust and Betrayal	39
Chapter 6:	Pain, Hatred, Ascension	48
Chapter 7:	Specter	57
Chapter 8:	Acceptance and Dominion	74
Chapter 9:	Restraint	83
Chapter 10:	Information	92
Chapter 11:	TREASON	97
Chapter 12:	Pandora's Box	149
Chapter 13:	Repent	160
Chapter 14:	A plea from the past	171
Chapter 15:	Bloody Sand, Pure Water, Tainted Beach	216
Prologue 1		231
Chapter 16:	Confrontation and Reacquainted	232
Prologue 2		247

Dedicated to:
Brigitte Marie Robinson &
Juanita Anderson

This is to you "Boss" and "Nita", because it was you two who always believed in me and pushed me to my limits intellectually and spiritually. This is a meager offering for the countless times you both have helped me. Thank you.

I would tell you who I am, but it matters not. If you are what I think you are, then you will only say the same. I wonder . . . Will you call me a Demon, like my father? Or will you call me an Angel, like my mother? Will you see the heartache behind my glare? Or will you see me as heartless beyond my soul? Will you see me as a weapon, despite my age? Or will you see a child, despite my mind? Will you see me as a Monster, regardless of my pain? Or will you see a Human, ignorant of my soiled hands? Will you trust me despite not knowing me? Or will you betray me because you do?

Prologue

The Seed

/ I'm not sure if what I have is photographic memory or not, but I can still recall the day that I was born into this world. My mothers' gentle smile and the warmth of her love flowing over me. Now that I think about it, my entire life seems to be planned out for me from the moment I was born. They say god has dominion over heaven while the devil has power over the earth. From the moment I was born I felt three pulls. I could feel Gods overwhelming love pouring over me. I could feel an even greater love coming from Goddess. But, there was an overwhelming feeling of lust from the devil for me. In life, I've learned a few things that have helped me in the long run. One of the things I learned over my life is how to manipulate. /

The hospital staff was rushing about like bees to a queen's call. White robed figures faded in and out amongst each other, almost as if they were a mirage and never existed in the beginning. Their excited chatter sounded of old wives discussing their husbands. Inside a white room, a woman sat on a bed ignorant of all of this. She was too busy screaming. Her stomach was round and bulbous. Legs in the air, she screamed again, louder than before as her legs stresses. The sound of loud whining assaulted the ears of the occupants of the room and she finally allowed herself to sigh.

Gently picking up the bundle, a woman dressed in white walked over towards the heaving woman. Gently, she placed the bundle in her arms.

"It's a baby boy." the nurse announced.

Breathing heavily, the woman holding the child smiled as she looked at the bundle in her arms. Nudging her nose against his little one, "My baby boy." she whispered. As the child opened his eyes, his small hands went up to grasp at her face. Smiling lightly, she kissed his forehead. "Everything will be alright baby." At the moment, she didn't care about anything. Not her mussed blond hair that clung to her sweaty face and would need a good washing once she was finished here. Not the exhaustion that filled her from the strenuous activity. Only the little bundle in her arms held her attention.

"You want me to let the father in now?" the nurse asked as she headed towards the door.

"Yes, please." the woman responded, not taking her eyes off her baby.

"Alright, please wait a moment." the nurse said as she left.

A few minutes later, the door opened to reveal a tall man with blond hair, brown eyes, wearing a black suit. As he walked in, he stood next to the woman lying in bed. Smiling down, he reached into his shirt and pulled out a white crucifix. Kissing it, "This is a gift from God." he whispered as he leaned over her side. Looking closer at the baby, he recoiled as the babies eyes seemed to glint in the lighting of the room. "Did you see that?" he asked.

/It all starts with a seed. Whether it's a seed of doubt, betrayal, or anger, they all start out as this. /

"What?" she asked, looking him in the face.

"The baby." he began, pointing at it. "His eyes, they, I don't know. They seemed to shine for a moment."

Chuckling lightly, she shook her head.

"Don't be silly Marcus." She said with a smile towards the bundle. "Young Sera's eyes didn't shine."

/And right then, the seed was planted in my fathers' eyes, heart and soul. /

"Right." he muttered as he took a seat to her left.

"I'm sorry, but I have some bad news." the doctor said as he walked into the room. "I'm afraid that your son suffers from an ocular mutation. We don't know how it happened, nor do we know if it's bad or not. But, it can't be ruled out that his vision, in a few years will be altered from normal."

"A mutant!?" Marcus exclaimed as he turned wide eyes towards his wife. "You gave me a mutant for a son!?"

Shaking her head furiously, she held the wrapped child closer to her chest. "NO! I didn't. I gave birth to a beautiful baby boy. My Sera." she reaffirmed. She paused as the room filled with wailing from the bundle. Looking down, she smiled lightly as she rocked the child back and forth. "Shh Sera, its okay, everything is going to be okay." she cooed.

"We would like to keep him here for observation to make sure nothing is wrong with his ocular nerves. We wouldn't want this to lead to blindness." the doctor suggested as he took a step forward.

"No!" she hissed. "I will not have my baby boy turned into some lab rat for you to study and test. I will take him home with me."

"No you won't." Marcus interjected. "I will not have that, that Demon in my house." he raged. His eyes filled with fury.

/And the seed sprouted from the soil. /

"What demon?" she cried. "The only thing in my arms is Sera."

"I don't care what you call that thing. It doesn't change what he is." he stated. "I knew his eyes changed. I wasn't dreaming it. He truly is a demon, a spawn of Lucifer." he ranted.

/And from the sprout, buds. /

"You will stop this foolishness right now Marcus." Maya ordered. "You are a man of God. Does he not teach forgiveness and love? Are you not even going to give your son a chance, before you sentence him to hell?"

He looked at her for what felt like hours, before he finally spoke. His words seemed to come out stressed and forced.

"Fine." he conceded. "I will give it the chance to prove itself. And once you see that I am right, and he is indeed the spawn of the Devil, you will let me dispose of him. He will leave my house."

"Fine, He will prove to you that he is the angel that his name represents." she said determined. Turning her soft gaze towards the now slumbering bundle, she smiled and lightly kissed his head. "Isn't that right Seraphim[1]?" she whispered. She smiled when his small head seemed to nod in answer.

/And in time, those buds would bloom into hideous roses of hate and malice. The devil was good at what he did, I would give him that much. In the course of a few minutes, he already began the sequence of events that would further define my destiny. The weird part was that the love of God didn't diminish as his lust for me over powered it. It was the love of the Goddess that was equal to his lust. My mother's love for me was oddly similar to the Goddess's own. It never wavered for a moment. /

---

[1] Seraphim: means "The burning ones." Or the "Fiery Serpents." Highest choir of Angels.

Chapter 1

Soiled

White is the purest color of all. Snow is the purest of elements. But, it doesn't take much to soil purity. Only a drop of crimson.

/The moment my mother died, I knew that there were powers at work that were bigger than I could possibly imagine. I loved my mother dearly, more than life itself. Nothing in this world mattered more to me than her. Not money, not toys, not even my life. She was indeed my everything. It was in that moment that the pull from the three gods further distanced themselves. /

The birds and cicadas were letting their selves be heard on this day, October 10th. Sera didn't know what to do first. Today was his birthday and he wanted to do something fun with his mother. Looking up towards his left, he spotted his mothers smiling face looking down at him. She was always smiling when he saw her. Never has he ever seen her with a scowl that the other parents have on their faces when he sees them. It was his sun. Her beaming smile was his light in the darkness. Looking back towards the way they were walking, he was reminded of why he brought her here today. Not that they didn't always visit the garden. They both made it after all. He spotted a baby snake in their garden a few days ago and he wanted to show his mother the little guy. He's read books about snakes before and he knew them to be dangerous, but they never seemed dangerous to him. They never attacked him. They haven't even so much as hissed aggressively at him before. But, even so, he knew them to be dangerous. Some had poison in their teeth. He hoped the little guy wouldn't bite his mother. She was too nice to be bitten by a snake. He was sure the snake would see that and not bite.

"Come on mamma." He urged as he tugged on her arm, nearly in a jog. "I want to show you the baby snake."

She nodded her head and smiled at him, always full of energy whenever they came to the garden. It was the only real alone time they had together. She knew he was a good child, but she couldn't understand why others were so blind to the fact. No, she took that back. She knew why. They refused to accept the truth. They followed the words of a man who refuses the truth. She felt her heart breaking as she watched his smiling face. He would never smile at any of the other people. Not any more. He's learned the hard way that people don't like him and won't accept him the way he is. As his golden eyes twinkled in joy, and his hair swayed about his shoulders, she felt herself on the verge of tears, before she pushed them back by sheer will. His eyes were the reason why no one would accept him. Why no children would play with him. Why mothers called him hurtful names. Why they glared at him. Why he was almost . . . she cut the line of thinking off, before tears started to fall from her eyes. She didn't want to go down that road again and she didn't want him to be worried about her like he always does when she cries. He always thinks it's his fault when she cries and tries to do everything to make her stop. The simple sight of it made more tears spring forth. Such a pure child didn't deserve to be treated the way he was. But she knew the world was not fair.

"I'm coming darling." She said with a smile. Today was his day, and she would do anything he wanted. "I have a story to tell you about a Serpent when you get him." She told him softly as they made it into the field. The large cherry blossom tree in the middle of the field was slowly beginning to lose its petals, having just over two thirds of the blossoms left. Walking over, she picked him up and fell onto the ground, rolling through the petals. As he giggled and laughed, she laughed with him. After all, you were supposed to have fun on your birthday. As she let him go and rolled off of him, he pounced onto her stomach, laughing all the while. Scooping him up in her arms, she went beneath the tree. Breathing heavily, she sighed happily as she held him close to her chest.

He always loved to play around with his mother. She would always roll with him on the ground and throw him around. It was fun. Lying on her chest, he caught his breath. Her warmth was always comforting to him. This was his safe place, besides the garden. No one could hurt him while he was with her. Looking up slowly, he smiled at her.

"I'm going to go get him now." He told her.

She nodded her head.

"Go on. I'll be waiting here for you."

He jumped up and ran off into the surrounding bushes. He slowed down as he got a few yards away. His chest was hurting him again. Moving a hand to grip right above his heart, he grimaced. His mother said the doctors said he would feel pain for the first few months, 18 tops. He hated this pain. It was a reminder of how much other people hated him. How one he expected to love him regardless of his appearance stabbed him when his eyes were closed. He didn't know how long he was walking, but he came upon the same place he found the baby. Getting to his knees, he crawled under a few bushes. He spotted the reptile curled into a ball sleeping with a smaller one next to it.

"Come on Silky." He said softly as he poked the snake with his small finger. "Momma is here and she wants to see you."

The serpent looked at him blankly with its green slit eyes as it was aroused from its rest. It knew who this was. It was the same creature that came to her a few sun rises ago. She knew that this thing before her was not a human. Humans didn't have eyes like hers. But he did. His eyes were similar, but different. His eyes were filled with light, but she could see the darkness in him as well. That was the reason why she didn't attack him the second she saw him playing with one of her hatchlings. He was unique, and she was curious about him. Her previous mate left after the birth of their young. This new arrival was a welcomed change. Perhaps, since the young were receptive to him, she could have him as a mate. His words drifted into her mind as she regarded him. Judging by his body language, he wanted her and the young to come out. Slithering towards his open hand, she crawled her way up his wrist, before coiling around his neck, resting her head next to his.

As he picked up her young, and turned away, she felt a disturbance in the air, along with the scent of blood. This scent was similar to his, but belonged to a female. She looked towards him to see if he noticed, but he kept walking on. As they made it closer towards the scent, she began to feel slightly aggravated.

As he poked his head through the foliage, she could see a human female and a male talking. She couldn't understand what they were talking about, but she felt the human female becoming irritated, judging by her body heat rising. The male gripped her forcefully and punched her in her stomach. She would hand it to the human; she could take a hit and keep standing. Turning her attention from the two in front of her, she focused on the rising panic coming from her potential mate. She could see his eyes clearly. They were wide from his surprise and apparent fright. But, she could sense his anger rising, see it in his soul. As a burst of blood hit the air, she turned her head back towards the humans. The female was on the ground with the male no where in sight.

As she lies dying on the floor, she slowly motioned for him to come closer. As he took slow uneven steps forward, his body shook with tears that refused to fall. Finally reaching her, he dropped to his knees.

"Momma." he whispered.

/She was even beautiful in her last moments on this earth. Despite the blood, the wrinkled clothing, the raged breathing and her mussed hair, she still was a sight to behold./

"Shh baby." she cooed. "There is something I need to tell you. Okay sweetie?" nodding his head, she smiled lightly as a trickle of blood ran from the corner of her mouth. He was such a good boy. A little angel. Always doing as his mother asked. "Good boy." she said softly. "I want you to be strong. I want you to do something with your life. Don't be like me and spend your whole life wanting. Please, for me will you do something?" she asked, voice getting weaker and weaker with each word.

"I will momma. I'll do it. I promise." He whispered softly as he gripped her hand. "Just don't go. Please."

/And I meant every word of it. I would do anything she asked of me./

"That's my Sera." She rasped. She knew that she only had a few more seconds left to live and she wanted to set him on the path of his destiny. Wanted him to become what he was fated to become. "Make something of yourself. Find your grandfather at the church I took you to once. He will tell you everything. Make me proud." She breathed as her chest finally stopped moving. Her remaining thoughts were of what might happen to him now that she was gone. She knew she was the only person that kept him safe from the others. She knew that now that she was gone, her husband would try and get rid of him once more. She also knew that her death would forever change him, and the light that he only showed her would never be seen by anyone anymore. Her heart and soul cried for him, because she knew that once the day was finished, he would never be able to shed tears again.

"Mamma?" he questioned softly as he placed his small hands on her shoulder. She was talking to him, and then she stopped. "Mamma, wake up." he told her, giving her a nudge. Surely she would get up if he kept nudging her. She always did. "Come on. This isn't fun anymore. I still have to show you Silky. Come on." he said, grabbing her hands, tugging. "Come on mamma. You said you would tell me a story when I showed you." he whimpered as he gave up and collapsed onto his knees. "Don't go to sleep." he whispered as he placed his head between her breasts and hugged her tight. "Don't go to sleep."

After an hour of lying on her cold body, he stood up and wiped his tears. She was his world. She was his safe place. She was a guardian angel. And now, she was gone. Now that he was standing, he couldn't feel his legs. He couldn't feel anything. His entire body felt light, almost as if he wasn't really there. His heart was a very distant thump in his ears as he felt an overwhelming sense of cold settle over his body. His heart didn't hurt like he thought it would. Instead, there was a void, a dark, cold void where his heart was supposed to be. His eyes were caked with dry blood and red from his tears. He didn't pay any attention towards the blood that stained his white shirt, or the little snake that slithered towards him. Looking down with vacant honey eyes, he nodded his head. Turning on his heel, he walked out of the clearing. If he would have turned around, he would have noticed the snake slithered onto her chest, curled into itself, and died.

> ***And if a drop falls onto a sheet of snow, it seeps through out the pure white. Deeper and deeper until there is no white left. Only pale crimson . . .***

Chapter 2

Truths and Revelations

The truth and a lie are subjective to the individual.

/I thought I was ready for, what my mother called, the endless slumber, but I wasn't. It took me an hour to come to terms with the fact that she wasn't going to wake up. A part of me died that day, and I thought I was never going to feel complete again. Sometimes I would wonder if she was proud of me now, with everything that I've done. But when I begin to doubt, I can feel the love that I know can only come from a mother to her son flow over me, followed by the acceptance I know only comes from the Goddess. I heeded her words and went to my grandfather after her death. The old church was still standing and so was he, outside the doors. Almost as if he knew I was coming./

"Seraphim." Matt greeted solemnly as he watched the small figure wearing a bloody T-shirt and shorts.

"Grandfather." Sera whispered as he nodded his head, keeping his eyes on the ground.

Turning slightly, he held out an arm going into the church.

"Follow me my boy. You look absolutely dreadful." he said gently as he waited for him to walk.

Walking silently, he followed him into the church. Walking past the empty pews, he turned into the back room where his mother took him once. He still remembered when she sat him on the bed and hit him with a pillow. They fought for what seemed like hours before he fell asleep from exhaustion. Sitting down on the bed, he kept his eyes downcast.

"What ails you son?" Matt asked as he sat next to him and placed an arm around him.

Sera choked as his mouth opened, but nothing else would come out. He still couldn't believe what happened. It was just too surreal. Too fast. Flinging his arms around Matt, he wailed loudly into his chest.

"Mamma!" he cried.

"Shh, my son." Matt soothed as he rubbed his back lightly. "Tell me what has happened to your mother."

"She was-was taken from Me." he hiccupped as he wiped his tears, breathing heavily.

"Taken?" Matt questioned.

"Uhuh." Sera nodded his head. "Some man came and killed her. She will never wake up again."

Matt was silent for a moment. He felt something wrong in the air, which is why he decided to go outside for a minute. He had no idea that what he felt was the life of his daughter fading.

"She told me to come to you and you would tell me everything." Sera continued as he looked upon his face. "What did she mean?"

Matt broke out of his thoughts at his question. She talked to him about his trails not long ago, when they last visited. He smiled lightly. Now, it seems, it was time.

"Come with me." he instructed as he stood and began walking out of the room. Walking into the backyard, he approached a statue of a beautiful woman. Pushing it, it slid back to reveal a stone staircase. Looking behind himself, he spotted the slight wide eyes of Sera. Turning back, he began descending into the darkness, listening to the foot steps of his follower. Reaching the ground, he took out a lighter and lit a torch that hung at the bottom of the stairs. Picking it up, he walked along the wall, lighting up the remaining torches. The dark room became alit with the amber glow of flames.

Looking around the room, he couldn't help but become slightly giddy at the sight. Books. Hundreds upon hundreds of books lined the walls. Looking towards Matt, he tilted his head.

"What is all this?" he asked as he continued looking. Slowly walking towards a shelf, he allowed his fingers to glide over the covers.

"Son, what would you do, if I told you that you were special?" Matt began as he slowly paced the floor.

"Special?" Sera repeated as he stopped to look at him. "I have the eyes of a serpent."

"Indeed, but that's only a part, a rather important part, of what makes you special." Matt said with a smile. "You were born into a special clan." he began. "Your mother, my daughter, was also apart of this clan."

"What clan? We have no last name, so what is this clan?" Sera asked, not quite getting the connection.

"No my dear boy, we have a name, but it's only reserved for the unique ones in the clan. The last name of Angelus."

"Angelus." he repeated in a whisper as he looked down.

"A set of prayers to commemorate the Annunciation and the Incarnation. That is our last name. The arrival of God. That is what we are." he sighed as he took a seat in a chair that was nearby. "Over ten hundred years ago, our ancestors were normal god fearing people, when one day, a group of vandals entered their village. They wreaked havoc on the towns' people as they killed, raped, and beat anyone they pleased. The Clan heard all of their prayers from their church. The people wished for everything to stop and for it to go back to normal, but their prayers weren't being answered. The Clan seeing this decided that if the Gods weren't going to answer their calls, then they would do so. But, they didn't get a chance to, as the vagrants left of their own accord to another village. So, they all decided that they would assign the duty to the young ones. They said that in order to accomplish this, they would have to have a heart that was black, yet with a soul that was as pure as white snow. They were to be called Noir and Blanc. But over the centuries, they have gone by other names as well, Raven and Dove, Angel of Death and Demon of life. They were to be a pair of assassins to do the Gods work on earth. In the beginning, the first born was to be Noir[2] and the second, Blanc[3]. But as time wore on, they decided that it was better if a

---

[2]   Noir is the color Black in French
[3]   Blanc is the color White in French

male was born, then he was to be Noir and the female was to be Blanc. If you remember, Noir was to have a heart of black, but Blanc was to be the embodiment of his soul, and keep him in balance so he would not go insane from the heavy burden that was placed on his shoulders, for that is what happened too many of the others. After seven hundred and fifty years, I was adopted into the clan at the age of twelve. They taught me everything they knew, and I was assigned to a Blanc, who happened to be the one who suggested the idea in the first place. Over the course of my training, I wanted to protect her, because I fell in love with her and her with me, so I perfected a way to keep my mind in balance."

"How?" Sera questioned as he listened intently to the story. Never did he think he belonged to a family that was so strong.

"Remember what I am about to say, because it will save your sanity." he said seriously as his eyes bored into his.

"Yes grandfather."

"The world has, is and will forever be covered in blood and by death, even in the presence of light. You must never hesitate, show fear, or show sympathy. You must strike true and without mercy. Never think. When you think, you pause. When you pause, they move. When they move, you die. To live you must kill. As long as you remember that, then you will become the next Valkyrie[4]."

"Valkyrie?" Sera asked with a tilt of his head. He remembered when his mother told him stories of warriors that would fight on the battle field and pray to the Valkyrie to watch over them.

"Yes. She was one of the best, besides me. She was the first Noir that has ever earned that title. There was a war, a secret war that took place here in the states. One hundred and fifty years ago, a male that was born Blanc got tired of being the one to protect his Noir counterpart. He decided to revolt against the old ways and reign over the world with the knowledge and influence that the clan has gathered over the centuries. Over half of the clan shared his views and tried to destroy the old. Remember, when

---

[4] The word *Valkyrie* derives from Old Norse *valkyrja* (plural *valkyrjur*), and is composed of two words; the noun *valr* (referring to the slain on the battlefield) and *kjósa* (meaning "to choose"). Together, the compound means "chooser of the slain". Old Norse *valkyrja* is cognate to Old English *wælcyrge*.

you will kill your family that has not crossed you, you have betrayed everything that you have been taught. Valkyrie led the rest of the clan in the fight against them. She killed countless traitors and protected his own with everything she had. So much so, that she died to protect a group of Blancs. Her last words were to announce that she would be reborn again when the world needed her."

"Was she ever reborn?"

"She was born with the eyes of a fiery serpent, gold as the clearest sun's rays and as sharp as a razors edge. You tell me."

Sera stood stock still as he heard his description. He couldn't be what his grandfather was hinting at.

"No." he whispered with wide eyes.

"Why do you think your mother didn't shun you when you were born, like so many of the others?"

"I can't."

"Why do you think you were named after an angel? Why she was so adamant about you learning to read and write at such a young age and why she was so happy and proud of you?" Matt continued with a soft smile. "Why do you think she died so readily when she had the skills to kill her pursuer? There was a reason to her death, that she accepted the moment it arrived. It was a test, of which you and she passed. The Goddess[5] was testing her love and dedication for you and your love and devotion to her."

He collapsed onto his knees, a vacant expression on his face. *It's my fault.* He whispered in the back of his mind.

"The world is not nice my son." Matt said gently. "There are trials and tests for all of us to partake in. Your mother died protecting you, the only hope the world has at a better future, by giving her life and having you witness her sacrifice. Will you allow her sacrifice to be in vain, or will

---

[5] Generalization to Goddesses in Mythology and pagan Semites. Specifically the Goddess Astarte, also known as Ishtar to Babylonians and Assyrians: goddess of Love, fertility, maternity and war. Aphrodite in Greek mythology, the goddess of love and beauty. Venus; Roman mythology, the goddess of love and beauty. Athena; in Greek mythology, the goddess of wisdom and warfare.

you live up to your destiny and become the Angel of Death, Valkyrie, once more?"

Reaching up towards his neck, he gripped the chain his mother gave him on his birthday. It was a five pointed star with a snake biting its own tail. On the other side it had the words, "One who fears nothing, should fear everything." She had the same one. His mother embraced her fate, and even though he didn't fully believe in fate, or understand it, he was willing to do anything to ensure he kept his promise. Looking up with hardened amber eyes, that seemed to flicker in the lighting, he nodded his head.

"I will do what needs to be done."

"Excellent my son." Matt said as he stood up and walked towards the bookshelf. Picking up the first book at the beginning of the row, he tossed it at Sera's feet. "Read that book. It's the history of the Angelus Clan and the morals and values of becoming Noir and Blanc. You have forty-eight hours." with that, he began his ascent up the stairs.

Nodding his head, even though he knew he couldn't see it, he picked up the book and began reading. He didn't know what he was supposed to do. When his mother told him to come to his grandfather, he didn't know what to expect. The truth. That's what his mother told him before she went to sleep.

He didn't show it, but he was scared. He no longer had his safe place. He no longer had his mothers comforting embrace. Her soothing words. Her bright smile. Her loving eyes. He only had the memory of her. And he would cherish the memory for eternity.

As his grandfather left, he grew more aware of his surroundings, or rather, lack of surroundings, due to the lack of light.

Right after his release from the hospital, he grew to hate the dark. He didn't know what was beyond it, and the thought frightened him; frightened him more than he knew. It was in the dark that he saw the hatred in his father's eyes. It was in the dark that he saw the silver glinting in the dim moonlight that flitted through his window. It was in the dark that he died.

But the light. Oh the light. The darkness frightened him, but the light downright terrified him. In the light he was bare. Everyone could see him. Everyone could see the Demon that his father preached. Everyone could see his eyes. He was relieved when his mother gave him the sunglasses. The shade they provided him gave him the comfort of not being seen. Not being noticed. Not being stared at as if he was an abomination. But they didn't shield him from the words. Their hateful, spiteful words. To him, they didn't matter much, but they hurt his mother. Her pain was his pain. Her tears were his. And when she would cry on the silent nights, when he would hear her distant sobs of sorrow, he would go to her and try with all his might to stop the tears. To make her feel better, but it only seemed to make it worse. In the end, he cried with her. His bloody tears would stain his and her shirt until he passed out from exhaustion.

Mother.

He was resolved to do as his mother said. As she bid. As she ordered. He would drown himself in the knowledge that the family possessed. He would do what was expected of him. As he opened the book, the first page was a list. A list of edicts. He stared at them for a moment, before looking at the top of the page. *Noir.* The word was written in Sanskrit. Below it, were three phrases that were numbered by roman numerals. *I: Noir serves a just master. II: Noir condemn those who sin. III: Noir protects the weak and young from harm.*

The words stuck him, even in his young mind, as being more than what they were. He knew they were important. He knew them to be his saving grace. Reading them over several more times, he felt himself even more resolve. This is what his mother wanted him to become. This is what she would be teaching him if she was still alive. He would do this, if only for her. Because, in the end, it was only her. And now, it was still her, but she would live through him.

Only when you have accepted what you discovered as fact can you ever come about a Revelation.

Chapter 3

Sprouts and Bloom

> *A sprout that is allowed to grow, longer than it was destined, blooms hideous flowers that should never have seen the light.*

/I knew the reason that my father was giving my mother a funeral. He didn't want anyone looking into her death which is why he acted so fast. But, I know one thing he wasn't planning on; my attendance with my grandfather. /

The church was filled with the sounds of mourning. The organ played a gloomy tune as people filed in and took their seats. In front of the stage, inside a beautifully crafted and decorated coffin rested an angel; a beautiful, blond haired, blue eyed angel that went by the name of Maya. She was dressed in a simple white ensemble that looked radiant on her person. The people that took their seats had faces of stone. Many of them questioned why they were there in the first place. But, this woman was something that they all had a common connection with. They all shared the same feelings towards her. Resentment.

They all quieted down as the organ began to soften and the father was stepping up to the podium. They were all listening attentively to what he would say concerning this matter.

"My wife was taken from me by the demon that she housed, the demon that she loved so much." His words were soaked in hate. So much so, you could have felt it. "The demon that she knew loved her." He was being condescending. "But, in the end, the serpent has destroyed another life, another Eve. We should not allow this to continue!" Marcus announced. As a chorus of amen's were yelled, he continued, "We should not let this go unpunished. I warned you all that this demon would take lives and ruin families, but you didn't listen. Well, now is the time!" he paused as the doors opened to reveal an old man and a small boy. "Excuse me; are you here to pay your respects?"

"We are here to indeed pay something, but respects isn't It." the old man replied slowly walking down the aisle with Sera at his side. As they came further into light, they were both wearing all black suits, with sunglasses on. Finally making it towards the casket, they both stopped. "My poor daughter." he whispered as he gazed at her body. "You did not deserve the end you have received."

"So, you are family?" Marcus asked as he walked from behind the podium and approached them both. "I'm sorry for your loss. I feel it was my fault for not killing the demon when it was born."

Sera stepped forward and looked up at him with his covered eyes. How could he blame his own son for this? It was ludicrous. Golden slits sharpened as they regarded him with hatred. The emotion itself was new to him. He's never felt it before. He would dare pin the blame of his beloved mothers' death on him? *You will regret this father.*

"And what demon would that be?" Sera asked as he slowly reached for his shades. Taking them off, he focused his gold eyes on his shaking figure. Whether he was shaking because of fear or hatred, he didn't know, but he knew which one he would be doing if he had a say in it. "You wouldn't happen to be referring to me now would you *Father?*" he finished in a sneer.

"What do you think you are doing here *demon*? Here to ensure that you have taken her soul to hell?" Marcus asked with venom as he glared at his son.

"I'm here to mourn my mothers' death." Sera answered truthfully as he walked past his father and up to the stage. "Unlike you whose only wish is to tarnish her memory."

"You ungrateful little-!"

"You might want to refrain from speaking to my grandson in that way Father Marcus." Matt suggested as he looked at him over his shades. "Now, my grandson is about to say a few words."

Sera looked out at the assembled masses with a blank look in his honey eyes, as they all looked at him with the utmost hatred as some clutched their children closer. Although, his eyes caught one person who looked at him with surprise and happiness, he didn't dwell on it. The fools believed his father's words without any protest and condemned him to hell before knowing him. How he hated them. What they were.

"My mother was a wonderful person." he began softly as memories of his mother flooded into his mind. Her holding him. Her singing to him. Her kissing his head before he went to sleep. The stories she told. "She was my everything. When I was hurt, she would heal me. When I was sad, she would do everything in her power to make me smile. My mamma once told me that stupid people are like sheep. Easily moved to believe what one with power decides. You all are nothing but livestock," the assembled glared at him as one looked on questioningly. "And I am the one pestering your Sheppard's fields. In time you will learn of your mistake and beg for forgiveness as you stand before god. But he will not hear you, for you have not heard Me." he walked down and stood before his mother's body once again, and kneeled. "Goddess that watches over us, please guide my mother, your sister, into your embrace. For she was taken by mistake, one that was meant for me. I humbly request your help in helping me keep my promise to my mother. If you grant me this one wish, I will dedicate my life to you." he whispered to her. Standing, he turned towards Matt with a nod. Nodding in return, Matt picked up Sera and held him over his mothers' body. Leaning down, he placed a kiss on her lips. Looking at her, his eyes softened and glassed over with unshed tears. *I will keep my promise momma. I swear it.*

/As my grandfather and I walked out of the church, I could hear my father telling them of how I see them as nothing but animals, food for me to eat. He was turning my words around to suit his own needs of control. But, I didn't care. When he stands before the Goddess, she will look upon him in disgust before she sends his soul to an eternity in purgatory. She doesn't look kindly on those who kill her sisters, nor does she like ones who treat her servants with anything but respect./

XXX

/The things people used to say about me and my mother used to anger me beyond anything in this world. She was a Goddess, a pure being that never hurt anyone. Yet, these people continued to tarnish her memory with slanderous things about her death. They knew nothing about what happened, and yet they continued with their lies. I would sit on the swing at a park where she used to bring me all the time and think about her. /

Sitting on a swing, dressed in black shorts and a red shirt, a little boy swung back and forth. Couples walked by staring at the little figure as he swung, children holding their hands. Upon closer inspection, there were bits of white in the clothing, hints at what the original color was before.

/Back. /

Mother used to bring me here all the time in the night.

/And forth. /

Higher and higher she would push me, until I got scared and asked her to stop. He smiled lightly at the memory of his mother holding him afterwards and soothing him with her soft words. He stopped momentarily when he noticed a few people standing across the street. Sighing to himself, he started swinging again. This would never stop. They would never stop.

/Back. /

What do you want from me?
"Look at him." One woman whispered to another that was standing by her side. "Is that him?" she asked.

The other woman nodded her head.

"It's the Demon." She hissed, a sneer gracing her face as she glared at him.

/And forth. /

Just like the others. He thought as he shook his head slightly.

"I heard he killed his mother." The first woman said as she watched him

Lies.

/Back. /

The second woman nodded her head in affirmation.

"I heard the same thing." She said. "I heard she was bitten by snakes that he called on."

The other woman shook her head.

/And forth. /

Mother, help me.

"I heard that he bit her himself. That he secretes some kind of poison from his teeth." She urged.

"Someone should put him down like the animal he is." The first woman stated with venom.

/Back. /

What should I do?

"Mommy who is that?" a small girl asked as she tugged on her hand.

The woman looked down at the girl.

/And forth. /

Tell her.

"That is a monster, an abomination to the human race, a killer, and murderer. He kills little girls and eats them." She replied in a sickly sweet voice.

That's right. He smiled sardonically as he remembered his mothers' words about stupid people.

/Back. /

The small girl hid behind her mothers' leg as the small boy turned his head in their direction. Gold glittered as it caught the suns rays.

/And forth. /

"Mommy!" the girl screamed. "What's wrong with his eyes?"

/Back. /

"Come on sweetie." The woman urged sweetly. "We have to go. The demon won't be able to hurt you once we get you home."

/And forth. /

He continued to swing as they all walked past. Some didn't even bother with hiding their disgust and openly threw things at him. He kept his eyes on the ground partially closed, and allowed the garbage and rocks to hit him.

Mother . . . where are you now? Are you happy? He asked himself as he turned his eyes towards the sky. *Do something with yourself. That's what you told me to do, but what am I supposed to do? How?*

The answer never came as he continued to stare into the darkening sky. He sighed to himself as he walked over towards the slide. Crawling under it, he curled into a ball and allowed his body to finally rest. He would never allow his eyes to rest. Having one's eyes closed was a bad habit.

Chapter 4

Clipping of Leaves and Releasing of Seeds

The grotesque flowers that have taken root within hearts sometimes need to be clipped, pruned and destroyed in order for the new seeds of life to take root.

/My training went off without a hitch. In only two years I've read every book and learned everything needed to become Noir and Blanc. I didn't want to waste any time. My muscles ached every day, but I pushed beyond to the point where I could no longer feel my limbs. I put into practice the morals as well. My heart was to be black, which wasn't hard to do. My mother was my heart. When she died, she took that as well. My grandfather gave me his personally designed weapon of choice for an assassin, a bracelet filled with wire. It didn't fit correctly when he first gave it to me, but he told me that I would grow into it, and it would never come off unless I broke my hand. I found his present to be one of my most cherished possessions. But during my training, I was forbidden to visit my mother's grave. When I finished, that was the first place I went, but I didn't expect to see my father there. /

As he exited the study, as he grew to call the library beneath the ground, he squinted his eyes as they adjusted to the light. Before, where he would hide behind shades, he displayed his eyes proudly. He was no longer going to hide behind the safety of the glass's shade. If people wanted to stare at him, then he would simply ignore them. He could still vividly remember the day he went into the darkness of the study. How his heart raced with each passing second spent alone in the room. After all, it was the first time that he was alone, truly alone, in the dark. But soon his eyes began to adjust. He could see things clearly. His heart slowed, like the books taught. But as time wore on, he found himself wondering the circumstances around his mothers' death. If the books have taught him anything it was to always be in the know. Always know the answer. Questions only lead to uncertainty. Uncertainty leads to pause. Pausing leads to death. He couldn't die just yet. He promised his mother that he would live his life and always want.

And at the moment, he wanted to visit his beloved mothers' grave. It's been two years since she passed, and he wanted to pay his respects to her. He didn't want her to think that he forgotten his promise to her. Or the love that he still had has, for her. Resigning himself to his search, he stepped out into the dark streets of the city, relieved that no one was out, and walked down the street towards the cemetery that was a few blocks away.

Walking into the cemetery, Sera stopped as he spotted his father standing before a grave. Stepping softly, he came up behind him.

"What are you doing here?" Sera asked softly as his eyes trained on the name of the tombstone.

"I should be asking *you* that." Marcus replied as he looked at him out the corner of his eyes. He was angry that it had to come to this. That it had to come out this way.

"I'm here to see my mother." he said plainly as he looked up towards Marcus. "But, I find myself wondering why you are here. What is bringing you here every year?" It was one of the questions that burned his mind in the darkness of the study.

"I loved my wife." Marcus growled as he turned to face him completely, glaring angrily.

"Why you seem so down and depressed." he continued as if he hadn't heard him say anything.

"It's not something I expect a *demon* like you to understand."

Kneeling before the stone, he bowed his head in a silent prayer.

"Why you seem so determined to pin the blame of my mother's death on an innocent five year old child." he muttered as he passed his hand over her stone in a five pointed star. "A child you claim, since birth, was a demon, a snake, a serpent and a spawn of the devil."

"She was a mistake." he ground through clenched teeth. His hands fisted themselves.

Standing fully, he kept his eyes on the stone. His fists balled hard enough to draw blood, cracking his knuckles. It was all going to plan. A plan that was originally meant to be executed in his father's home, but going to plan nonetheless. He was intentionally angering him by ignoring him, but he thought he trained his emotions better than this. He could feel his blood literally boiling in his veins. His heart was beating quicker than he wanted and it took the pain of breaking the skin in his hand to bring it back under control. His mind mentally repeating the codes of Noir. *Noir is an instrument. An instrument of God. Instruments have no emotions, ergo, Noir has none.* It was all a matter of control. Mental control, he told himself.

"How my killing her could be misconstrued as a mistake?" he asked softly.

"You were supposed to die, not her." Marcus whispered as his eyes darkened. It wasn't supposed to be that way. "She was not supposed to be there. He was supposed to kill you and save her from further sins. He asked her where you were, but she didn't speak; only said something about not giving up humanities last hope. How the Angel has come to watch over once again. He stepped out of line by beating her, but she wouldn't tell him where you were. She told him to kill her, because she would never break her oath."

His golden eyes sharpened and flashed as he listened to him rant. He remembered that day clearly. How could he forget? He took his mother to a place where he spotted a snake a few days before. It was a garden that he and his mother made when he was four. That's how he knew where to find him. After playing around in the grass for a few minutes, he told her of what he found. She smiled and told him to go and fetch it, because she had a story about a snake to tell him. Smiling, because he liked her stories, he ran off to retrieve the snake. During that time, the man must have come for him. Coming back, with the snake in hand, he spotted the man beating her. Ducking behind the surrounding bushes, he peeked through. He couldn't hear her words while she was on the ground, but she saw his eyes through the leaves. He was going to yell, but the sight of her eyes stopped him. After the man stabbed her and ran off, he walked up to her.

He could hear something in the depths of his mind creak, and then snap, like a pencil that was bent too far. But as quickly as he heard it, it was gone. He was distantly aware of his body shivering. He knew it wasn't from the cold. It was from the anger building within him. He wanted to push it back, like he was taught, but he desired to release this feeling. The resentment towards this man, who not only took his mother away, but also tried to take him away.

"So, he killed her. When he came back and told me of what happened, I was angry and glad at the same time. I was angry because it was you who were to die and not her, but I was happy because since she was out of the way, there would be no one to hinder me in getting rid of such an abomination a second time." his voice gained a hint of insanity as he continued to rave. "I was going to kill you the same day, and make it look like another act of mindless violence, but you were nowhere to be found. I assumed you were lost and would die of starvation. Imagine my surprise when you showed up with her father the day of her funeral. You disappeared for two years after that day."

"Why are you telling me this?" Sera asked as he closed his eyes. He wrestled with his conflicting responses. On one hand, he could allow his anger to control him and kill the man who has brought him so much pain. Or, he could suppress the urge and leave. The sounds of his fathers' footsteps coming closer were loud in his ears. He tensed his muscles as his left hand twitched. He made his decision. Or rather, his father made it for him.

"Because," Marcus hissed as he looked down at his much shorter person with a visage of malice. "I am going to do what I planned on doing the day she died." he placed a hand on his shoulder and squeezed. "I'm going to kill you *Demon*."

Turning his head slowly, he looked up at him with blank eyes.

"You're too late." Sera whispered as he readied his muscles. His words drifting on the cold, clammy breeze that decided to drift through the tombstones. "I died with my mother." he finished as he pulled his arms apart. Marcus screamed in agony as his hand was severed from his arm.

Falling back, he began scrambling away from Sera. Allowing the blood to shoot onto his face, he watched his father fall back. His father was so set on killing him that he didn't mind his surroundings. Twitching his hand, he sent a loop of wire around the hand he could see through the slits he left in his eyes. Turning fully, he slowly advanced on his screaming person. He could hear his fathers' heart beat, louder than before. It was only out done by his screams, which seemed to have become a wail. He could smell his fear and anger, even though he wasn't sure how he knew what it was he smelled. He could even vaguely taste the scent of his fear. He was distantly aware that his vision had become sharper, the colors more vivid. His eyes shifted from honey gold to angry vermilion as he glared at him. "You wished to kill me father?" the question was rhetorical. The manner in which the question was posed made one more than opposed to answering the question, simply because they valued their lives.

/Step. /

"Stay away from me!" Marcus screamed, scrambling backwards. He was a shell of the man that he feared in the night.

/Step. /

The leaves tussled in a light breeze and danced to unheard music. As some of the dancers mis-stepped, he stopped them short with his foot.
"Why? Because my mother loved me more than you?" he continued as he brought his hands together.

/Step. /

"You are a demon! You deserve to die!" he rambled as he glared at him, holding his stump of an arm. There was his father. Showing his true colors. The boogeyman.

/Step. /

"Because of the way I was born?"

/Step. /

"You are an abomination, a mistake that should have never seen the light of day! God missed you, but I will not!"

/Stop. /

"I was a Demon Father." Sera conceded with a nod. All things considered, he was. "I was an angel. But, now I am both. I am an angel, after my mother, and a demon by my father." bringing his hands apart, the dim light trailed along the wire as if it were rain, in the shape of a five pointed star. "You have no idea of how right you were. But, I loved my mother and would never harm her. But you," he paused as he threw the wire around his neck and pulled until he heard his father choke. "I have no qualms about killing."

"You damn demon!" he gasped as he gripped at his neck, trying to remove the wire that was cutting into his neck.

Walking closer, he kneeled before his gasping form as he looked into his blue eyes. Blue eyes that were a mere imitation of his mothers true blues. A cheap knockoff.

"You hate me because of my eyes. My mother loved and cherished me because of them. You live in a dream where you are right and everyone else is wrong. The eyes you use to judge and criticize are tainted beyond use." taking his hands slowly, careful to keep the pressure on the wire, he placed his thumbs over his eyes. Pressing forward, he continued to talk softly over his screams of pain, and the fluid that leaked from the sockets. "I believe you don't need them anymore."

It amazed him how easily he could do this with no regret. He didn't feel anything, save for the slight thrill that coursed through him as he gouged out his eyes. He knew that a normal person wouldn't do this to another. He also knew that a child would be even less likely. But there was a major difference between them and him. He was neither normal, nor a child. He was Noir. And Noir was he.

"I'll kill you!" Marcus screamed as he clutched at his eyes. "I swear I'll kill you!"

Letting the wire go slack for a moment, he looked at him for a moment with gold eyes, before turning and walking away. Hearing his father standing, he stopped. In all honesty, he would have allowed the person to live. He would forever be reminded of the Demon he constantly preached about, whenever he woke up and couldn't see. Whenever he went to grab something and was painfully reminded that he lacked the appendage. It would be the ultimate irony. The hand that tried to kill him lay on the floor. His own eyes were the reason why the hand tried it in the first place, which is why he popped them out like bubbles. Poetic justice. But as he heard his constant claims of vengeance, he felt himself give in to his impulse.

"No you won't." he whispered as he closed his eyes, listening to his father's steps as they grew closer. The air grew tense with a feeling that only the residents could identify. The feeling only increased as the steps got closer towards their intended target. Turning around, he pulled his arms apart. Opening his eyes, vermilion slits glared at him as his head fell from his body and topple to the floor. The breeze that was gracing the graves with its cool reprieve died. The leaves that found joy in frolicking in the wind ceased. The sun that shed light on them even seemed to shy away from the burning fury in his eyes that seemed to eclipse and out shine his own. Following it, he looks at his feet. The sound of the body hitting the floor was distant to him. In such short amount of time, he's grown accustomed to doing things that normal people wouldn't do. After all, he was not human. Kneeling down, he placed his lips to his ear. "Because you were already dead. You just didn't know it yet." he whispered as he kissed his father's lips lightly. The newly departed glared once, before the muscles in the face relaxed into a stern look. "Good bye father." standing, he turned and walked away. Licking his lips, "Bitter." he muttered with a scowl. "Just like you father to leave a bad taste."

Because once they take root, they will forever be rooted into the soil of the soul. And the roots will need to be stripped from the ground and the soil salted so nothing ever grows again.

Chapter 5

Trust and Betrayal

Trust is easily broken, but hard to mend.

/I was surprised that someone would want to adopt me in the first place, which was a mistake in the first place. I should have known that whatever she was offering would cost something so much more, but I didn't think about that. I only cared about getting another chance at a family again. It started out rough, and for the first few years, I hated Susan. Hated her so much, that I contemplated killing her many times. I knew that if I were to do it, I would get away with it without even being considered a suspect in the crime. But, there were so many things that still remained to be done and I didn't want her out of my life. Before I knew what was what, she wormed her way into my routine. I was originally going to use her and leave, but instead I ended up staying. Her love for me was real and I relished it. It was foolish of me to do so, but I couldn't help it when the chance presented itself, I couldn't pull the trigger. But, things have worked out for the best with her alive and well and under my guard./

The streets were filled with people walking and talking and otherwise going about their happy little lives. Their white shirts and dark pants were nondescript and were impossible to tell one from the next. All of it was nothing more than inconsistent chatter amongst ants. He took that back. Ants had a purpose in life. They served the queen, protected the colony.

These things did nothing. Simply existed. None of them took the time to look into a nearby alley to see a child with rags sorting through the garbage. And if he was honest with himself that was the way he liked it. If they were looking at him, it was only with the utmost contempt and hatred in their eyes. He understood that the only person he could count on was himself. He had to figure that out quickly, or else they would have killed him a long time ago. He didn't have a reason to go back to his grandfathers after his training was complete. It was pointless. So, he decided to head out on his own. He knew that what he was doing, if he was a normal child, would surely be suicide. But one thing he knew about himself, was that he was not normal. His parents made that obvious. And he hasn't been a child in a long time. He bit back a curse as his finger caught a fish bone in the garbage bin he was sifting through.

"Concentrate." He reminded himself. If he wanted to eat, then he would have to focus on the task at hand. And eating was the main focus at the moment. As he heard a gurgle he looked down and growled audibly at his stomach. "Quiet." He hissed. He didn't need his stomach to remind him of what he was painfully aware of. It's been two days since he's eaten and he was starting to become irked. Sighing, he resumed his search through the bin. Finding nothing, he went over to another and began his search anew. Deciding that simply sifting through the trash while still in the can was a stupid rout to go down, he tilted the can over and began riffling through it.

He paused as his ears picked up on a set of footsteps that stopped in front of the alley way. Looking up, he spotted a young woman, no older than 25 years old looking at him. He knew to be weary of people that he didn't recognize. That was a painful lesson learned. Not on his part, but the part of the party responsible. As she took a step closer, he stilled. What was this woman thinking? Was she simply here to watch him like he was an animal in a zoo? He didn't want to go through the pain of neglect again because of childish dreams that he was too foolish to let go of. He tensed his muscles in preparation for a quick getaway.

"Hey." she said softly. "It's okay. I'm not going to hurt you."

He didn't move. Simply stared. Her tone was disarming, but he wasn't going to let sweet words get to him. That's how it always started. With such pretty, pretty words.

"What are you doing out here by yourself?" she asked gently, stopping 10 feet away.

He stood slowly. Eyes never leaving her form for a moment.

"What do you want?" he asked. He knew she wanted something. People dressed as nicely as her didn't simply walk down alleys and up to homeless children and ask them questions.

Quirking an eyebrow at his tone, she smiled slightly.

"I don't really want anything." she replied.

His eyes narrowed.

"Don't lie to me. I know you want something. Every living thing capable of cognitive thought wants." he said quickly. He was still ready to bolt if she made any sudden movements.

Looking at him, she paused.

"Fine. You're right. I do want something." she conceded.

"Well?" he asked with a raised eyebrow. "What is it?" she conceded to quickly for it to be something simple.

"You." she said simply.

His eyes opened wide for a moment. That was straight forward. So straight forward that he was momentarily stunned. But as he got over his surprise, his mind began working over the reasons as to why she would want him. He knew he would have recognized her if he had seen her before. She was a beautiful woman and stuck out like a sore thumb in this neighborhood, only to be compared to his mother. She's certainly never heard of him before, because if she did, then she would not be talking to him. And if she was talking, it would only be hateful words. He began to frown, before it tapered off into a light glare. He couldn't understand. And he didn't like it when he didn't understand.

"Me? What for?" he asked, tone brimming with suspicion. Humans were easy to read. But this person was not.

"I have a job offer for you."

He quirked an eyebrow at her reply. She wanted him for a job? That was a new one. Was it possible that she was a hidden Blanc and knew of his lineage? He shook his head. To his knowledge, they were all dead. And judging from her tone and eyes, she was honest about what she was offering him. Would he dare take a chance?

"Really?" he asked. His voice had a minute amount of hope before he was able to squelch it.

She smiled lightly.

"Yes. I run a business. And, I need some more help in order to get it off the ground. I'm sure you don't want to live on the streets for the rest of your life. I can adopt you." she offered.

She was offering to adopt him. His mind only processed that portion of her explanation. As he tried to piece together what she said, he was constantly coming up with a blank. He had no real reason as to why he shouldn't take her up on her offer. And even if she turned out to be like the others, she would, in the end, end up like the others. His eyes stared blankly at her.

"Sure." he finally said. Walking towards her, he looked up. His black bangs falling to frame his small face. Sometimes he disliked his hair long, but if people thought he was a girl, they were more than likely to be nice to him. "So, what's your name mom?"

She smiled.

"My name is Susan, Susan Roth. And what's your name?"

He considered telling her his name, but thought better of it. If she knew his name, then maybe she would change her mind about him.

"Don't really have one. Haven't used it in years." he lied with a shrug. Well, he wasn't lying completely. After all, what was a name other than a way to differentiate between different persons of the same species? So in essence, he wasn't lying. His name hasn't been spoken, uttered, or thought of in years. Only a title. Only a rank. Only a shadow.

"Alright then, what do your friends call you?" she asked.

He mentally sneered at the thought of friends. He's never had any before. All the children that were his age or even close were taught to hate him with a passion only shadowed by their parents.

"Don't know. Don't have any. They don't really want to hang out with a boy who has eyes like mine." Near the end, he wasn't able to hide the sullen tone his voice took, and it irked him to know he slipped, but didn't let it show. For all she knew, it was the reaction to being alone.

As she grabbed his hand, he fought the urge to smile and repressed the warmth that filled him. A relapse from when his mother did the same thing. He needed more control.

"Well, I think I'll call you Suen. I always wanted a boy."

He looked up at her with a questioning look. He's heard the name before, in one of the books he's read, but couldn't recall what it meant.

"Sue-n?"

"Yes. It's pronounced Sin. It's the name of the god of the moon in Mesopotamian faith."

He hummed lightly. A small smile adorned his face. *Mother was named after the Goddess of the Moon.*

"I like it." he finally said.

"Good."

As they both walked out of the alley, he kept his eyes hidden behind his hair. Beneath the shadows that his hair provided, he found comfort in the shade. Even though he grew to tolerate the glares, he still didn't like them. It shielded him from the hateful glares that were undoubtedly being sent his way. On the outside, he was placid. But within, he was livid. They still hated him without reason. They still wished death upon him. They were still spreading their slanderous filth. *Filthy humans. All of them. Sinful creatures.*

XXX

Glaring at her figure as it retreated the way they both came from behind the bars; he mentally cursed his lapse in judgment when he met the woman. *I knew something was off about her from the moment I laid eyes on her.* Sitting back in the cell he sighed aloud. Looking about the room, it was painfully obvious that there was no way out of the cage she left him in. Looking at the cage closer; he tried to find any rust on the bars. *I can tell this thing has been down here for a while now. I only have to find a weak point, then I'll get out of here and the first thing I'm going to do is cut that bitch's head off.* He looked left then right. Up then down. *Nothing.* His shoulders slumped and he pushed himself closer towards the bars, only to hiss as he made contact on his previously forgotten welts. *Damn that stings! I am so going to enjoy taking her life when I'm free of this place. Call her Mistress my ass. I will never call her that.* His eyes landed on the small bundle of fur that was only a few feet away. The small pup was simply sitting there looking at him with its wide eyes and wagging stump of a tail. *I guess it's just me and you dog.* He thought wryly to himself as he motioned for the dog to come. Pulling the dog into his lap, he curled up and allowed his body to rest. But his mind, he would keep alert. This is how it always started. Their sweet, sweet words were used to lull him into security, and the bitter truth of the matter is that they all seek the same thing. His pain. His suffering. His life.

XXX

He came to, yet again, to the sound of the door opening and the footsteps of the one who trapped him down here in this cell. He didn't know how long he has been here, but he knew it was longer than what he would have liked. But, he was grateful that she fed him at least. She stopped at the bars as usual and deposited a cup of water and some bread. *Same old, same old.* He thought sardonically to himself as he slowly reached for the offered food. The water always felt great going down, and the bread tasted so sweet on his tongue.

"So are you going to call me what I asked?" Susan asked as she stood above him like the many other times.

He didn't answer her. Just simply turned his head and continued eating. He knew what was coming next. If he had a watch, he was sure that he could set it to the next action. Even though he knew it was going to come, he couldn't stop the quick inhalation as he felt the belt across his stomach.

That bitch!
Crack!
I am going to kill her!
Crack!
And I'm going to enjoy it immensely.
Crack!

Always three lashes. Always on his stomach. Always painful.

She didn't say anymore as she turned and left without a moment's hesitation. He watched her leave with fire in his eyes. The sound of the door closing was his cue to speak again.

"I'm going to kill her." he whispered to the empty room. He looked over towards the dog, which was eating as well in a corner of the room.

The dog always ate everyday in the same corner. He would have eaten some of the dog food, if it were within reach. *But, I'm sure that's the point.* As it finished, he motioned for the dog to come. Holding it in his hands, he pets the fur. "She thinks I will call her Mistress Dog." he said aloud. The dog perked its head up almost as if it were listening. "She thinks if she beats me, then I will crack. But, she doesn't know Seraphim Angelus. I don't cower. I never back down. And I always get what I want." the dog wined as he assaulted the small animal to stronger pets. Stopping, he looked down and patted the dogs head lightly. "Sorry. I was just wrapped up in the moment. I didn't mean to hurt you." the dog barked once as if saying okay and laid back down on his lap. *I swear I will get out of here.* It was in that instance, a plan formed in his mind.

XXX

Now his body was getting thin and weak. The measly bread and water every now and again just wasn't enough to sustain life. He needed solid food. Looking up at the door opening, he looked back towards the ground. She was only going to give him bread and water again, ask him to call her mistress and beat him when he didn't. He didn't see a need to look up at her.

"So how are we doing today?" she asked kindly. He didn't answer. "Are you going to call me Mistress like you are supposed to do?" her tone was sickly sweet. He contemplated if he needed a visit to the dentist to check for cavities. Condescending.

He shifted a little. Picking his head up, he mustered up what was left of his defiance and looked upon her with narrowed golden eyes. As she kneeled down, he kept his eyes on her figure. This was different than her normal behavior, and it threw him off. He really disliked variables that weren't in the equation.

"What? You don't want to talk to me anymore? Do you only speak to the dog?" she asked mockingly. His glare intensified with her correct assumption. "The dog isn't your friend." she stated, slowly bringing her hand out of her pocket. "He doesn't have loyalty." slowly the dog shifted. Standing up, it walked over towards her hand. He kept his eyes on the dogs figure as it moved. *It won't come to you.* He thought to himself. As the dog moved he felt his heart leap into his throat. *He wouldn't.* He tried to move, but his body was weak. The dog slowly trotted closer towards her open hand and began nibbling on, what he thought was a treat. *How could he?* He could feel the weight of his situation fall onto his shoulders. He wanted to open his mouth, but the lump in his throat stopped any sound from escaping.

Taking the treat, it nibbled gleefully on its snack. "You see? It will turn its back on you in an instant." as she moved her other hand behind herself, he tensed.

How could he do that to me? He thought as his eyes became downcast. The sound of metal hitting the floor brought his gaze up. *A knife.*

"But, that won't happen with us. Here in the Spirits, you are blood."

Blood. The word echoed into the depths of his mind. Attached to the word was a fuzzy picture that he couldn't make out.

"We never turn our back on blood. Honor, loyalty, and family. Those are what we hold above everything else." slowly his hand reached for the blade. "You want to be family don't you?" she asked. Her voice was distant to him. Like it was a distant memory coming back. An image of a beautiful woman standing over him with a gentle smile. *Mother . . .*

As he gripped the blade, he could feel the presence of another's hand on his. "Then strike the one who betrayed you." she prodded.

An image of a man with broad shoulders and a sneer on his face entered his mind's eye. *Father . . .*

"The one who sold you out for a treat."

He was my only friend in this hell and he sides with the enemy. Slowly he approached the dog on his hands and knees. *A traitor to the clan is a traitor to the cause. One, who bites the hand that feeds, is one who is destined to starve.* The blade of the knife scrapped across the concrete floor as he drew near. *The enemy of my enemy is my friend.* His hand raised with the sharp implement poised above the hapless animal.

"The one who was so easily swayed to betray you." she whispered as he got closer towards the puppy.

As he stopped two feet away from the ignorant pup, he looked up towards her face. Golden eyes glazed over as he looked upon her form. *Goddess who watches over us, allow my hand to strike true. Guide this confused soul into your waiting arms to be escorted to his rightful place. I am but your humble servant, and you are . . .* the dim gold brightened.

"Yes Mistress." he replied in monotone. He brought the blade down fast and hard onto the dog's stomach.

She gently opened the door, and beckoned for him to step out. Slowly he complied, with the knife in hand. On uneven footing, he stood before her as straight as his body would allow.

"Hand over the knife." she ordered.

"Yes Mistress." he answered swiftly. Turning the handle of the blade towards her with practiced ease, he allowed it to be taken.

"Good." she turned. "Now, come with me. It's time to continue your training."

He walked silently behind her. Looking over her shoulder, she smiled lightly. Finally coming to an open clearing, she turned towards him.

"Alright. You want to be useful to the Spirits? Useful to me?" she asked, looking him in the eyes.

"Yes." he replied. *I will be useful to my family. Useful to my Goddess. Useful to my mother . . .*

Swiftly, she punched him in the stomach. His eyes followed her movement, but he didn't guard himself. *Noir never flinches, never backs down, never shows fear.* He repeated to himself as the air in his lungs was forced out. He fell to one knee holding his stomach. She was stronger than he expected her to be. Stronger than most of the males he got into fights with. *Strong.*

As he lay gasping for breath, she spoke. Her words were like ice. Her tone made him, forced him to look upon her with respect.

"If you want to be of use to the Spirits, then you will have to become strong. Stronger than you are now. If that's what you want, then come at me with the intent to kill." she stated. Brown eyes boring into gold. As he stood up, he resolved himself to do as she asked, as she ordered.

But betrayal is easy to give, but hard to take back.

Chapter 6

Pain, Hatred, Ascension

Human suffering is painful. Humans hatred is pointless.

"Again." Susan ordered as she chambered another round.

He readied himself. The sweat building on his forehead rolled down and into his eyes. He didn't blink as the salty secretion made its way into his line of sight. He needed his vision. Looking at the barrel of the gun, he began the calculations in his head. The training thus far has been brutal. The work on his mind was relatively complete, it was his body that she was working on and she was pushing it beyond its limits.

The room was large. The common color, on the ceiling and walls, was gray. Normal, nondescript gray. The vast space was filled with a cold chill. It was late afternoon, but you could never tell with the petulant gray sky. The room held the scent of old blood and was currently being filled with the scent of sweat.

The barrel is pointing forward at a slight downward angle meaning it's aiming for my thigh, given my distance.

The gunshot was loud and thunderous. Within this room, everything seemed amplified. He dodged to his left, but wasn't quick enough to avoid a graze of the rubber bullet.

"Not good enough." Susan reprimanded as she trained the sights on him again. "Again."

He stood, ignoring the stinging sensation in his right thigh. She was right. She was always right. It wasn't good enough. He needed to be faster. Needed to anticipate. Needed to predict. Needed to *know*.

The average human only uses five percent of their brain capacity. Noir is able to access the rest. I need to open my eyes and see.

Another gunshot.

His right arm hangs useless at his side. He grits his teeth. It hurts more dead on than it does in a graze. He has yet to accomplish splitting his attention. That would become a problem if not settled.

Goddess that watches over us, please grant me the power to see what needs to be seen. He focused his eyes on the position of her arm. *Slightly to the left.* His sharp eyes looked towards the gun. *Pointed more to the left.* Moving slightly down, he locked onto her finger. As the muscle twitched, he tensed his muscles. He knew what was wrong.

She pulled the trigger.

He was moving ahead of time. Moving before the trigger was being pulled.

The thunder roared in his ears.

He never factored in the trajectory of the bullet once it left the barrel.

He moved.

Didn't take into account the distance from his person to the other.

He could feel the slipstream near his right ear.

The sound of the rubber bullet hitting concrete echoed through the room.

He didn't watch her eyes.

"Good Suen, very good." Susan praised with a clap of her hand. "If you hadn't of dodged that bullet, then you would be unconscious right now and without dinner."

"I wasn't timing it correctly." he began. She always wanted him to explain what he figured out and in explicit detail. Wanted to document his findings and progress as it steadily increased. "I was moving before you pulled the trigger which gave you time to correct and adjust. I wasn't watching your arm. The manner in which you held the gun determined the direction of the bullet. Your hand also played a part in its desired location. But, the critical thing I missed was your eyes. You have to see where you want to bullet to strike in order to ensure it would hit its mark. That along with the twitch in your finger tells me when you are going to pull the trigger."

She nodded her head.

"All of that is very true, and I'm surprised that you found all of that out after only three shots fired. Impressive. But, you will need to do so again and again and again until it becomes second nature to you." she said as she raised the weapon again, sights trained on his head. "Now, let's continue."

"Yes Mistress." was his response as he dodged yet another bullet. She was never one to warn him, and he never expected one.

XXX

Standing before Susan, Sera stood at attention. His training under her was finally finished and he was to get his first mission tonight. He could feel the expectation buzzing in his mind. Like a hive of killer bees waiting to defend their hive from a threat. He pushed the emotion back and out of his mind as the buzzing dimmed to a distant hum, before it was gone completely. It was his training at work. As she walked towards him, he looked her in the eyes.

"Suen," she began. "You have far exceeded my expectations. I never thought you would become what you are now. You have become strong. Stronger than I was at your age. And because of that, you are to become my first Hell Born." reaching behind her back, she pulled out a red wrapped object. Slowly un-wrapping it, she presented him with a blood red mask of a fox. He smiled as he spotted the animal face. "From now on, when you put on this mask, you will be known as Fox." she announced. Voice filled with pride.

Looking up, his eyes flashed as they landed on the blood red mask. Gently taking it from her hands, he placed it on his head. It was a perfect fit for him. Looking up towards her, he awaited her next orders.

"Now, your first mission is to go here." she handed him a file. As he opened it, she continued. "You are to get rid of everyone inside. But, leave one alive. Your ride is waiting for you out front. The supplies you will need are in the car. Dismissed."

Turning on his heel, he walked out the door. Walking the halls, he was slightly giddy at the thought of killing. These people were interfering with the Spirits and pestering Susan, meaning they were the enemy. Walking outside, he spotted the car, the back passenger side door open. Climbing inside, and closing the door, he picked up the vest that was lying in the seat and put it on. It was red in color and made him smile at the color scheme. It reminded him of blood. Strapping the dual holsters onto his thighs, he checked both guns before loading them. Picking up two silencers, he pocketed them. No need in putting them on them now. Looking up, he noticed the car has stopped while he was preparing. Opening the door and stepping out, he was not surprised that the car left. Looking around, he spotted a small house shaped object a few hundred meters out in a vacant part of town. *Target sighted.* He mentally reported to himself as he quickly stalked his way through the light cover of the trees. Finally reaching the rather small, in comparison to the base, shack, he spotted two men guarding the front door. Both of them armed with a simple handgun. Nodding to himself, he walked out slowly after withdrawing a gun from his holster and twisting the silencer on. He would kill these men. He was ordered to kill these men. He wanted to kill these men. They were the enemy. They were the opponents. They were Human.

"So she was all like-" the first man paused as he spotted Sera's small figure walking out of the shadows. "Who are you?" he demanded.

Quickly raising his hand, he shot him in-between the eyes. He didn't want to hear the man talk; didn't want to hear his annoying voice. It would only aggravate him further than he already was by simply being in their presence. As the mans friend fell back, he attempted to raise his hand and fire upon him, but was stopped short as a bullet found its mark in his head.

Walking up towards the door, he offered a final glance at the two bodies. *"Disgusting."* he sneered. Opening the door, he spotted four men working on bagging up, what he knew was cocaine from the mission statement. Raising his hand again, he shot each one quickly and efficiently. It was so easy, came so effortlessly, like breathing. Turning his head quickly at the sound of feet rushing towards another door at his side, he pulled his second gun and charged the door as it opened. He could feel, even hear, his heart thumping in his chest. He knew it was over 60 beats per minute. He also knew it wasn't beating so quickly out of fear. It was purely expectation. The first man that he spotted had an A-K 47, poised and ready for use. Coming up on him, he jumped onto his figure, sending the man toppling backwards. Placing his gun to his throat, he pulled the trigger twice. The resulting torrent of blood that shot onto his masked face was lost on him as he spotted the remaining three trying to get back up. Moving his left arm, he shot one in his stomach and chest. Leaving the gun in the first's throat, he shot the one in front of him through the hole in his neck. As he poised his gun on the third, he was forced back by the force of the shot he got off. He didn't move as the man came over to inspect his body. He didn't even move as the man kicked his body to ensure that he was dead. Being so close to the ground, he could hear other footsteps coming closer to inspect the noise. As he could see the men surrounding him, he held his breath. The man, who shot him, leaned down and gripped his mask.

"Let's find out who this little fucker is!" the man growled as he tried sliding the mask off.

"Are you sure this is the one who killed our guys? I mean he couldn't be more than a child." a second man asked.

"Why won't this mask come off?" the first growled as he shook the mask.

Gripping his guns, Fox smiled beneath his mask.

"Fools." he whispered softly as he prepared his body. Humans were all fools. They were so confident that they were at the top of the food chain, they have forgotten about the animals. The animals that were around before their pathetic race inhabited the earth. They were so sure that they were the best; they were all about to be butchered, because they have forgotten about the animals. Possum.

"What the-!" the man screamed as he felt something grab his legs.

Hooking his legs behind the man that stood over him, he brought up both arms and pressed both barrels on his forehead.

"Die!" he growled as he pulled both triggers. As his blood rained on his face, he flexed his leg muscles and used the already slippery floor, from the blood, to pull himself from underneath the man. Turning over quickly, he pushed the man into the group as they opened fire on him. As they cleared a way for the body to fall, so they wouldn't be trapped underneath, he ran over the body, shooting two in the chest as he ran by. Running back into the main room, he hid behind the table they were using to bag their drugs. The sound of the bullets hitting his cover was lost on him as he focused on the footsteps of his prey. Closing his eyes, he mentally plotted their positions. As they all stopped shooting, his eyes sprung open. Standing quickly, he trained his sights on where he knew them to be. He smiled viciously as each body fell to the ground. Turning, he walked through the remaining rooms to ensure they were all empty, before heading back towards the main room. Hearing a man groaning painfully, he walked slowly towards him. He stopped before him, tilting his head slightly.

"You son of a bitch!" the man screamed as he raised his gun. He screamed again as a bullet tore through his wrist.

"Human, I am not a son of a bitch. I am no dog. I am a fox." Fox said softly. The human vocabulary at times seemed limited to simple profanity.

"Just kill me." the man pleaded pathetically.

Shaking his head slowly, he walked closer towards him. He wondered, for only a second, if everything was supposed to be this easy, but passed it off as nothing. They were weak. He was strong.

Simple as that.

"Even my father didn't beg when I killed him." he commented idly. "He was the worst human I have ever met. A disgrace to the race. And you are even more pathetic." placing his gun towards his other wrist, he pulled the trigger. He drowned out his screams as he continued to look at him impassively. "I cut off my father's hand, before I gouged his eyes out with my fingers. He didn't even cry. He continued to curse my name and swear death upon me before I cut off his head. He was entertaining. You," he paused as he placed his gun in the mans open mouth. "Are not." he finished as he pulled the trigger. He sighed as he felt a shiver pass through his body. Standing fully, he looked out at the bodies that littered the floor. Such an interesting sight. The dark red liquid seemed right at home on the cement floor. He could feel his body shuddering in euphoria. He didn't try to hide it this time. No one was around to see his lapse in control. His ear twitched as it picked up on a sound to his left. Tensing his body, he turned, gun raised, towards the intruder. As he sighted Susan standing before him, he felt his trigger finger twitch. *"I've been waiting for the moment when I would put a bullet in this bitch's head."* he growled to himself. *But she has taught me more than anyone else.* His finger eased on the trigger. *"I promised to kill her."* The pressure reapplied. *But I never said when.* It receded once more. *"Just kill her!"* More pressure. The hammer eased back slowly. *She could be helpful in the future. With all the connections she has, she can so easily give me a helping hand in keeping the promise.* The hammer paused in its movement. *"Grr . . . fine."* His finger completely left the trigger. Lowering his arm, he looked at her.

"They bored me." he said finally, lowering his gun. "They were not entertaining." And that was the truth. They were not entertaining. Not really. The last one was interesting, but only mildly so.

Slowly, Susan walked towards him and placed a hand on his shoulder.

"Let's go." she suggested as she gave him a nudge.

Going with her, he allowed her to lead him out of the building and towards a car that he knew was hers. Climbing into the passenger side, he closed the door. Taking off his mask, he laid it in his lap. The mission was over, but he still felt a tingling sensation coursing through his body. Hearing the drivers' door closing, he turned towards Susan.

"Can I go hunting again?" he asked eagerly. Perhaps he could find a human that was entertaining. One to compel him to stop and observe as the fear eats away at them like thousands of termites eating away at an old house.

She turned towards him and smiled gently.

"You can only hunt the big game." she assured.

Nodding his head with a smile, he closed his eyes as the car began pulling off. Hunting the big game meant that he would be facing better opponents. Perhaps, more opponents. The thought made him truly happy.

"Good." he whispered, riding out the adrenaline high.

As they made it back to base, he quickly got out of his seat and followed behind her into the dimly lit hallway. Making it towards a room he didn't recognize, he followed her in. He quirked an eyebrow at her as she pushed a bed to the side and opened a hidden passage beneath it.

Following silently, he walked down the stairs. As they reached the bottom, he was slightly surprised to find a fully furnished room. In front of him, was a bed that he was sure could hold four people comfortably. It was covered in a crimson bed spread and black sheets with black pillows at the head. To his right, he spotted a small room that was sure to hold a bathroom. He stopped at the bottom of the stairs, because he wasn't sure as to what he should do now.

She stopped at her bed as she felt him stop walking. Turning, she looked at him with a small smile.

"What are you doing?" she asked as she watched him.

He tilted his head slightly.

"This is your room." he pointed out calmly.

She nodded her head.

"Yes, but you didn't answer my question Suen."

"Why am I here? I thought I was to continue sleeping with the dogs." he sounded genuinely perplexed. He didn't like the dogs, but their fear kept them away from him when he rested. And they alerted him to any intruders on his territory.

"Come here." she said gently.

Slowly, he complied with her request. Standing before her, he looked up at her face. She still held a gentle smile. He had to restrain himself from smiling back. She was so similar to his mother that he almost forgot she was gone. As she situated herself on the edge of her bed, she motioned for him to come closer. Heeding her call, he stood between her legs. As her hands went for his neck, he didn't flinch. *So, she will kill me here and hide my body to forever be in this tomb.* He surmised calmly. *If this is my fate for not taking the chance I was given, then so be it.* He was mildly surprised when she unzipped his vest and took it off his shoulders. Her hands then found the holsters to his guns and un-strapped those as well, before placing them on a side desk. As she sat back up, she placed a hand on his head and pets it lightly.

"This is where you are to sleep from now on." she answered his unasked question. "Now that your training is complete, you need a bed in which to rest. I have more than enough room here for the both of us." she continued as she picked him up. Placing him down on the bed, she laid back next to him. "I will not have my son dying of pneumonia."

He could feel himself being affected by her words. *So, she really plans on being my mother.* He said to himself as he looked into her eyes. Smiling lightly, he nodded his head, before wrapping his small arms around her body and planting his head between her breasts. *It feels like mother.* He thought drowsily to himself as he snuggled in closer to her warmth. *"This is the perfect time to kill her."* No. she is willing to become mother. *"After everything she has done?!"* Even more reason to not kill her. *"She deserves to die!"* And she will, but not now. Now, she is mother and as long as she is, she will not be harmed under my watch.

"Lullaby and good night, with roses bedight. With lilies o'er spread is baby's wee bed, lay thee down now and rest, may thy slumber be blessed. Lay thee down now and rest, may thy slumber be blessed. Lullaby and good night, thy mothers delight. Bright angels beside my darling abide, they will guard thee at rest, thou shalt wake on my breast. They will guard thee at rest; thou shalt wake on my breast." Susan sung softly as she wrapped her arms around his smaller body. She held him tighter as she felt dampness on her chest. Looking down, he was already asleep. Kissing his head lightly, she closed her eyes.

> **But, to become something more, something more than Human, requires you to rise above what makes them so pathetic. You must ascend.**

Chapter 7

Specter

Remorse is simply your memories aware. Becoming aware of them creates fear.

The room was dead silent, as it should have been while bodies were at rest, but there was a presence in the air. One of sorrow and grief. It was thick in the air and one would be hard pressed to wade through the depressing bog. A low, high sound penetrated the dimly lit room before it was absorbed by the walls. Again it sounded, and again it left. The whimper was soft, and almost not audible. If it wasn't for the disturbing silence that settled over the room, one was sure to have ignored it.

He tossed in his slumber. Sweat built on his face as his features contorted into pain and grief.

"Mamma." he whispered mournfully as he shook his head. "Don't go to sleep." he pleaded weakly. His voice, so tiny, one would mistake it for a breeze. "Don't go to sleep." his body began to shudder and quake as if having a seizure. Opening his eyes with a start, he looked both ways in panic.

"Mamma!" he screamed as his head turned. He almost jumped out of his skin when he felt arms encircle him from behind and a hand in his hair.

"Shh. I'm right here." Susan cooed as she gently pet his hair. As he relaxed in her grip, she pulled him closer towards her. "It's alright. It was only a bad dream."

"Mistress?" he questioned groggily as he turned his head slightly. His heart was still pounding in his chest. The dream was one of the worst ones he's ever had. He knew what it meant though. It only happened when that day was coming again.

"Shh, darling. Everything will be okay." she continued to sooth. "I'm here."

He nodded his head and allowed her to continue. He welcomed the warmth and love she was giving him at the moment, even if it was all an act, it was welcomed. It's been too long since he's ever been held like this. He knew he was being selfish and childish, but he didn't dwell on it.

"What happened in your dream?" she asked gently, as she placed her head next to his. "Maybe I can help you."

He shook his head lightly.

"I don't want to talk about It." he said softly. "And you already have."

Nodding her head, she gave him a final squeeze before letting go.

"I'm glad I could help." she said as she stood. "Now, come along. I have something to show you."

He nodded his head mutely as he followed her lead and stood up. Following her towards the smaller room, he stopped at the doorway.

Turning from the shower, she looked back at his still figure.

"Why are you standing over there?" she asked.

"I'm to guard the door while you shower." he answered as if it was obvious.

Shaking her head, "Come over here Suen." she said with an amused smile. "You need to clean yourself too. You are covered in blood."

Nodding his head, he slowly walked towards her. Not that he minded the blood. He stood still as she began taking off his clothes. He didn't feel embarrassment for being bare to a woman. After all, his mother used to bathe him all the time. He tilted his head as he watched her undress. As the last of her clothes hit the floor, he couldn't deny that she was beautiful. Just like his mother. As she stepped into the shower, he followed closely behind. As the warm water hit his skin, he sighed. It's been years since he's felt warm water on his skin. His grandfather told him that cold water was to build stamina and the mistress, during training, would only hose him down. He flinched slightly as he felt hands on his back. He relaxed as he remembered that he wasn't alone in the shower. As her soapy hands came around his front, they stopped at his chest. He knew why she stopped, as he felt her hands trace the scar.

"What happened?" she asked gently.

"My father tried to kill Me." he answered truthfully as his hand went towards his chest. His fingers ghosted across her hand in the shape of an X. Oh how vividly he could remember that fateful night that he died. His father was constantly watching him in the darkness of his room. Glaring at him. Silently cursing his very existence. Every night he would stand in the doorway and watch Sera as he lay in his bed. Every night there were three glimmers that he could see coming from his father. Two from his eyes. One from his hand. He never wanted to sleep while the man was in his room. For hours they looked at each other. Then he would turn away and close his door. But that night, after a day filled with playing with his mother for his birthday, he was exhausted. He awoke to a painful stab in his heart. He opened his eyes wide and screamed for his mother. Screamed for someone to save him. Screamed for the pain to stop. And soon, it did. As if the goddess had answered his prayers, he was granted eternal darkness. He awoke in a white room, bright with white light, and alone. He didn't want to be alone. He began panicking. He thrashed in his bed and was afraid. The door flung open to reveal his mother's happy frantic face as she went to him and hugged him close. His sobs subsided. His shivers abated. His eyes filled with tears of joy. He was not alone anymore. His mother was still here with him and he was happy. And his crimson tears that stained her shirt were proof of that. "An ice pick to the heart was his way of killing me while I slept. It broke off inside. They said that it was a miracle that I lived."

She growled in her throat.

"I will kill him." she hissed.

He was slightly surprised at her reaction to his scar. She did beat him repeatedly for two months, then proceeded to beat him whenever he did something wrong for another three months. But, then again, she always left how many lashings he was to receive up to him and his progress, and she never took it too far. Her protectiveness was a welcomed feeling.

"There is no need." Suen said softly with a shake of his head. "He is dead."

He could feel her slight disappointment at not being able to end his life, but she was also happy that he was no longer alive.

"That's good. Anyone who is willing to do that to family should be killed and sentenced to hell for the remainder of time." she stated with a nod of her head, as she moved to lather his hair. "Now, close your eyes, because you have a lot of blood in here and I don't want to get it in your eyes."

He nodded his head as he felt her massage his scalp. He let a content purr escape his lips as he pressed his head into her fingers. It felt good to finally have his hair washed again. Having so much, it was a hassle to clean it himself. Her fingers were hitting just the right spots and he felt himself drift off slightly.

"Sing me a song mamma." he whispered distractedly.

"Sing you a song?" she questioned.

He snapped his eyes open, but squeezed them back as he felt soap rolling down his face.

"Never mind." he said with a shake of his head.

"You are my little one, you are my son. My heart my joy, my shining sun. If you were to leave, I think I would die, from not having you by my side. The darkness would scare me, without you beside me. Please stay as my light and to home, you guide Me." she sang softly as she rinsed the soap from his hair.

Turning in her grip, he looked up at her with a small smile.

"Thank you for your help." he said gratefully, before he motioned for her to turn around.

"What?" she asked.

"I have to clean you now." he said evenly as he tilted his head. "It's what you do to one who washes yours."

She nodded her head as she turned and sat down on a stool she grabbed from the back of the tub.

"Close your eyes. I need to wash your hair." he told her. As she nodded her head, he began lathering her chocolate tresses. Threading his fingers through her hair slowly, he began humming. Her hair was as long, if not longer than his mothers, but it was just as smooth. He smiled as he heard her hum in relaxation. "I use to wash my mother's hair before she died. She would let me play in her hair until we began to become wrinkled from the water." he commented idly. "Your hair is just as smooth."

"Thank you Suen." she said gently, relaxing further into his touch. "What else can you tell me?" she asked, hoping to get him to open up.

"She was a beautiful woman with blond hair as bright as the sun and eyes that matched the clearest of skies and put the ocean to shame." he answered with fondness as he worked on her body. "She always had a smile on her face and never let me leave her side for too long. Always overprotective."

"What was her name?" she asked.

He stiffened slightly. Shaking his head, he reached for the hose and rinsed her hair out.

"I believe it's now time for us to get out." he said monotone as he pulled back the curtain and waited for her to follow.

Nodding her head, she followed out after him. Grabbing two towels, she handed one to him as she dried herself off.

Wrapping the towel around his waist, he waited for her to finish brushing her teeth. As she gargled, she handed him a black tooth brush.

"Brush." she ordered after she spit. "I will not have your teeth falling out because of neglect."

"My teeth will fall out regardless. I have yet to grow into my permanent set." he pointed out calmly.

"Just take it." she said as she placed it in his mouth.

Nodding his head, he began brushing. After he finished, he walked back into her room, where she was waiting, dressed, holding another pair of clothes. As he walked out, he took his time to admire her beauty. Her brown hair was feathered down her back. Her lips were lightly glossed with a cherry gloss. Her eyes were lightly shadowed and the rosary around her neck was situated comfortably between her breasts. Her simple black blouse and black jeans accentuated her figure. Tilting his head, he awaited more instructions.

"I want you to put these on. The place I am taking you, you need to look presentable."

He took the offered clothing mutely and began putting them on. Finally finishing, he looked down at himself. He was wearing a long sleeve version of what she was wearing.

"Let's go. I have some people I want you to meet and some things that need to be taken care of." she said as she began walking up the stairs.

Following closely, he walked behind her. Reaching the outside, he closed his eyes and squinted. The sun was bright and it hurt his eyes after being in the dark for so long.

"Come Suen." Susan said as she got in the driver's side door.

Nodding his head, he moved around to the back passenger side, before she told him to sit up front. Doing as he was told, he sat silently as the car began to pull off. Taking his eyes off the front, he looked out at the passing scenery. They were going further and further away from Chicago. *Good.* He thought to himself as he relaxed. *I would not like to see those faces of the ones who condemned me. I might kill them.* And he didn't doubt that, if he were to see any of them, he would indeed kill them. He knew he could only hold back for so long.

It was three hours before they finally stopped. Looking at the house, he wasn't surprised that it was rather big. As the front gate was opened, and they drove in, he sat upright in his seat. Finally stopping at the front door, he looked over towards Susan.

"Why are we here?" he asked.

"I have to see someone about financial business." she answered.

He shook his head.

"I should have asked why I am here." he corrected.

"That's simple." she said as she opened her door. "I want to introduce them to my son. It's been a while since I've seen them, and they have been asking me to come and visit for some time now. Now get out and be presentable." she finished in a joking manner.

Opening his door, he got a better look at the house. In his opinion, it was a mansion. The four floors, the enormous perimeter, and the tall white columns before the door were a dead giveaway. As the door opened, he tensed his muscles.

"Ah, Susan!" a fairly older gentleman greeted as he opened the door said. His gray hair was slicked back and his face held the signs of age.

"It's so good of you to come." he paused as he looked down at Suen. "And is this the young lad I've been hearing so much about?" he asked as he went to pet his head.

Side stepping the hand, he moved closer towards Susan. How dare this man assume that he could lay a hand on him. And in a degrading manner no less.

"Don't touch me." he stated calmly.

"Suen," Susan began to scold as she looked down at him. "That was rude."

"He has not earned the right to touch Me." he said evenly. "When he has proven himself, then he may shake my hand. I am no dog to be petted. I am a-"

"Child." she interrupted him. She had a feeling where he was going to go with that. "That is still no excuse to be rude."

"I apologize." he mumbled with his head down. It wasn't his goal to anger her. He simply didn't want anyone besides her touching him.

She placed a hand on his head.

"Just make sure it doesn't happen again." she reminded.

"Yes Ma'am." he nodded, allowing her to pat his head.

"Well," the man said. "He is certainly a ferocious little guy isn't he?" he finished with a smile. Turning on his heel, he began walking into his house. "Come, come. My grandkids are here visiting, so the little one wont be lonely while we discuss business."

He followed the light pressure on his shoulder from Susan, as he walked beside her into the house. The inside was larger than he expected it to be. They followed the man into a room that he took for a study. As the man sat down behind a desk, Susan took the seat in front of him. Walking over to her side, he stood beside her.

"You can have a seat my boy." the man said as he watched Suen.

"I am alright. Thank you for offering though." Suen said softly as he shook his head.

"Well, let's get started." the man said as he reached into his desk and pulled out a gun.

Moving quickly, Suen positioned himself between them both as he threw a wire around the man's neck. Pulling it only tight enough to restrain him, he sneered at the man. She told him they were here to talk to the man, and he was going to shoot her? His mother? Not while he still had a breath in his body.

"Human, you have made a grave error." he hissed as his golden eyes thinned.

"Enough Snake." she ordered from behind him.

He paused. She was ordering a threat to be allowed gratis? It didn't make sense to him. His job was to ensure that she was safe and this human was in the way. Surely she couldn't be serious. But, replaying the tone of voice in the order, he thought better of taking off his head. Easing up on the wire, he allowed it to recede back into the bracelet. Standing fully, he turned towards Susan with a blank expression.

"I saw him as a threat and sought to dispose of him quickly." Suen said coldly.

"He is one of our gun supply men. I will not have you threatening our source of weapons."

"It's quite alright Susan." the man said as he rubbed his neck. Turning towards Suen, "Those were some quick moves and a very impressive weapon. Can I see it?" he asked.

"No." Suen answered quickly.

"Suen." Susan said warningly.

He turned his head towards her and leveled her with a glare.

"I will not allow one who is not of the clan to inspect my weapon." he told her seriously. "I will defend it with my life."

"Well, it's a shame." the man said finally, breaking the tense atmosphere. "But, I think we should be getting to business now."

"Yes." Susan agreed.

Going back to his previous position, he turned slightly as he heard a knock at the door. Turning as it opened, he spotted two boys, who looked to be in their early teens.

"Grandpa, we were going to go to the park with some friends." the first boy said.

"Alright Steven." he responded as he turned towards Suen. "How about you go with them and enjoy yourself while we discuss business?"

Suen looked at him blankly. He didn't want to go with them. His job was to stay at her side as protection, not go out with some kids and play. Besides, he wasn't sure how to play with others. He's never done it before with anyone other than his mother. He's never even thought of playing. It was for children.

"Suen," Susan said, gaining his attention. "Go with them and enjoy yourself."

He looked towards her, about to object, but resigned himself to a nod when he saw her eyes. She honestly wanted him to go and play. Turning back, he kept his head low as he followed the two out the door. Walking down the hallway behind them, he looked towards their backs with a sneer. *I do not wish to be here.* "Kill them and return to her." He could feel his wrist twitch. *I cannot do that.* "Who says? I was never given an order to not kill them." That much was true. He was never given the order to not kill them. As his wrist twitched again, he forced himself to stop. *Silence.* He was brought out of his thoughts as one of them asked him a question.

"Excuse me?" he asked. So immersed with controlling the voice, he wasn't paying attention to the boy.

"I said get in the car. We have to get going, before the rest of the guys leave." Steven said rudely.

"Kill him for his rudeness." Silence you. He thought to himself, even though he was sourly tempted to teach him some manners. His right hand flexed in response.

Following silently, he climbed into the back seat. As they sped off, he was contemplating if he should have put up a bigger argument. Surely this couldn't end well. For who, he didn't know. But he knew he would get the short end of the stick.

As they pulled up to a vacant park, he noticed five others standing around. To him, they looked like the common thugs and lowlifes that he tussled with before he came to the Spirits. Getting out of the car, he kept his head down. He was distantly aware that he was avoiding eye contact.

"Hey Steve, what's with the kid?" one boy asked.

"I was roped into looking after the kid Bobby." Steven answered with boredom.

"Well, let's just ditch the twerp and go hang." a female said to his left.

"Frankie is right Steve. Let's just leave the kid somewhere and pick him up after. Hell, we don't even have to pick him back up." another guy said.

Suen looked up at him as he finished. If they planned on leaving him, then it was fine. He memorized the way here and wouldn't have any problems finding his way back. By his estimation, it would only take him fifteen minutes to reach the mansion if he ran.

"Whoa!" Bobby said as he took a step back. "Those are some freaky looking eyes man."

The others looked closer at him and various looks of shock flashed across their faces, as one had a look of recognition.

"Those are some cool contacts kid." the second guy said.

"Yeah." Steven said as he finally got a look at his face. "I've never seen anything like it before."

"They kind of remind me of the eyes of that kid in your story Francine." Bobby said as he turned to look at her slowly retreating figure.

He kept his eyes on her, because she knew who he was in his past life. That wasn't good.

"Those aren't contacts." she whispered with wide eyes as she shook her head slowly.

"What are you talking about?" Steven asked, turning towards her as well.

"You aren't real." she whispered as she shook her head. "You can't be. You are supposed to be dead."

Turning fully towards her, he slowly began walking towards her.

"You know me." he said softly. "And I know you." he remembered now. "You were with the kids who picked on me as a child." He heard a growl, and he wasn't entirely sure if it was internal or external.

"No." she whispered as she hit a wall. Frantically, she ran her hands across the brick, but found no escape. "You died the day your mother died. Everyone saw it. Your stone is next to hers." she continued to ramble.

Stopping a few feet before her, he looked at her with narrowed eyes.

"I should kill you human." he stated as he flexed his hand and wrist. "You tormented me as a child when I did nothing to deserve It." he could feel his temper boil. The growling intensifying. He could almost feel it vibrating in his bones. *"Kill her. She deserves it for all the things she put me through."* He could feel his muscles tensing, ready for a fight. He was eager and angry. His blood was boiling. *But*— *"How mother had to listen to the taunts and whispers that they all passed as she walked the streets. The names she was called, even by children."* "My mother was a good woman, and you all slandered her name as if she were a whore."

"You are a demon, and she gave birth to you, which means she is a whore." Francine said defiantly.

His eyes flashed as he reached for the hidden ring in the bracelet.

"What did you say?" he asked softly. He was completely ignoring the shocked and slightly scared faces of the others present. They didn't matter. The human in front of him had his sole attention.

"Your father was right." she said, gaining confidence. "You should have never been born. You should have been put down like the animal you are."

His eyes transitioned to vermillion slits as he glared at her figure. The words were eerily similar to his father.

"Human, retract your words, before they are your last." he said hoarsely. He was barley restraining himself. His blood was beyond boiling. It felt like molten lava coursed through his veins. The growling had increased to a loud roar. He tried, although not as hard as he knew he could, to restrain himself and he could feel the feeling regressing.

"Fuck you Demon!" she screamed as she glared at him.

Bowing his head lightly, he chuckled. He released his hold on his impulse and allowed the searing hot blood to course through his veins, into his heart, and throughout his body.

"The words of a dying woman." he whispered with humor. Looking up, he quickly charged her. Jumping up, he gripped her neck with both hands. Loosing her balance, she fell to her knees. Bringing her face closer towards him, he glared at her with hatred. "You Human piece of meat. You are nothing but food. You are undeserving of the tongue you use to speak such hateful and slanderous words." he said as he gripped her cheeks hard, forcing her mouth open. "I don't think you need It." he slowly moved his mouth, into hers, as he kept a firm grip on her neck and cheeks. Grabbing her tongue with his teeth, he readied to pull out as he felt a disturbance in the air. Placing a foot on her stomach, he used her to push off to avoid a tackle. Turning around, he was mildly surprised to see Susan standing up, and helping the girl. What was she doing?

"What are you doing Suen?" she asked as she steadied the girl.

"Move out of the way." he growled as he tensed his muscles. His sole conscious thought was of ripping out that simple girls tongue.

She looked at him once, and the moment she saw his eyes, she knew she wasn't going to get to him this way. Settling herself in a fighting stance, she invited him.

"This does not involve you woman." he growled in aggravation. He was restraining himself, with the last of his will, to keep from attacking her. "Get out of the way, before I force my way through you."

"Then come." she offered.

He felt his resolve waver at her challenge. As his eyes settled on her person, he felt himself lost to the rage. He could see everything from a third person's point of view. He wasn't even sure if he could stop it now. Growling aloud, he charged her. As he went for a punch to her stomach, she sidestepped and kicked him in the back. Falling forward, he rolled, only to spring up and slide a few more feet on the hard soil. Standing fully, he slowly walked towards her, both hands open to claw. Getting within reach, he swiped one hand towards her hip. As she dodged to her right, his left leg came to kick her rib. Grabbing his leg, she swung him around, before letting him fly. Turning in mid air, he landed on hands and knees in a crouch. Growling one last time, he stood and dusted off his clothes, before folding his arms across his chest and turning his head.

"Fine." he growled. "She lives. For now anyway." he finished in a sneer as his eyes faded to gold. Sighing, he looked back at Susan, who was walking towards him. Lowering his gaze, he avoided eye contact. *"I should have killed her."* He pushed the voice out. *No. She is not to be harmed under my watch.* It whispered through his defenses. *"I could have cut her head clean off with my wire."* *Silence you. You know I will not allow that.*

"Suen?" she asked as she looked down at him.

"Let's go home." he said softly as he headed towards the car. He didn't look behind himself to know that she was behind him. He felt himself at odds with himself. The first edict of Noir was to serve a just master. He attacked his.

XXX

The car ride back to base was long and silent. Susan looked about to say something, but at the last minute decided against it, and Suen looked cold as usual. The silence that would have put anyone else on edge seemed to settle around him in a comfortable blanket. As they entered the base, and to their room, Susan stopped at the stairs as Suen stopped a few steps ahead of her.

"What was that all about?" she asked.

"Nothing." he said calmly. He didn't want to talk about what was going through his mind. Nor did he wish to discuss why he was so easily irritated. Walking towards the bed, he began taking off his clothes. "She simply said some things that she shouldn't have. That's all." he finished as he climbed into bed and succumbed to exhaustion and allowed his eyes to rest.

When he opened his eyes, he was no longer in the room he shared with Susan. He recognized the room instantly for what it was. He could never forget the room. He died in this room. He looked around himself, and was greeted with the dim light of the moon cascading into his room. This was the first time that he ever had a dream that involved his room. Turning his attention back towards his front, he noticed his father standing in the doorway. This was also the first time that he has ever seen his father in his dream completely. Normally, he was only a pair of eyes in the dark. But now, he had his entire body. Well, most of his body. His eyes were still missing, but he could tell that he was glaring at him. And his arm was still missing a hand. As a child he was unnerved by his eyes. Now, he was simply irked that he wouldn't say anything.

"Hello *son*." Marcus greeted with a twisted smile as he looked down at Sera. How he knew he was looking down at him, he wasn't completely sure, because a blind man couldn't possibly see, but he could feel his stare through those empty sockets. See his nonexistent eyes on his person, judging him with bias.

"You are dead." Sera said softly. He could feel something trying to push through the surface of his emotional barrier, but he ignored it.

His father shook his head as he chuckled.

"Silly demon, you cannot kill a worker of god."

He bristled at the title that has been with him since birth. If his mother never called him by his name, he would have thought that he was really named Demon.

"My name is Sera, and you are no worker of God *father*." Sera sneered. "I will show you the true implements of his work." reaching for his wrist, he paused as he couldn't feel his bracelet. This was his dream. He controlled it. Why wouldn't his bracelet be here?

"Don't be foolish." his father chastised. How he hated the way his father talked down to him. As if he was nothing more than an insect. "Your foolish string will not help you here. Now you are mine." he finished as he lunged at him. As he wrapped his hand around his neck, he smiled sinisterly. It was the same smile he was the night that he killed him. "You see? You are supposed to die by my hands. And now you will, now that that meddlesome woman is out of the way."

Glaring hatefully at him, "You are mistaken father." he growled as he reached his hands around his father's neck. The pressure pushed through the barrier. "My mother was a wonderful person and you do not deserve to speak of her in any context. I killed you once, and I will do it again!" he growled as his grip increased. How dare he call her meddlesome!

He smiled amused at his attempts as his breathing was cut off.

"You can try son," he spoke as if he wasn't having the life choked out of him by angry hands. "But you can never kill me."

"You bastard!" Sera shouted, as he forced himself on top of his father. "You are dead!"

"No, you can never kill me."

"You Human lump of meat!" he howled as he added more pressure.

"Suen!" Susan yelled as she looked up at him in shock as her hands grip at his wrists.

"You will die Human!" he shouted, as he gripped his father's neck harder. "La vie est Ember. L à mou est Enfer. Enfer est le Ciel. Permettez-moi de vous accompagner au paradis et vous soulager du purgatoire[6]. I will ensure that the Goddess knows of your transgressions."

"Suen, stop this!" she pleaded as she listened to him speak in a different language. She moved one hand behind her pillow. "Please!" she insisted.

---

[6] Life is Hell. Love is Hell. Hell is Heaven. Allow me to be your escort to paradise and relieve you from this purgatory.

"Die!" he hissed as he prepared his hands to snap his father's neck. If he could kill the man in the real world, then he could kill him in a dream. He yelped aloud as he felt a painful shock course through his body. He jumped off his father's body as he curled into himself.

"Suen!" Susan said as she got out of bed and ran to his side.

"I will kill you father!" he growled through his teeth as his body shivered. "I don't know how you did this, but I will kill you!"

"Suen! It's me! Susan!" she screamed to his crawling figure.

"I am the burning one that will take you to Hells fire." he whispered hoarsely as he fell flat on the floor. "I swear I will take you with Me." he said softly as his eyes faded to gold. Breathing heavily, he slowly began sitting up on his knees. He didn't know how he got on the floor, but he assumed it was from tossing in his dream. He could still feel the lingering of the rage that filled him in his dream. It was a tingling sensation in the back of his mind. Looking up, he spotted Susan with a concerned look on her face and something in her hand. "Mistress?" he questioned groggily as he wiped the sweat from his forehead.

Walking quickly, she dropped to her knees and pulled him into an embrace, placing his head between her breasts.

"Suen." she whispered as she planted her head in his hair.

He could feel her distress, and slight fear, as she held him close. Something was bothering her and he could feel it. And it bothered him that he could. *Mother . . .*

"Mamma?" he questioned in a soft voice. "What's wrong?" he slid his arms behind her and gripped her shirt tightly. "Mamma, you're scaring me."

"Shh." she cooed as she began rocking. "It's okay Sera. Everything is going to be okay. Nothing's going to hurt you anymore, I promise."

"Mamma?" he whispered, as he looked up towards her face. He stopped at the small bruises on her neck. "Did Father touch you?"

"You were just having a bad dream, that's all." she assured as she shook her head. "It's over now."

He stilled at her words. She has bruises on her neck in the shape of small hands. In his dream, he was strangling his father. His hands gripped her clothes tighter.

"I did it." he said softly.

"No, you were having a bad dream."

"Yes, a bad dream." The tingling returned. *Silence.* It subsided.

He shook his head, as he buried his head further into her.

"I was not asleep." he began. "At least, not completely." He was still unsure about how he knew this. But he *knew* he wasn't completely asleep. "A part of me was trying to kill you just now." he was tempted to lie about it and let her think of it as a simple dream, but he couldn't risk her dying any time soon.

"What do you mean?" she asked as she looked down at him.

He didn't want to tell her about the voice, he's been hearing more frequently as of late, but it seems that fate has other plans. *Either that, or Goddess is really trying to test me.* He thought bitterly to himself.

"Ever since the time I was training with the dogs, I've been hearing a voice." he began.

"A voice?" she asked as she looked at him.

He nodded his head.

"I've heard it before then, but it was not as often as it is now. It normally only made itself known on October tenth."

"What's so special about today?" to her it didn't sound like anything important happened on this day.

"It's my birthday." he answered softly. Blood flashed before his eyes, before it was gone just as quickly as it came. Like a mirage in the desert it dissipated.

"That's wonderful!" she said happily as she hugged him again.

"And my parents death." he finished, voice filled with grief.

She immediately stopped smiling and looked down at his face. It was so vacant, that she felt herself shiver despite their close bodies.

"Each year, the voice gets louder and louder. What it says, are things I would rather not do. I find myself increasingly more agitated and angry with each passing year. What my grandfather has predicted has begun to pass." he finished in a tone that could only mean a revelation.

"My poor child." she cooed as she began rocking again. "I'll help you get through this."

He released her shirt and began to stand.

"No." he said lowly, shaking his head. His words were distant and vacant, as if talking to the wind and hoping it would give him solace.

"You can't help me, but I know someone who can." turning on his heel, he began walking towards the stairs with purpose.

"Wait!" Susan said standing. "Where are you going?"

"I need to do something. Something that only one man can help me with." he replied with his back turned. He still remembered the way back into the city. "I promise I will return. And when I do, perhaps," he hesitated on his words. It's been so long. "Perhaps we can do something together."

She nodded her head.

"I would like that very much, Sera."

He turned slightly at the name.

"How do you know my name?" he asked. He never told her and it bothered him slightly that he didn't mind her calling him by it.

"You said it in your dream." she pointed out. "It's a nice name."

He turned back around and nodded his head.

"I'll be leaving now." he whispered as he ascended the stairs. He had a long walk ahead of him and a lot of time to think.

Everything that he has been trying to prevent, everything that his grandfather has taught him, was starting to go to waste. He could feel his defenses crumbling.

Becoming afraid gives memories form. The forms they take are specters of your heart.

Chapter 8

Acceptance and Dominion

> *Emotions are what make Humans Human. The lack of them makes them something else. You cannot force yourself to become what you are not. You must accept yourself as you are or suffer being pulled apart from the inside out.*

Walking back to his grandfather's church took him longer than he first expected. The streets of Chicago were the same as the day that he left. As he looked around the dark street, he released a sigh he didn't know he was holding. He didn't want to run into anyone that would recognize him. One person who wasn't even there anymore was more than enough. Reaching towards his neck, he felt a growl in his throat. Around his neck was a solid black leather choker. He knew he couldn't get it off, because he felt a metal hole in the back, which was most likely for a key. He wasn't happy about finding out that she now had a literal leash on him, but there was nothing he could do. After the display he put on when they were out on their little trip, he wasn't that surprised. After all, he did attack her and then threaten her life twice. She needed a sure way to keep him in line. Because if and when a third time comes, he wasn't sure he would stop. *And what better way than to lock my muscles when I step out of line?* He could feel the tingle in the back of his mind again. "She tags me like a dog! She deserves to be killed for this insult." She will *not.* He pushed it back, but was met with resistance. *"She deserves it!"* it persisted. *Silence.* He separated himself from the voice. *"You can not keep doing that."* It whispered beyond the barrier. *Silence!* He squeezed his eyes shut as he gripped the pendant around his neck. He was happy that she didn't take it from him while he was training. She must have figured it was nothing that would interfere with his training and left it and the bracelet alone. Finally calming down, he looked at the church and sprinted across the street.

Walking up to the door, he knocked three times.

"Coming." Matt said from behind the door. As he opened it, "Seraphim! Where have you been young one? I have been worried sick about you." he fussed.

"What you have warned me about." Sera said softly as he looked up towards his grandfather. His eyes flashed once. "It's happening."

Matt looked at him wide eyed for a moment, before ushering him inside. Looking both ways, to ensure that no one has seen him enter, he closed the door. Taking him by the hand, he quickly began walking into the back room. Letting his hand go, he turned back towards the door and locked it. Sitting down across from Sera, he sighed.

"I must honestly say, I never thought this would happen so soon." Matt began as he looked at Sera's disheveled features. For the child to come to him in this manner, after thinking him dead for half a year, something must have happened. "Something big must have happened for it to have progressed so far, so fast. Tell me, what you have been doing ever since you left here two years ago."

"After I left here to visit my mother's grave, I saw my father." he began. "I killed him with the wire you gave me."

Matt nodded his head.

"I knew as much, when they said the cuts were not made by a blade. But, why did you kill him?"

"He killed mamma." he stated in a growl as his eyes shifted once. He reigned in his temper and relaxed. "After, I decided to live on the streets full time. I stole to eat, and whenever I was approached by another who wished to harm me, I beat them into submission. A year and a half later, I was found and adopted. She took me back to her house, where she locked me away in a cage with nothing more than what I had on my body and a dog as company, for two months. After which, I was taught hand to hand for a month, before being forced to fight for my food with wild dogs for a month. After which, I had to do marksman training for my food and I had to learn how to use a sword in two months. When I finished my training, I was issued my first mission. I killed twenty men at close range." he finished as his body twitched.

"I'm assuming that the collar around your neck is from her, correct?" Matt asked.

His eyes shifted to red as he was reminded of his restriction.

"That woman is going to die." he hissed as he reached for his neck. His voice was clipped and sharp as a razors edge. "She deserves it for putting this confounded contraption around my neck."

"First things first." Matt said seriously as he glared at him. "You will watch how you speak to your elders. Have you forgotten the edicts and morals that I have taught you?"

As his eyes shifted back, "No grandfather, I have not forgotten." he said softly. In his lapse of control, he lashed out at his grandfather. He didn't want that. "But, it has been happening more and more frequently, these lapses in control. They all are tied with the day of her death."

"Son, I'm sorry to tell you this, but I cannot help you with this problem." he said mournfully.

"What do you mean?" Sera asked. He walked for over two weeks to get his help, and now he is saying that he can't help him. He could feel his heart rate increase, but he wasn't worried about that. He was more concerned about what this could imply.

"I mean, it's another test." he answered simply. "Another test from the goddess." he paused as he leaned back in his chair. "You know, I find it rather ironic that you and I have both found our life partners by serving them."

"She is not my life partner." Sera stated calmly. He didn't know where his grandfather got the asinine idea that she was his life partner. Maybe his old age was starting to get to him. Former Noir or not, one couldn't escape the ravages of 'old age'. "She is my new mother, and Mistress."

"And that's how it started out for me as well child." Matt assured. "But, one day, she is going to approach you and you are not going to be able to say no to her. I'm sure she is beautiful, smart, kind, ruthless, and strong."

"She is." he nodded his head. Those were some of the traits that he admired and respected of hers. In so many ways she was just like his mother.

"You see? Already, you are smitten with her; you just don't know it yet. Either that, or you won't recognize it as thus."

"Grandfather, this is not why I came here." Sera said as he shook his head. It must be old age, because his grandfather was so easily sidetracked. He needed an answer. "How am I to get this other side of me in control?"

"You go back to the one who holds the key. Only they can help you lock away the fury. And only they can unleash it." Matt said cryptically.

Sera stood and nodded his head. He knew that he wouldn't get a straight forward answer. He never got a straight answer from the man. Always riddles and weird proverbs to explain important messages. He got the general message that his grandfather wanted to impart. Walking out the door, he began his long trek back to the place he called home. After all, she was like his mother. And if she was like her, then she would undoubtedly be worried sick at this point.

Coming towards the huge gate, he felt nostalgia as the gates opened up to him. They reminded him of the gates he saw when he was three. He pushed them aside and began walking towards the door of the church. At first, he found it rather coincidental that the two places he knew as home were churches. A church was Gods house and his angels the servants. He was named after an angel, so it was only right that he was to live here. As he got closer towards the doors, he noticed Susan standing in the doorway. He would have questioned how she knew he was coming, but it didn't really matter. She seemed to have a sixth sense when it involved him. Walking towards her, he collapsed a few feet before her. He neglected eating in order to cut his trip down to only a few days in order to make it back as quickly as possible. He never did want to worry his mother. She already had so much to worry about. As he hit the ground, he was barely able to see her rushing to his side and placing his head in her lap.

"Mistress." he rasped as he tried to sit up, only to fall back onto her lap.

"Shh. You shouldn't talk." she said as she picked him up bridal. "You're so thin!" she gasped as she began walking towards the doors. "When was the last time you ate anything?"

"Nine days ago." he answered weakly. The only thing he was sure to continue doing was drinking. The body could survive for two weeks without food. But, without water, you could die of starvation in only three, four days tops.

"I could have dropped you off . . ." she began, but he couldn't keep his eyes open long enough to catch the end of her sentence as he drifted off into unconsciousness. He also neglected sleep. Only allowed an hour of rest a day.

XXX

Waking up to a beeping noise, he blearily looked around the room. He didn't know how long he's been out, but it felt like he's been out for years. All he heard was a constant growling in darkness. He looked all around himself, but he couldn't see where it was coming from. He felt that it was the voice, but he couldn't locate it. Looking around now, he noticed he was in an all white room with tubes connected to him. The beeping increased as he ripped the tubes from his skin and threw his legs over the edge of the bed. The resulting flat line only reminded him of what he already knew. Standing, he quickly realized that he was out longer than he thought. Falling to his hands and knees, he gasped. For his muscles to be so weak, he had to have been out for more than 7 days. If he wanted to get out of this room, he had to get his legs to work again. He sent a mental command to his legs to stand. It took longer than he planned, but he got them under his control after thirty minutes of trying. The mind was a very powerful thing. Taking a moment to regain his footing, he stood fully. Walking towards the door, he slipped behind it as it opened. Taking the wire from his wrist, he readied to throw it around the persons neck.

"Sera?" Susan said as she entered the room. As she noticed the empty bed, "Where is he?" she asked herself.

Stepping out from behind her, he stood at her side as he released the wire.

"Mistress." he greeted calmly.

"Sera!" she yelped in surprise as she turned around. "Don't do that."

"I wish to go to our room." he said softly as he gripped her hand. "I do not wish to spend any more time here."

"Of course." Susan agreed as she ushered him out of the room.

After taking him downstairs, she settled him into bed. He didn't think they had a hospital in here, but then again, he hasn't been around the place yet, despite his time being there.

"I rather dislike hospitals." he confided as he looked at her.

"I can understand that." she said as she took a seat beside him. "I don't really like them that much either."

"They remind me of my death."

She shifted slightly, so she could lean over him while petting his hair.

"You were malnourished when you came back. Your muscles were exhausted and your mind was in no better shape. You were out for more than a week. We had to put you on a feeder, so you wouldn't waste away anymore." she leaned down and placed her forehead against his. "You scared me for a second." she confided. "I thought I would lose you."

He could feel warmth worming its way through his body, starting in his chest and spreading outward. She was honestly worried about him.

"I will not die from simple lack of food." he pointed out as he pushed the feeling back and out of his mind. He couldn't allow the warmth control. "I have gone longer without."

"That doesn't mean that I should not be worried about my son dying on me, now does it?" she asked as she gave him a smile.

"No." he whispered, entranced by her smile. It was similar to his mothers, but stronger. He wasn't sure how it was even possible. "But, I do have news." he began, as he remembered his reason for traveling in the first place.

"Really?" she asked as she sat up. "Did he help you?"

"In a way, yes." he nodded his head. "But, he couldn't do anything for me."

"I'm sorry to hear that." she said as she placed a hand on his shoulder.

He moved a hand to grip the one on his shoulder as he looked at her with a small smile.

"But, you can." he finished.

"Me?"

He nodded his head.

"Only the one who holds the key can lock the rage away. And only they can release It." he repeated the words of his grandfather. "You had me collared." he began as his fingers traced the leather binding. The growl that persisted in the depths of his mind was ignored.

"I wish there was another way, but I couldn't risk you going off on every person we met." she said with remorse.

He shook his head. It wasn't his goal to guilt her and condemn her for her actions.

"You hold the key." He confided. "Only you can help me cage it away. You are my Mistress, my owner. It is your job to train me," he paused on his next words. His mind was in shambles and he knew it. And his body was at a point where he knew most would have died already. But, this needed to be said. "And break me."

"Break you?" she repeated.

"Yes. Only you can do it." he confirmed.

"Why me?"

"Because, it was meant to be." he answered cryptically. During his walk back, he had plenty of time to think. Think about how he was going to get back. How long it was going to take. Whether or not she would be worried about him. How everything happens for a reason. How life was not normal. He knew more about the human psyche than any other being in existence. *Sin is Human. Human is Sin.* He could kill without remorse. *Something like that should not be possible. I should feel a twinge of guilt.* Feelings could and would be repressed. *At my age, it shouldn't be possible. I shouldn't know what emotions I feel.* He was beaten and starved into becoming stronger. *I should have died from starvation. I should have died from the hits. But, instead I grew stronger.* Saved from a life alone by a woman offering to become the one thing he missed most. *I loved her dearly.* He beat the street thugs that were trying to take his food. *They were humans trying to bully me because I couldn't hide behind my mother anymore. Such foolish thinking they have.* He killed his father. *He was a despicable human being and was deserving of his death.* He was tortured and driven to the brink of insanity by his grandfather. *I went for the truth, but didn't expect to learn the truth. The truth about myself.* His mother was murdered. *It was my fault that she died. My fault that she was so willing to give her life for me. My fault for being so weak that I couldn't protect myself and constantly hid behind her.* He could read and comprehend by five. *She read to me every day for hours until I knew the dictionary and definitions by heart.* He was killed at three. *And was never revived. I saw what awaited me on the other side. Cold, empty, hallow darkness behind rusted gates, only eclipsed by burning red eyes staring at me longingly. Morning Star*[7]. He could talk at one and a half. *She urged me to speak. She wouldn't accept any gestures from me. Only words would satisfy her. And I would do anything to satisfy her.* He could walk at nine months and run at twelve. *She would guide me up and allow me to walk. When I fell, she would not pick me up. I had to learn to do it on my own.* He heard and saw his father's rage at three minutes. *Even when I was a new born he hated me. Despised me.* He saw his mothers face for the first time at one minute old. *A Goddess that gave birth to me.* He was born with golden eyes of a fiery serpent. *And my sorrow was my blood.* He was reincarnated nine months prior. *Valkyrie.* He was not normal. *I am not Human.* "You must chain the beast to your will." *You must control me completely.*

"Suen." she began seriously. "What you are asking of me is dangerous. If I am to continue, then there is a chance that you will die."

That was something he wasn't afraid of. He's died twice before.

"I know."

"Very well." she said calmly. Standing, she walked over towards the candles and began to blow them out. "But, I want you to have a good night sleep. I still have many things to teach you."

He nodded his head as she began walking over towards the bed. Turning, he buried his head in her chest and sighed. He wasn't truly

---

[7] a planet, especially Venus, seen in the eastern sky around dawn. Another name for Lucifer, meaning light bringer.

looking forward to the trials she was going to set forth to break him, but he wouldn't turn away. Noir never backs down, for it is a sigh of vulnerability. Noir never quits, for it is a sign of weakness. A Noir never shows fear, for it is a sign of Humanity. *Noir never shows fear.* He said to himself as he felt his eyes becoming heavy. A distant whisper assaulted his ears, before he lost consciousness. *"I stopped being human the moment I was born."*

Once you accept what you are, you need control. For without control, one is no more than a simple beast.

Chapter 9

Restraint

Some things cannot be controlled. Some things require a lock and key. Knowing how to free it becomes harder the longer one waits. At times, one needs help to learn restraint.

Standing before her, Suen tilted his head and allowed the dim candle light to display the raised letters that spelled '*Release*' across the collar. During his year and a half of working with her, he's grown accustomed to her calling on him to handle mundane things around the base and missions that were only a few miles away. He recalled her teaching him about the different cities and how to act towards certain people when in their company. Simple educate stuff.

"Suen," she began, in what he knew as her mistress tone of voice. She would occasionally alternate between them depending on the circumstances. "I have to go to a meeting with a local mob, and I want you to accompany me."

He nodded his head.

"Yes Mistress."

"And while we are there, I don't want you to go off on them like you did the first time I took you to an associate."

"I saw him as a threat and sought to eliminate him." He reminded. He wasn't going to apologize for something he knew to be the right course of action.

"I told you he was not an enemy." she stated.

He growled in his throat.

"I told you of my reasons." he said. He could feel his temper rising at her accusation. The tingling in his head returned.

"And you know them to be wrong."

"Listen." he began as his eyes shifted once. The simple tingle turned into a full blown seizer within his mind. "The Human was posing a threat."

"You will listen to me." she said as she stood.

His temper was already at its limit because he was reminded of how old he was. He didn't want to deal with this. And the order he was given was the last straw.

"Human, you will lower your t-" he cut himself off as he felt himself compelled to collapse onto his knees, grinding his teeth. He momentarily forgot the collar around his neck in his rage. It's been a year since she shocked him last. He lost sight for a moment as he felt the shock hit him. Regaining his sight, he looked around. He was no longer in the meeting chamber.

XXX

The room he was in was dark. He's never seen this place before. Deciding to stop standing still, he began walking. A rolling stone gathers no moss. His ears perked up when he heard the sound of a growl. *That has to be the voice.* He thought to himself. Following it, he came to a cage. It was taller than anything he has ever seen before, reaching into the darkness of the sky. Even larger than 'The Gate'. The bars were a dark bronze in color and seemed to have rusted over with time. Walking closer, he could see a small opening in the gate, where it looked like something broke out. Peering into the darkness, he could see a pair of ruby red eyes staring back at his gold. The growling intensified as he found himself drawn towards the bars. In an instant, he found himself eye to eye with a shadowy figure behind the gate. He couldn't move as he felt a small hand, no bigger than his own, cup his cheek.

"So beautiful." the voice growled as it ran a thumb across his cheek. The voice was gruff, but held a distinct carnal edge. The way it flowed from the darkness and streamed over him, made his body heat rise.

Who are you? Suen asked as he felt his body become lax under the attention. It felt sinfully wonderful.

The voice chuckled lightly as it closed its eyes.

"*Silly little Sera.*" it chortled. "*I am you darling.*"

You can't be me. He replied, almost in a trance. His mother called him that. *I am me. There is no other.*

"*Oh, but you are wrong.*" it stated as it drew him in closer towards the gate. He was distantly aware of another arm wrapping around his waist. The feeling of this, thing, holding him was very calming. As if it was always there holding him in this manner. "*I am indeed you. Another side of you, but you none the less.*"

Are you the one who has been speaking with me? Suen asked as he tried to move his cheek away from the offending hand, only to have it grip his chin lightly.

"*Yes, I am. I am only trying to give you what you want.*" It whispered seductively as he felt its lips graze his own.

But, I don't want to kill needlessly. He argued weakly. The conviction that he knew should have been in his voice was vacant. Warm breath ghosting his lips made his quiver. He was feeling warm.

"*That's what you truly believe, isn't it?*" the voice asked rhetorically. The silence between them stretched on for what seemed like hours. The figure didn't remove its hand, or its arm that was still around his waist. It seemed it was perfectly comfortable with the position they were in. "*What are the edicts of Noir?*" it asked suddenly.

Noir never hesitates. Noir shows no fear. Noir never questions orders. Noir serves their master faithfully until death. When in the face of death, hold head high, so the grim reaper will know of your courage. He recited on reflex. He stiffened slightly, but relaxed as he felt its lips touch his gently. They were the scorching heat to his ice.

"*Very good.*" it purred as it backed away slightly. A pleased look in its red eyes. "*Noir is an instrument of God. Meant to kill indiscriminately. Meant to rid the world of sins. This entire world is covered by the sinful creatures called Humans,*" the word was forced out with what he could see of a sneer. "*And you are compelled to kill them.*"

But, mamma was a human. He argued with a shake of his head. He felt something soft and slightly fuzzy flick beneath his chin, before forcing it up.

"Yes, she was. The only pure human on this disgusting planet." the voice agreed. *"But, the humans took her away, because of their fear. Their fear of us. Humans are the cause of all our pain, why shouldn't we rid ourselves of their punishment?"*

"You will listen to me." she growled as she stood over his convulsing figure. Her words drifting into the back of his mind. "I am your Mistress. I am your owner. Suen I will not have you constantly undermining my orders. You have to restrain yourself. You have to get this other side under control."

They are all nothing more than cattle. Suen whispered as his eyes became half lidded. Its words were so sure. He melted as it kissed him fully on the lips. He was overwhelmed with the passion behind it. So much so, that he found himself holding onto its arms to keep upright. He didn't know when he made it to the floor, or when the voice came out of the cage, but he knew it was now on top of him. And the fact that he was at its mercy was not president. Only the feeling that it was giving him.

"Yes." it hissed as it broke the kiss. Finally getting a look at it, he realized it was another version of him, only with red eyes and a tail, which seemed to wag with excitement. *"They are nothing more than a source of food. You said so yourself, that they were the cows and you were the pest, harassing them."* he leaned down and nibbled on Suen's neck. He felt himself tilt his head a little to allow more access. *"So, why are you listening to a human that not only lied to you, but has beaten you repeatedly? She is just going to use you and then dispose of you."* he licked his neck to his chin, as he allowed his tongue to slide over Suen's lips. *"Stay with me, and I will ensure that that doesn't happen. Let me kill her."*

"Human, I am in control." he growled.

"No you are not!" she shouted as she pressed the button again. "Get a hold of yourself Sera!"

Suen heard her yelling echo in his mind. His eyes snapped open, glaze gone, glaring at his copy. His name acting as a key to opening a door, long lost and forgotten.

Get off of me. He stated softly.

"I don't think so." his red eyed copy grinned. It was of the cat that caught the canary variety, and he had no delusions about which one he

was. Or which one the other 'him' thought him to be. *"I don't think you want me too."*

I said get off me. He repeated as he pushed him off slowly. Standing upright, he regarded his twin. *I am Noir. I am bound to obey my Master(s). And she is not only my master. She is also my mother. I will not allow any harm to come to her.*

"How can you-"

Silence. He interrupted in a cold tone. *She is as genuine in her affections towards me as mamma was. She only treated me like that, because it was for training. She has already begun to regret her actions. She doesn't deserve to be grouped with the other humans.*

"But you swore to kill her." He said in a cocky tone, as he smirked at the glaring Suen. *"And you and I both know that you can never break an oath."*

Suen nodded his head. He remembered the oath he swore the instant she imprisoned him in the cage.

And I will. He confirmed with a nod of his head. At that instant, his copy's hands were bound behind his back by an unseen force. The water rippled and tossed. *But it will be when I have decided.* The copy's upper body was bound by leather straps. *Not when the impulse decides it.* The water settled.

"Fine." he relented with a twitch of his tail. He sounded of a petulant child that couldn't get his way. And for some reason, despite the rather attractive, yet dangerous visage, it suited him. *"I only ask that something be done about this. You should know that these bindings won't be able to hold me forever. I will require an offering. It's only a matter of time before the past comes back and when that happens . . ."* he trailed off as his smile grew to a predatory grin; a look that seemed more at home than the irritated glare earlier. *"Although, I must admit, she is a rather strong woman. Strong indeed."* he finished in a growl.

Suen quirked an eyebrow at the comment, but didn't say anything. The past events were beginning to catch up to him and he was relieved that they were. His vision began to fade to black as heard another whisper. *"It's about time you shut him up. I was really beginning to worry about her well being."* turning his head, he spotted a gray area that he didn't notice before. Standing in the center was a white figure; he could only guess was another version of himself. *"Fox was dangerously close to getting us killed. You can only walk the line so long before you step over."* And who are you? He found himself asking calmly. After being seduced by another version of himself, and not becoming disgusted with the action, he found this other to be quiet pleasant. *"Let's just say that I'm a different you."* the white one whispered as his vision faded back to the missions' room.

He found himself breathing heavily on the floor in the fetal position with his head in Susan's lap. Looking up at her face, he offered her a small smile. It was thanks to her that he was able to snap out of the trance. If she hadn't of yelled his true name, he would have submitted.

"Fox is locked away." he whispered.

She hugged him close to herself as she kissed his forehead.

"I was worried you were dead." she said hoarsely, as a few tears escaped her eyes.

"Your heart stopped beating after the second shock."

"You did it, but there is one stipulation." he paused, a little uncertain as to what she would say to his suggestion.

"What is it?" she asked.

"If I don't find a way to release the feelings I have inside, then I will revert."

"And what do you propose?"

His eyes transitioned to crimson as he shot her a grin.

"I require sacrifices." he answered lowly. He was vacantly aware that it sounded dry and underused. Nothing like it did in his mind. "My master." he finished in a seductive growl.

"I believe something can be arranged." she agreed.

"Good." he said as his vermillion orbs continued to stare at her in hunger. "Because, I am famished and in need of nourishment." he slowly turned in her grasp and leaned up to her face. It was more beautiful now. Riddled with fear. "Will you feed me now?" he asked huskily as he grazed his lips across her cheek to her ear. "Will you sacrifice yourself to sate my thirst?" his lips kissed her ear lightly, and he smirked at the shiver that ran through her body. He had to restrain himself from biting. "My insatiable, voracious thirst."

"Fox I presume?" she stated with a slight tremble.

"At your service *my* master." he replied flirtatiously.

"How do I get Sera back?" she asked.

He chuckled lightly, with a shake of his head.

"That cold hearted snake is simply sitting back and watching the show, because he has given me full, well almost, full reign until I have been sated. But, there are two words you should know and never forget." he began. "Release and Seal, for that is the purpose of a key, correct?"

"Seal." she said.

He clicked his tongue in a not amused fashion as his eyes gave her a glare that would have frightened any lesser person to a trembling, blubbering lump of flesh.

"I'm sorry, but until I have been fed, there will be no locking me away. I have been dying to get a drink ever since my first mission." standing fully, he gripped the fox mask that rest on his hip and pulled it free. Placing it on, he tilted his head slightly. "So, what poor souls do you wish to be offered master?" he asked softly through the mask.

Dusting herself off, she stood and walked over towards her chair, where she kept files waiting on the arm rest. Leafing through a few, she walked back with one.

"There is a small meth lab in southern Illinois. I want you to kill every single one." she ordered.

Gripping the file, he turned for the door, before stopping at the handle.

"Where are the swords you and I practiced with when I first arrived?" he asked idly.

"They are in the same place we practiced, why?" she asked.

"Snake wanted to ensure that I enjoy this." he answered as he opened the door.

Susan walked back to her chair and slumped as she sat. His red eyes were extremely unsettling, and the way he talked made her think he was talking about killing her to ease his pain. She shivered at the thought.

"A fox and a snake." she mused silently. "An odd combination. One is the supposed prey and the other the hunter. The Yin and Yang. Good and Evil, but I wonder which one is which . . ."

But, be careful of the one who knows how to restrain you. For they may wish for total control.

Operation: Cover

"We should get you in school soon." Susan said as she watched him read, yet another book. "Soon you will have to go."

"No." he answered, eyes still on the page. "I will not go to school."

"Why not?" she asked, quirking an eyebrow at his insistence.

"At least not yet." he continued, as if he hadn't heard her. "The people will still remember me from last year. I can't risk them recognizing me. I need to wait until they have forgotten about Me." *they no doubt will still be wondering what happened to the 'Demon brat'. I'm sure they are wondering what happened after my father's death.*

"Alright then." Susan conceded, knowing when he wasn't going to budge. "I guess I can home school you for a while-"

"Fourteen." he interrupted, turning a page.

She raised an eyebrow at his statement.

"Fourteen?" she asked.

"Yes."

"Why at fourteen? I'm sure you are smart enough to only need two years of schooling and you'll be on, if not above their level."

He folded the page he was on and looked up at her. She wouldn't know what happened to his father or his mother while he was still there. She knew nothing about what, or how he lived before she found him on the streets.

"I am currently above their level." he answered in a monotone. "I am positive that I am, at least, at an eleventh grade level at this point in my studies. My education level is not why I wish to wait until I am fourteen to enter school. When I start, I would much rather be a ghost to everyone that I encounter. If anyone notices me and recognizes me, then my position here will be compromised. When you found me, there were plenty of people that knew of me and saw you leave with me in tow. If I were to simply show up again, so soon, then they would no doubt put two and two together and know that you are here. If what you have told me is of any value, then many people that you would rather not know of your location, will know that you are still here in Chicago. They will then come for me, in an attempt to get at you. This is not acceptable. When I reach the age of thirteen, puberty will have begun to kick in and I would have changed dramatically from the time I was eight. When I do finally go to high school, it will have to be a place where I can stay on campus. Doing missions for you will be easier from there, because I will already be on the outside. There will be no need for me to bring them back here. As for your spot for me in your actual business, I will simply pose as a go to guy. I will be your eyes and ears during meetings and anything else that doesn't require your immediate attention."

Throughout his explanation, she didn't speak. Her mind was replaying, and analyzing his words. He spoke the truth. If her enemies got wind of her with a child, then they would undoubtedly use him against her. Not that she was worried about him defending himself. But in defending himself, he will reveal his true identity. This would be worse. She didn't want to reveal him unless the situation was in need of dire attention. After taking his advice on a few problems and having them turn up in their favor, she knew to take his word for it.

"Alright." she said after a moment. "You can continue to stay and continue your studies while here. In three years time though, you are to attend school. I want you to be the best of the best while there. Create a profile that will only show that you are an exemplary student."

He nodded his head, before returning to his book. He would have done as much anyway, even if she hadn't told him to. Having a profile like that would make it even harder for anyone to believe that he was a killer in disguise or even a trouble maker. They would only believe that he was an ordinary student who was gifted and worked for a security firm. But, now there were two things on his mind. One, he needed to get another book, because he was finished with the one he had. And two, he needed 'His' books. He put it out of mind for the moment. He could always tell Susan of the books later.

Chapter 10

Information

Curiosity killed the cat. But, it wasn't the searching that killed it. It was suicide from not being able to come to grips with the knowledge it acquired.

Sitting in a lotus position, Suen kept his eyes closed. He's been trying to understand his mind better, so he wouldn't break like so many others he's read about, in the Clan and outside. He didn't want that to happen to himself. His grandfather told him that once he was able to restrain the part of him that wanted to do nothing but kill, he was to meditate in order to calm himself and control himself. The cool breeze that swept through the clearing ruffled the blades of grass and tossed his hair slightly as if encouraging him in his task. Other than the wind, no other creature or element, attempted to impede on his progress. Almost as if knowing it would invoke his ire.

Finding himself in front of the bars of the gate, he stood, looking into the darkness. The darkness seemed to be an old lover in the way that it caressed and contoured to his very form. The black outfit he wore blended, and yet stood out from the darkness itself. The ruby eyes within regarded him calmly. Like two candles in the night, lighting his way through the darkness. Deeper into the darkness. He didn't move, because he knew that his other self was ambiguous and flirty.

"*So, you have come, yet again, to see me.*" Inari said softly as he neared the gate.

Yes. Snake answered calmly with a nod. He could hear the footsteps coming closer towards the gate and the soft splashes of water as each step hit ground. As he came from the shadows, Snake quirked an eyebrow. Before him stood a female version of himself. Her long ebony hair contrasted with her porcelain skin as it flowed back and forth with each movement, just above her waist. The finest of silks couldn't have captured how soft and delicate her hair seemed. Her lips were covered in, what he thought, was a blood colored crimson, and were quirked in a smirk that he had no doubt would set any hot blooded male into a frenzy if passed their way. Her mid sized chest was accentuated by the blood red kimono she wore, only accentuated by the opening in the top that displayed a considerable amount of cleavage. *Can I ask why you have taken the form of a woman Inari?*

"*My darling,*" the female doppelganger giggled. His spine tingled as if tickled. "*I have taken this form, because it is me. Or rather, another side of me. But my name is no longer Inari.*"

Fine. He conceded. With all the things he's been subjected too, this was not shocking. *What is your name then?*

She walked closer and gripped his chin lightly. As her eyes danced with amusement, she planted a kiss on his lips. Pulling away, "*My name is Benehime.*"

He simply quirked an eyebrow. He was use to this type of greeting. But, the name seemed oddly fitting. Crimson princess. Bloody princess. The name its self was as beautiful as the creature in front of him was, but it also held the terror that one should fear from such a person. He thought it suited her.

I'm here to find out more about myself. He began as he took a seat on the flooded floor. His declaration echoed in the empty space, but was soon swallowed by the darkness itself.

She nodded her head, before walking over towards his side. Taking a seat as well, she folded her legs beneath herself. Placing a hand on his shoulder, she gently guided his head down onto her lap.

"*And what can I do to assist?*" She asked as she began combing her fingers through his hair.

I want to know, just what is going on here. He began. *I still don't know what this place is called, or what it is.*

"This place is your mind. Well, a representation of your mind, but your mind nonetheless. Here you can control what happens. It's like a vacant landscape waiting to be built upon."

So, this is like a mindscape. He stated as he looked into her eyes. Now that he got a closer look, her eyes seemed to be a brighter shade than Inari's.

She nodded her head.

"That would be the correct term to use to describe this place, yes."

And exactly what are you? He asked.

She smiled lopsidedly.

"That depends." she began. Her eyes were trained on a distant horizon that he couldn't see in the darkness. "Are you referring to me, Inari, Widow, Snake, or Seraphim?"

All.

"Well," She began coolly. "I guess you could call me and Inari your subconscious. We are the desires and wants that you, yourself, long for, but will never act on consciously. You, Snake, are a part of the collective consciousness, which comprises of three aspects; Snake, Fox, and Sera. Sera, is what you originally are and will forever be. We are all simply a portion of what makes you, you."

And what about Widow?

"That is something else entirely." she said calmly. "He is what most people would consider a normal person, born and raised in a normal, healthy family."

But what is he? Snake interrupted.

"I was getting to that, before you interrupted." She said calmly as her eyes flickered towards him for a second, and then returned to the darkness. "Now, as I was saying, Widow is a construct of what you see a normal person being. A construct of the original, pure base of your being. He isn't so much as a part of you as we are, but an invention of yourself. A defense mechanism if you will. You have created him for the sole purpose of being able to simulate a normal Human and to help assimilate into Human Society."

I think I understand that.

"Good." she said as she nodded her head. "Now, as for us, it gets complicated. Fox is aggression and hatred. I am simply another part of him, *the blood lusting, seductive part. We only wish to grant your deepest darkest desires."* She purred as she bent her head down and kissed his forehead. The darkness seemed to try and smother him with her words for emphasis. *"And we will do anything to do it."*

And what of me, Snake.

"Well, Snake is simply your way of coping. Honestly speaking, you are nowhere near normal, and by your definition, you aren't Human. Snake is a construct of what a Serpent is. Lying, seductive, calm, collected, manipulative, and the list goes on and on. When a normal person kills, they are affected severely mentally, whether they want to admit it or not. Snake, on the other hand, simply cares less. The reason is that ever since you locked us away, the blood lust and pleasure you would normally experience from a kill would be diverted towards us, so it doesn't affect you directly, until the time of offerings. At that point," he could feel her blood lust ghosting over his skin like the gentle strokes of fingers in his hair. He suppressed a shiver of excitement. *"It's open season."*

So, he began. *All these different versions of me are simply my way of coping with the environment around me.*

"Yes. A version of isolation if you will. You genuinely feel emotions, but as to how to identify and express them, is where Widow falls in. After so much observation, you have developed a way to imitate them, but not generate them." She paused. *"After all, something can't be made out of nothing, and nothing cannot be created out of something, the basic law of physics. Nothing can be destroyed, only broken down into smaller, more basic, components. Not to mention that your base emotions are so low, they might as well be non existent. The only true emotions you display constantly are hatred and calm. There really is no in-between."*

Bipolar[8].

"Not precisely, but close enough." she agreed as she continued combing through his hair.

He didn't mind her doing so. Susan loved to do it too, for some odd reason. Slowly fading away from the cage, he kept his eyes closed from

---

8 psychiatric disorder with extreme mood swings: a psychiatric disorder characterized by extreme mood swings, ranging between episodes of acute euphoria mania and severe depression

the outside world. The conversation he had with himself seemed to have cleared his mind further. It made sense to him, and if it made sense, then it was true if supported by facts, which she gave. Opening his eyes, he looked up at the moon and sighed. It was still as beautiful as the last time he's seen it. It was something he would never tire of.

"Mother, Father please believe me every word is true. I am not the Demon that you say I am, it's true. Mother please believe me I am an angel here for you. But father I am what you say, for you, your date is due." His soft voice carried the melody through the night and into the surrounding darkness. He wasn't sure where the melody came from, but he felt it described him fairly well.

Chapter 11

TREASON

"glutTony, avaRice, pridE, wrAth, luSt, slOth, eNvy"
The most horrendous lies within the horrors.

Walking down the streets of Chicago, Sera was concentrating on the task at hand. Over the years of being with Susan, he figured it was time that he took the family books back with him to the base. It was only right that they should be with him. He was the new Noir and the next heir, so they should be where he is. He was mentally preparing himself for the argument he would have to put up with his grandfather. He wasn't sure, but he knew he was going to be met with some resistance to the idea. Looking at the church that lay up ahead, only a few blocks away, he felt something stir within him. It's been a whole year since he's seen his grandfather and he was curious as to what he would like to talk about. No doubt he would like to know what he has been up to lately. It seemed that all old people were fascinated with the lives of others, especially their families.

Finally coming to the stairs, he strode up them with purpose. He was going to get his books. Knocking on the door, he awaited an answer.

"I'm coming." He heard Matt say from the other side. As the door opened, he saw his grandfather looking at him blankly. His face was blank. Turning, matt began walking back into the church without a word.

Tilting his head slightly, Sera followed closely behind.

"Grandfather, is something wrong?" he asked, watching his back as he reached the stage of the church. Finding his grandfathers lack of response slightly troubling, he walked to his side. Following his eyes, he came upon the crucified Jesus Christ. "Grandfather," he began. He wanted to get the business out the way so he could talk to his grandfather about what was bothering him. "I wanted to request that the books come back with me to base. They should be with me seeing as I am the heir. I promise nothing will happen to them."

"Some things we can never change." Matt began eyes still on the crucifixion. "Jesus Christ knew that he was to die by the very people that he held dear and tried to help. He knew his fate, and yet he still stood and allowed it to happen. He allowed stones to hit him and his peers' condemnation. He did it all so he could save the people of their sins. He died for their sins. He died because of their sins. The sins of envy, greed, and wrath."

"Grandfather?" he didn't know where he was going with this. The whole conversation about Jesus was a new one.

"The thing is, he could see into their souls, and instantly knew who his traitor was, and yet he did nothing to stop or alter his fate."

Sera was going to ask him why he was talking about Jesus, but he jumped back on reflex as his grandfathers arm swung around to strike him in the chest. Skipping a few steps back, he looked at Matt with wide eyes.

"What are you doing grandfather?" he asked. He was under the impression that he finished his training under him. As he received no answer, he flicked his wrist and claimed a knife that he kept on his person at all times. He turned it into a reverse grip as matt charged him quickly, despite his old age. Bringing up his arm, he deflected the strike meant for his neck and skipped back another three steps. "Is this training?" again, he received no answer as his grandfather rushed him. Deciding that this was yet another test he was being given by Matt. Turning sideways, he dodged the stab that was aimed for his stomach and brought his hand down on the outstretched arm. Matt saw it coming and kicked his legs out from beneath him. As he fell, he sighed. Apparently, his grandfather was still as fast as he was when he began teaching him. His eyes widened slightly as he saw the knife coming down over his heart. Shifting slightly, the blade found its place in his shoulder. He grunted in slight pain. Kicking his feet out to strike his shins, Sera forced himself from under matt, turned over and jumped up and behind a pew. "Grandfather!" he called out. His voice echoing in the empty church. Looking into matt's eyes; he felt a tingle in the back of his mind. *"He has betrayed me."* He listened, because he couldn't find anything to say. He didn't want to believe it. Not him. *"Yes. It's true. He is just like father. He secretly hates us. He's wanted to kill us, but he held back."* The tingle began to make itself known in his right hand as it began twitching. *"He's Judas to our Christ. He pretends to be there for us, but turns us over to the wolves."* His knuckles crack under the strain of being balled. *"No one can be trusted."* His golden eyes gained an amber hue as an unseen breeze flitted through the stone walls. *No one can be trusted.* He finally found words. *"Alone. Always and forever alone."* *Always alone.* The amber hue darkened into blood crimson as he glared at his grandfather's figure. *You are the same.* He wasn't aware of the blood stopping from the wound on his left shoulder. He wasn't aware of the people talking and moving outside the church walls. The only thing that held his attention was the man in front of him. Growling in his throat, he rushed forward, hands open and ready to claw. Matt brought up the bloody blade in an attempt to deter him, but he simply pushed past it, ignorant of the slight cut that broke the skin on his right arm. Grabbing Matt's outstretched hand; he jumped and pulled him closer. Kicking his feet out, he drove them both into his stomach. Turning over and landing on his hands and knees, he looked at matt as he began standing up. He sneered at his form. Pouncing up and over the side pew, he ducked beneath the wooden bench. Bringing a hand over to his left wrist, he gripped a hidden ring. Listening to his grandfathers steps as he approached the bench, he flattened himself against the floor and silently waited.

XXX

Watching the bloody eyes of his grandson, he knew he was beginning to get serious. As he rushed at him though, he began to reconsider if he was thinking rationally. But was surprised by the move he made. Landing on his back, he was sure to get up quickly. Looking at him, crouched down on the ground on all fours reminded him of a fox. His eyes were piercing and angry as he watched him. They reminded him of pools of blood. Of blood that he so needlessly spilled. As he jumped up and over the first and second pew, he found himself comparing the move to one a fox would do to avoid capture. Standing slowly, he considered his options. Standing here to wait him out would be pointless. The boy had the patience of a saint. He could stand here all day, and Sera wouldn't budge an inch. Slowly, cautiously, he took steps towards where he saw him land. From the look in his eyes, he wanted to rip him to shred with his teeth and he didn't want to be eaten. Finally coming five feet away from the pew, he stopped. Preparing his body, he jumped the final feet only to look down and find the spot empty. He knew Sera couldn't have been behind him, because he would have seen him on his walk over. That meant he had to be further back. Taking a step forward, he was unprepared for the fist that hit his chin. Regaining his balance, he turned to deliver a strike of his own, only to have it blocked. Kicking his leg out, he tried to distract him, only to have him grab his leg in a grapple. Kicking his other out to strike him in the head, he missed as Sera ducked. Using his hands to break his fall, he braced himself. Turning around, he spotted nothing but air. His eyes shifted each way, looking for the elusive creature. As he heard a slight scuffle of cloth, he turned to the front of the pews. Walking quickly, he spotted him just in front of the stage. Cocking his left arm back, he sent a haymaker towards his face, only to have him turn on the spot as he slipped between his defenses and gripped his arm with both hands. He was going to grab him in a bear hug, but Sera ducked and jumped out of the way. Taking a step forward, he felt something restricting his legs. Trying his arms, he found them to be in the same predicament.

XXX

Sera looked at Matt as he tried to step forward with a grin of satisfaction. He wasn't going to fight someone who was physically stronger in hand to hand. That would be foolish. Pulling out his wire, he set about his web. Each and every strike, block, dodge and retreat was specifically meant to further ensnare him into his trap. Sprinting forward, he kicked matt in the chest, sending him sprawling back into the first pew in a seated fashion. Running his tongue along the steel in his mouth, he calmed at the metallic taste that entered his mouth.

"I honestly hated you." Matt said evenly as he looked into the bloody eyes of his grandson. "From the moment that I found out that it was your fault that my only daughter died, I wanted to kill you." Sera's grin widened. "I promised my daughter though that I would teach you the family ways. The first time you came back, I was so shocked that you had changing eyes that I was momentarily distracted from what I wanted. I tried to love you as a son, but I couldn't. I just couldn't. Every time I look at you, I am reminded of her. You are her twin. You have her face, her long hair, though a different color, even some of her mannerisms. And even though her eyes were blue and yours are gold, they have the same shape. Her ghost that haunts me. So, when you were to come back a second time, I was to give you the test. The final test of all Noir's. You were to kill your predecessor. I saw it as a chance to finally kill you without breaking my word to my daughter."

Sera didn't say anything throughout his talk. He was trying to refrain himself from tearing into his flesh with his wires. This man wanted to kill him because of something he couldn't control. *Or could I?* He found the question halting him in his actions. *I couldn't.* He reaffirmed. Glaring at him with a smile on his face, he prepared to pull the wires taut, before he was stopped by a question.

"Will you keep the family traditions alive?" matt asked softly.

Nodding his head, he prepared his body for the resistance.

"There are some things in the back waiting for you."

Not offering any acknowledgment, he pulled the wires as he jumped backwards. He watched with morbid fascination as each ring of wire cut through his clothes first, before he spotted the first sign of crimson. He could practically hear the wire biting into his flesh, through muscles, and finally singing as they severed bone. Matt's torso sat in the pew, bleeding out and onto the floor. His face set in resignation. Walking closer, Sera leaned in close as he watched the life slowly fading from his body.

"Au revoir grand-père.⁹" Sera whispered as he kissed his lips lightly.

"Good bye Noir." He breathed as his eyes closed for the last time.

---

9   Good by Grandfather.

Stepping back from his former teachers' body, he looked at him in disgust.

"In the end, you were still human." He said softly with honey eyes. Walking around the front right pew, he picked up both of the knives and placed them in his pocket.

Turning, he walked back into the back room where he knew his 'presents' were waiting for him. Walking into the same room he first entered nine years ago with his mother, he saw a black box sitting on the bed. Walking closer towards it, he spotted a small card taped to the top. *'To Sera'* he knew his mothers handwriting when he saw it. He could still smell the faint scent of pomegranates that his mother seemed to exude present on the surface. With trembling hands, he picked up the box. *Mamma.* He stood like that for a while, before he turned and walked out of the church without a backward glance.

Coming outside, he spotted Susan waiting in a car for him. Climbing into the passenger seat, he closed the door with the box in his lap.

"Why are your clothes bloody?" Susan asked as she looked at him.

He considered simply telling her it was a training accident, but decided against it. She deserved to know the truth of what happened inside the church.

"Sera?"

"I killed my grandfather." He answered.

"What?" she gasped.

He glanced out the corner of his eyes and saw her hand covering her mouth.

"I went to ask him about the books. He didn't answer me. When I asked again, he struck out at me. I thought it was another training session. But, when I lost my knife and he was aiming for my heart, I knew it wasn't. Before he died, he told me he hated me. Told me that I was nothing more than a ghost that constantly reminds him of the daughter he lost because of me. That he wanted to kill me for the longest time." He elaborated. Turning towards her fully, he wasn't shocked to see anger and sorrow in her eyes.

Slowly her hand reached out towards his face and cupped his cheek gently. It moved around to the back of his head, as she pulled him into a hug.

"I'm so sorry." She whispered into his hair. He found himself shivering from the warm breath that ghosted over him and the raw emotion that flowed from her.

"Can we go home now?" he questioned softly as he hugged her back. "I wish to rest."

Breaking away, she nodded her head with a small smile.

"Of course." She agreed.

XXX

Walking into his room, he closed the door with one hand while the other held the box. Walking over towards his bed, he placed the box in the center and took a step back. This was a gift from his mother. Something she left behind for him. He was overjoyed that she left him a gift. But he couldn't open it. He wanted to, but he just couldn't. His grandfather, someone who took care of him when his mother died, just tried to kill him, because of her death. A part of him hoped and wished there was something in the box that told him of her love for him, but another part, the rational part, told him that the contents of the box was something he didn't want to see. That inside the black box, that had the inscription *'Pandora'*, was the light of her heart that he never wanted to see. Picking up the box, he slowly walked over towards his closet. Opening it, he gently placed the box down in the back. Looking at it one last time, he closed the door. Staring at the door for a few moments longer, he sighed lightly.

"I suppose I should check on the Hell Borns." He muttered into the darkness. Turning around, he walked out of the room.

In the dark, cold closet, the box sat silently.

Operation:
Earth's Abortion, Hell's Children, Heaven's Error

Standing before Susan, he pondered why she would want him here. It was his day off and he was going to spend it in the study. Instead, he was told to come in full uniform, save for his masks and wait in her office.

Waiting for her to finish with her paper work, he thought about his new mask. He originally asked her why he would need a new one. She told him that Fox was to be a weapon. Something only in times of need was called upon. Then, she took out a white mask, with red swirls as scales. She told him his new name would be Snake. He found the name suiting. It would seem that fate was working its magic again in his favor. He was also promoted to the rank of Captain. That caught him off guard though, considering he was not even an officer.

Ever since he gained control over his 'other self', she's been asking him about decisions in the Spirits. He knew of the history between the Dawn and the Spirits. Their grudge and the lack of man power she's had ever since. He suggested that they create more Hell Borns, but on one condition. He knew his training would kill any of these people, regardless of age. So, the training would have to be toned down. She agreed.

"Suen." Susan greeted as she looked up from a file. "I've brought you here for a very special mission."

He tilted his head. He could feel his excitement building, before he pushed it back again. Was she going to let him go hunt?

"Yes Mistress?"

"I want you to create the new Hell Borns and lead them. It's time that we reestablish our work force." She confided.

He looked at her for a moment to ensure he heard her correctly. She wanted him to create the new Hell Born unit and be in charge of them?

"Are you sure?" he asked.

She smiled lightly.

"I am sure Suen. You are only a child in appearance. In spirit and mind you are far older and wiser than any of the soon to be recruits. I trust that you will get the job done."

"But, as you said, I am a child in appearance. Chances are that they won't even respond, let alone respect me. How am I to lead if they won't follow?"

Her smile turned sinister, and he was again reminded of who he was talking to once more. She was the leader of a criminal organization. Not a house wife.

"Then make them listen." She ordered.

He smiled at her suggestion. He was going to be given humans to train and make stronger. He was ordered to make them better than humans. Something of nightmares.

"Yes Mistress." He said as he nodded his head.

"They are waiting for you in the chapel."

Nodding his head, he turned and left to find the soon to be demons of hell.

There were only two types of people that would want to become part of the Spirits; Rejects to society who couldn't fit in. They were people that he categorized as 'Then'. All they thought about what the past, which was why they couldn't fit into normal society. They were unwilling to conform to the new ways. People who enjoyed killing and were a danger to those around them, and he classified them as 'Now'. That's what they constantly thought about. Not the effects of their cause, but the now. Not having the foresight to see when an action is against the social norm. But, there was a third type, for people like him. Classified as 'Then, Now, There'. Ones who knew nothing more than killing and surviving for the next day. Their pasts shaped their present, and their present would soon shape their future.

Walking into the chapel, he spotted roughly 60 men and women. They were all dressed in their normal attire, or what he assumed to be normal attire. Some of the faces he actually recognized as being from the Spirits own ranks. As he walked in front of the group, he took his time in watching their reactions. The majority were of what he expected. Scrutiny, questioningly, amused, confused, irritated. The list went on. He was sure the main question on most, if not all, their minds was what a child with a mask on doing here? Well, he was going to give them their answer.

"Listen up." Suen said as he walked back and forth before the assembled recruits. "You are all to become something great. This is an opportunity for you all to leave behind your mortal shells and become something more. Something immortal." he stopped before them. "We have assembled you all here to join the newest group of assassins."

"Is this some kind of joke? Why do we have to take orders from you kid?" a man asked rudely. "You don't know the first thing about being an assassin. We've been doing this since before you or your parents were born."

Suen looked at him coolly, before speaking. He knew he would encounter some people like this and was prepared.

"I have a question for you. No, I have a question for all of you. What do you fear?"

The men and women looked around themselves for a moment, not getting the question.

"What are you talking about kid?" the same man asked.

"My name is Snake, and I'm asking you what do you fear? What makes you shake in your boots, the hair stand up on your necks, the compelling urge to look behind you? What do you fear?"

"Kid, we fear nothing."

You fear nothing do you now? Snake mused with a mental smirk. *"Let's show them something to fear then shall we?"* Fox suggested. *Indeed. They know not of the Démon de vei's motto.*

"So, you fear nothing then?"

"That's right."

Suen looked out among the rest.

"Do you all fear nothing? Step forward if you have no fear." he ordered. As twenty men and three women stepped forward, he flexed his wrists and popped his joints. "Is this all of you? All of you that fear nothing?" he asked once more to ensure that was all. After no more stepped forward, he smirked beneath his mask. *Fools.* "Good."

Just as practice, he drew his guns with precision and speed worthy of a veteran. Each bullet found its mark in their targets skull. The shots were echoed by the body in which they reside. The stunned gasps of the group went unheard as the last of the ones who stepped forward fell to the ground in cold empty husks. Holstering his guns, he looked at the stunned and horrified faces of the rest.

"They were imbeciles." he began. "They are not worthy to become what we are creating. There is always something to fear. You should not lie to me, or question my orders for they come from the Mistress. If you do, then you will end up like those humans that are visiting the Goddess at this very moment. So, tell me now what it is that you fear." he ordered as he looked one in the eye.

The man shifted with obvious discomfort. Obviously, seeing a child kill over twenty people without batting an eyelash was a little intimidating.

"I'm afraid of death." he finally said.

Suen shifted his eyes towards another off to the far side.

"I'm afraid of what awaits me when I die." she said softly.

"I'm afraid of spiders."

"I'm afraid of drowning."

Suen nodded his head.

"I thank you for telling me some of your fears."

"I'm afraid of you." a voice said to his right.

Turning his head, he spotted a woman with brown hair and brown eyes looking at him with hesitation, fear and intrigue.

"What is your name?" he asked gently.

"Heath." she answered in a shaky voice.

He turned his attention back towards everyone else.

"What you are to become is Hell Born. Hell Born is the name of the new assassination squad that has been created. Your fears are what make you human. There is nothing that will get rid of that entirely. But, if you follow me, I will show you how."

"But, didn't you say that we can't rid ourselves of our fears completely?" Heath asked in a hesitant voice. She was obviously afraid of stepping out of line with someone who would sooner put a bullet in their head than take insubordination. He could tell that he would like her. She was smart.

"I did." he agreed with a nod of his head. "But, I will show you how to ignore your fears. How to suppress that impulse. When you are on the job, you will know no fear what so ever. But, remember this; "One who fears nothing, should fear everything." The ones that were just executed a few minutes ago were ones who thought they feared nothing. I showed them that they should always fear. Fear me." his eyes gained an eerie glow. "I am everything that you think you have gotten over as a child. I am the bump in the night when you were a child. I'm the monster in your closet. I'm the monster your mothers told you stories about when you were bad. I am not averse to showing you what you fear most, because I will show you regardless. This was the first test, and I have to say that I am disappointed with the turn out. I thought more of you would step forward." at this, more of them shifted. *Such pathetic little creatures they all are. "I told you that a long time ago."* Fox commented gruffly. "In any case, I will begin the elimination process."

"Um, Captain Snake, what is it that you fear?" Heath asked nervously.

For only a second he considered answering her question. This one seemed to be terrified of his presence, but curious about him as well. This little Q&A was more than that. She was showing courage.

"What I fear is not of this world, for what it is that I fear does not exist on this plane. Where you fear death, I embrace it. And while you fear what awaits you, I have accepted my fate because my goddess is a war loving one. What I fear is her wrath if what I am doing will not please her or my mother." he answered truthfully. "Now, you will all learn what it means to be a Hell Born. Someone, tell me what you believe a Hell Born is going to be?" he looked out at them and awaited their answer. For a few moments, none of them seemed to have any idea what he was asking, before he noticed the one named Heath raise her hand. "Yes Heath?"

"Does it mean born from hell?" she answered hesitantly.

He frowned for a second before it tapered off into a thin line.

"First, never define a word with the word." He began in a lecture, "Its bad grammar. And second," he paused as he allowed a small smile to grace his face, even thought it went unseen due to his mask. "You're correct. You all will become Demons born from hell its self. When people hear of you, they will quake in fear. When they see you, they will be blinded. By the time I am done with you, even you will not recognize yourself. Now, let us begin."

1st Lesson: Till death

The room was empty save for two occupants. The cold air shifted as a breeze found its way through the cracks in the cement and stone.

Looking into the eyes of the first recruit, whose name he knew was Joseph, he was prepared to lecture this human on the fine points of survival.

"Alright Joseph, I want you to come at me with the intent to kill." Suen ordered as he stood still. His golden eyes as blank as ever as he regarded the human. The slight flinch he noticed that ran through his body told him of the recruit's reluctance at the order. "I will not repeat myself. If you don't, then I will kill you myself." That was apparently enough to encourage him to attack. Remaining still, he allowed him to invade his radius. Turning sideways quickly, he avoided a fist that was aimed at his head. Kicking out his leg, he tripped him up and watched as he landed face first on the cement floor. He didn't say anything as he quickly got off the ground and rushed him again. Side stepping the haymaker that was headed towards his face again, he hooked his elbow into his, placed his right leg behind him, and pulled forward. As Joseph landed with a thud on the ground, he quickly positioned himself on top of him and landed a punch just below his throat. Jumping off of his body, Suen waited until he caught his breath. Watching the man stand, he could see wariness in his eyes. Apparently he didn't think he would be put on his back by a child. And now that he knew better, he was going to be more careful about his actions.

Two hours had passed, and Suen was contemplating whether or not he should simply kill this human. An hour into the exercise, the human was already on his last legs. He mentally scoffed at the effort. This person would be dead if he was out in the field. Such a disappointment. He knocked him out over forty-five minutes ago and was now waiting for him to awaken. As his figure groaned on the ground, and he began to shift, Suen slowly walked over towards his body and kneeled.

"You must never allow the opponent to render you unconscious. During that time, they could easily kill you, or worse, prep you for torture." He drawled in a low monotone. "If you ever allow yourself to be rendered unconscious again, I will kill you myself. I will not have weak underlings. Is that understood?" as the man groaned a yes sir, he kicked him once in the ribs. "Now leave here, before I decide to advance you to the top of my death list." He watched with hidden amusement as the man found energy that he didn't have prior to his lesson, as he ran out of the room. As the door closed, he sighed. He had a feeling that most of the recruits would be the same.

Ten hours into the training session, he was growing increasingly more aggravated. They were all simple street fighters. None had any finesse. Granted, in their line of work, simple kung-fu wasn't going to save your life. He wasn't looking for any advanced techniques. He simply wanted to see if any of them had foresight. The ability to read an opponent. Of course he could simply tell them, and hope that they would eventually figure it out, but he didn't want to give away the answer to the problem. He sighed angrily to himself. He only had one more to go, and then he could rest. As the door opened, he spotted Heaths nervous figure walking into the room.

"Heath, I want you to come at me with the intent to kill." He ordered.

As he expected, she rushed at him. He knew she wouldn't question his order or hesitate. She already knew that he was serious. That alone, made him move her up in his book. As she swiftly recovered from his counter, he couldn't hide a smirk that made it to his face. She was good. He only hoped that he wasn't setting his expectations too high.

Three hours in, and he could tell that the constant reversals and counters were beginning to take its toll on her. He was mildly enjoying himself. So much so, that he worked up a small sweat. She was blowing everybody's records so far, out of the water. Even though her body was bruised and fatigued, she constantly got back up, just as she was doing currently.

"That's enough." He ordered. As she stood, breathing heavily through her nose, she stood at attention. "You have displayed the will to continue fighting, even though you knew it to be a lost cause. You must never quit fighting until you are dead. If you still draw breath, then you still fight. I am proud to say that you have surpassed every last one of your predecessors. You have earned two days rest. After, you are to begin the training regimen that I have posted in the meeting room. Dismissed." As he watched her salute and turn out the door, he smiled lightly to himself. This human knew her place. Knew not to step out of line. Not to question orders. Speak when spoken to. Goddess, how he loved hierarchies.

2nd Lesson: Law

"Alright." Sera began as he looked out at the assembled masses in the chapel. "Today I wish to speak about survival skills. First, let's cover urban survival. Does anyone know the first rule in urban survival?" he asked.

"To blend in." Heath answered as she raised her hand.

He nodded his head. This Heath was rapidly becoming his favorite.

"That's right. In order to not be seen, one must become the scenery. Observe your surroundings and adapt to them. When you are in enemy territory, you must not attract attention to yourself. You must conform to their ways. What's the second rule?" he wasn't surprised that Heath was the one to raise her hand again. "Yes Heath?"

"To secure an escape route."

"Yes. Getting in isn't necessarily the hard part. It's always the get away. You must search for as many escape points as possible, because you will never know when one is not available to you. Now, what do you do when you have been discovered Heath?" he decided to ask the question directly, because none of the others seemed to be able to answer.

"You take out any, and all who get in your way." Was her immediate answer.

"Very good." He observed. "Now, let's continue to the Wild. Hypothetically speaking, what if your mission was compromised and you had to escape into the surrounding jungle to evade being captured. During your run, you slipped and fell down a steep hill. And as a result, you lost consciousness. When you came to, you didn't know where you were, or how long you have been incapacitated. It was night, and most of your equipment has vanished. The only things you have left are a book of matches, a broken flashlight, your first aid kit and your combat knife. How would you survive to complete your mission and make it back to base, before the enemy finds you?"

"You simply back track." One man in the back scoffed. He had a military crew cut and had a rather strong face.

Sera repressed a growl as he pulled his gun from his holster and aimed it at his head. These humans seriously needed to learn their place in the food chain.

"Heath, would you please inform the private as to what my rank is." He ordered gently as he glared at the cowering man.

"Captain, sir."

"And am I above or below his station?"

"Obviously above sir."

From the tone in her voice, he could tell that she was enjoying this to a certain extent.

"And how do you address one in a station, such as mine?"

"You raise your hand and wait to be acknowledged."

"Thank you Heath." He nodded. "Now, if you so much as step out of line again Shields, I will put a bullet in your head. I don't care what branch of service you've come from; you never speak out of line when talking to an officer. Do you understand me?"

"Y-yes s-sir." He stuttered fearfully.

Holstering his gun, he kept his eyes on him for a second.

"Now," he returned to his previous question. "Does anyone have an answer for me?"

"Sir."

He sighed. It seemed that the others were either too afraid to answer him, or Heath was the only capable human amongst them. And for some reason, he didn't doubt that it was the latter and not the former.

"Yes Heath?"

"First, you have to establish a drinking source. After that has been established, you find food. The enemy will most likely still be looking for you, so you don't make a fire in the day and you erase all traces of it by night."

"Let me interrupt you for a moment Heath." Suen calmly looked out amongst the class. She raised a very good point. "Can anyone here tell me why you would not make a fire in the day?" again he was met by silence. "Would you please tell them Heath? Because I don't think they are as educated as they should be in this matter."

"The smoke would be visible in the daylight sir." She answered.

"Yes." He agreed as he glared out at the rest. "Anyone with a pair of eyes could spot you from higher ground, and considering that you fell down a hill, everyone is on higher ground but you." Flicking his eyes back towards her, he nodded his head. "Continue with the explanation."

"Sir. After you have surmised that they have given up their search, which could take anywhere from 24 to 72 hours, you begin to head back towards their hideout. Since your weapons have been lost, you must use stealth and sneak into their base under the cover of darkness. You can use the alcohol in the first aid kit to cause a distraction away from your target. After slitting their throat, you leave while everyone is distracted by the fire. Once leaving, you simply have to get as far as you can in the next hour. The ideal thing to do would be to find a mode of transportation during the confusion."

"Thank you for that detailed explanation." He nodded his head. "Now that we have killed 45 minutes, I believe it's time for you all to return to your trainings." He turned and began walking towards the door. "And Heath, I would like for you to come to the clearing in an hour."

"Yes sir."

And he turned out the door.

"Well, look who's the teacher's pet."

Heath turned at the scathing remark. Over the last five months, she has gotten use to the usual barbs that the others would hurl at her. They thought that they were being ignored and mistreated and she was getting favors.

"Yea," a female said to the side. "I bet you wipe his ass when he gets up don't you?"

She ignored the hateful question. They didn't understand the importance of this mission. Some were still blind and ignorant to the fact that this was not a game and any who thought of it as thus would be killed sooner than the rest.

"You wouldn't be speaking in this way if Captain was here would you?" she asked calmly.

"He ain't here." The female pointed out hotly.

"And yet you didn't answer my question." She said softly.

"He's probably getting changed right now." A male joked. Some of the other males laughed at his joke. "I swear, he looks like a little girl. Anyone thinks he's on his period?"

"If I were you, I wouldn't joke about the Captain." She warned as she tensed her muscles. "That's insubordination."

These people were to be above humanity, and yet they digressed to their level. It was a mockery of what he taught, and what they all wanted.

"So what!" he said indignantly. "I could kick his ass any day of the week."

"I was under the impression that he kicked all our 'asses' once before, and you were not even able to stand up to him for more than an hour." She shot back.

The jibe at his skills must have pushed the wrong button, because he walked up to her face with a glare that would melt ice. She calmly looked at him in his eyes as he approached. He was nothing in comparison to Snake. Captain Snake was intense, and it wasn't his eyes that were the most intimidating part. Granted, his eyes did set one on edge, but it was the look in his eyes. One of a person who only lived for one thing and one thing only. Nothing else mattered to them. So, looking into this mans eyes was nothing in comparison.

"I dare you to say that again." He growled through clenched teeth as he flexed his muscles.

"I said if he kicked your ass once, he could do it again." She glared at him. "Now please leave my personal space. I have to meet with Captain in twenty minutes."

"Why you little bitch!" he raged as he cocked his hand back.

She prepared herself to counter the attack like Snake did so many times, but an unsettling feeling settled over the room and made him pause. To her, it looked like time had stopped. Everyone around her seemed to have been frozen in their previous actions. Now that she thought about it, she couldn't move either. And now that she tried, she found herself becoming afraid. Why couldn't she move her muscles? Why couldn't anyone else move either? She finally got her answer as she heard his voice.

"Were you about to strike a fellow Hell Born?" Snake asked calmly. Although she could tell that the tone was anything but calm. She wasn't sure, but she thought she saw a snake around his neck, looking dangerously at them.

"I-I was-"

"It doesn't matter." He said offhandedly. Walking over towards them, he stood next to her. "Because I will settle this little argument."

Now, the snake seemed to be hissing at him and ready to strike.

"Sir," she interjected with a soft voice. She didn't want to draw the snake's attention. But it seemed that her precaution was not needed. The snake's body twisted around to face her, but it was no longer glaring. The golden eyes seemed to look upon her in consideration, before she caught a subtle nod as it turned back around.

"Yes?"

"It is not necessary to reprimand him sir."

He hummed lightly as the snake slithered towards his ear. She thought it looked as if he was listening and understanding it. She couldn't believe that there was really a snake on his shoulder. She scanned the crowd and the rest seemed to be completely oblivious to it.

"I believe you are right." He finally said with a nod. She wasn't sure whether he was talking to her, or the snake. And the thought of him talking to a snake didn't seem out of the realm of possibilities. "I believe you should be the one to teach him a lesson."

Time seemed to have returned to normal at those words. Everyone gasped and the man stepped back lowering his arm.

"Sir." She saluted. She didn't know what that meant, but she would do as he ordered.

"Everyone to the field." He ordered.

As she stood in front of Stevens, she could feel Snakes eyes on her. Looking his way discretely, she was correct. His golden eyes were focused purely on her person, and she felt as if she was under a microscope. As if he could see everything.

"You two are to fight to the death." He announced.

"But sir-" the man began to protest but was cut of by a knife finding its way into his arm.

"Silence." Suen said calmly as he lowered his arm. "I do not like it when others interrupt me. Now, as I was saying, you two are to fight to the death. This is the way we deal with problems in our own ranks. Insubordination will not be tolerated."

"But sir, they are the same rank." A female pointed out.

"And I will put a knife in you as well Sam, if you interrupt me." They didn't seem to get that he was serious and it irked him. "Now, insubordination will not be tolerated. And it is punishable by death. But, an even bigger crime is going against the values that we hold dear. Sam, will you recite to me the three values of the Spirits?"

"Honor, Loyalty, Family."

"That's right. And which of the three did he break?"

"All three."

He turned his head as Heath answered.

"Correct. Honor was broken when he tried to lie to me. Loyalty was broken when he went against his Honor. And Family was broken as he tried to strike Heath. Here, we are family. I am the father; Mistress is the mother and you the children. We are loyal to our family. I will tell you all this now; I will fight for you to the best of my abilities because you are family. And in a family, you have the honor to go to the parent if you have a problem with your sister or brother. If you ever break these rules, these values, death is the only outcome for one of you." Going to his waist, he pulled out his dagger and threw it at Heath's feet, blade in the ground. "Begin."

She didn't hesitate as she heard the order to attack. Dropping to her knees, she picked up the blade and rushed at him while he jerked the knife out of his arm and prepared himself. Her thrust towards his stomach was avoided by a quick turn to his left. Stopping suddenly, she turned to avoid a stab in her side, but couldn't avoid the blade completely. Standing, they began circling each other. Like two predators trying to stake claim to the same territory. A part of her was seeing this as just that. This man has been the ringleader in the taunts and jibes and she knew he didn't like her. Ever since he's found out about her outlasting him, he's been outraged. The gleam in his eyes was malicious and yet lustful. In the depths of her mind, she knew he was lusting for her and it made her skin crawl. His hesitation wasn't because of fear. She knew it wasn't that. It was his prayers being answered. As he came at her with a punch, she blocked with her free left hand. Bringing her blade up, she poised it to stab his heart, but was met with steel. As his hand gripped hers tightly, she knew he wasn't going to let her go. And him being male made him physically stronger that her. Her theory proved true as he began pushing her blade back. Deciding that this would kill her, she kicked her legs out and caught his knee. As he lost balance, the pressure on the blade shifted and sent both out of their hands. Falling on top of him, she punched him in the face. But the hit he landed felt like a brick. Coughing to catch her breath, he took the momentary lapse in concentration to switch their positions. Blow after blow he began landing on her face, and even though she was trying to avoid the hits, she could see the sadistic joy he was getting in pummeling her. Each hit was beginning to take its toll on her and she thought he was going to beat her to death, which was probably the thing he was going to do. Bringing up her knee, she wedged it between herself and him. Putting all she had into the push, she kicked him off, sending him back a few feet. Sitting up quickly, she looked through swollen eyes as he began walking towards her slowly. He was over confident, and that was something Captain Snake has taught them to never become. Getting up, she stood on uneven footing and readied herself. He came at her quickly and she only had a moment to gain a quick survey of the surroundings. Blocking a hit that came from her right, she didn't see the kick aimed for her side. Falling over, she didn't get a chance to breathe as he jumped on top of her and began choking her.

"Teacher is going to have to get a new pet." He sneered as he increased pressure. "I wanted to do this for the last five months."

"There is—something—you should—know." She gasped as her sight was becoming weaker. The encroaching darkness around his face was beginning to become more apparent.

"And what's that?" he humored. His twisted smile left his face as he slowly looked down towards his stomach.

"Always—mind—your surroundings." She breathed as she twisted the blade. He was so preoccupied with killing her with his bare hands, that he forgot about the knives that he forced out of their hands. Moving the blade deeper, she smiled weakly as his hands slackened around her throat. "It can get you killed."

Clapping his hands, Suen took a step forward.

"Winner Private first class Heath." He announced. She couldn't keep her eyes open long enough to hear the rest of his announcement. The lack of oxygen was taking its toll on her body. Turning towards the sky, she watched the passing clouds as her vision began fading. Her final sight was of Captain Snake looking down at her. And even though she wasn't sure, she could have sworn she saw a small smile on his lips beyond the cloth as she passed out.

XXX

Waking up slowly, Heath looked around her surroundings. Her head was hurting and her eyes couldn't open all the way, so the only thing she saw was a sliver of light. Trying to move her body, she gave up as she groaned in pain. Having a full grown male pound into you with fists like brick was bound to leave a few bruises.

"I see you are awake."

She turned to see the person the voice belonged to, but all she could see was darkness. But, she didn't really need to see him, to know that it was Snake talking.

"Captain." She rasped as she tried to sit up, but was pushed back as a hand rested against her chest.

"Don't get up." He told her in a neutral tone. He could have been talking about the weather for all she knew, judging by his tone. "Your body is pretty banged up."

"He did a number on me sir." She confessed.

He gave a light chuckle and she thought the world was coming to an end. This cool, calm, and cold killer just laughed. She never thought she would see the day. She supposed it was the child in him coming out.

"That he did." He agreed as he composed himself. "During your fight, he had multiple chances to kill you. If he hadn't of been so keen on killing you with his hands, you would be dead."

The callous way that he told her made her cringe slightly. He was always clinical and non bias when he spoke. She thought it rather pleasant of him to not blatantly point out that he injured him before the fight.

"But," he continued. "You won, because of his over confidence." She couldn't tell with her vision impaired, but she could feel him coming closer. He seemed to exude a cool, yet deadly calm and it made the hairs on the back of her neck stand on end. "Now, lay still, so I can put the cream on. It will heal your bruises in twenty-four hours." He instructed.

"But I wasn't aware that anything like that existed."

He gripped the hem of her shirt, and began pulling it up to her chin. She blushed as she felt her shirt rise. He was really straight forward with a task. She blushed further as she felt his hair tickle her lightly. As he began administering the cream to her abdomen, she shivered despite herself. It was cool on her skin and it was already beginning to sooth her aching muscles. But, she found that his hands were surprisingly hot against her skin. As he made it to her bruised breasts, she flushed further. The combination of his hot hands and cool cream was beginning to have an effect on her body. One she didn't expect to have with one as cold as him. Let alone one of his age. But, he seemed older than he really was. This conflict was making her body confused as to what it should do. A light moan left her lips before she could check it and she held her breath to see if he noticed. It was embarrassing enough to have someone applying cream to her body, but to become aroused because of simply contacting was outrageous. And being affected by her superior officer was beyond inappropriate. After a moment, she allowed herself to breathe. He hadn't noticed. And if he did, she was grateful that he kept it to his self. As his hands moved from her chest to her eyes, she sighed. Soon he would be done, and she would be back to training.

"I'm finished." He announced calmly as he stood.

"Thank you sir." She told him gratefully.

"It's my job to look after my children." He said somberly. "Just rest and by tomorrow, you will be as good as new." With that, the chill she felt ever since his appearance disappeared.

Lying alone in the bed, she felt herself drawn to his words. His job to look after his children? The way he said it made it sound like they weren't his words. Like he was remembering and repeating what he's heard. And the feeling within it only made her envision a mother comforting her child.

"Captain, what would make you sound so sullen?" she wondered softly into the darkness of the room. Deciding to think on it later, she allowed her body to rest.

3rd Lesson: Me, Myself, and I

Three months has passed since she was promoted to her current position. Ever since the day she was promoted, the taunts had stopped and everyone was focused on their training. It was obvious that none of them wanted to be subject to punishment should they step out of line again.

Although, she was curious as to the final test they would have to take in order to become a Hell Born officially. The others, as they came out of the testing area, were quiet. A bit too quiet. She wondered what he put them through to make them change so quickly. A couple of them seemed to disappear all together. Her heart pounded in her chest. He called her in today for the final test, and she wasn't sure if she was ready for it. Whatever he subjected them too was too horrible for words.

As she walked into the base, she found him standing near the door. He was apparently waiting for her.

"Follow me." Was the only thing he said to her as he turned his back and began walking down the hallway.

Following behind, she noticed that she has never been down this hallway before. She was tempted to ask him where he was taking her, but the cold chill that she normally felt around him was full force. The only thing, besides the chill she was getting, that kept her from voicing her thoughts was the fact that he was her superior and subordinates weren't supposed to ask questions.

Coming towards a room, that was only obscured by the light overhead that seemed to have chosen to die, he opened the door. As she stepped inside, she could feel something off about the room. A part of her wanted to take the lights way out and simply die. This room was bad. Evil. Something about it just seemed not of this world. Following him in, she was surprised as the door closed behind her. Turning quickly, the only thing she caught was darkness. Rushing towards the door, she found it locked. Her heart pounded in her ears as she fumbled with the knob.

"Captain!" she screamed, only to have her own voice answer back in the form of an echo.

"You are to stay inside, until you have realized." His voice was soft, and it seemed to come from all around her.

"Realize what?" she was confused. She looked all around her, but only saw inky blackness. He's never told her the purpose of this test.

"Not until you realize."

Resigning herself to her fate, she walked a few paces into, what she thought, was the middle of the room. Standing, she tried to focus on what she could possibly be looking for. A small chill passed through the room, and she found herself searching for the source. The room was pitch black. Nothing could be seen here. No. she took that back. This was beyond pitch. It was an abyss. She shivered as the temperature seemed to have dropped a few more degrees. This place was not meant to be visited by humans. It was not meant to exist in the mortal world. This was a place only demons were allowed entrance without consequence. This was a place where it only seemed to become darker and darker the longer she stood in the darkness. This was Stygian[10].

She trembled in fear.

Darkness wasn't supposed to get darker. It was impossible. You couldn't make black any blacker by adding more black. But then again, this place wasn't normal. It wasn't even abnormal. The term normal didn't even deserve to be in the same context as this room. But, could she really call it a room? There were no walls, no ceiling, no nothing, of which she could see. Only the floor. Her stomach dropped as she felt the sensation of falling. She screamed at the top of her lungs, but this time she was not met with an echo. The darkness its self seemed to have swallowed her pleas for help with its unyielding form.

Her heart was pounding, faster than it was when the door closed. Faster than when she watched Snake kill the twenty recruits. Faster than she ever thought possible. But this was something that shouldn't be possible. She was standing in a room. She knew that. A room consisted of four sides and a ceiling and floor. She knew that as well. But, now

---

[10]   pitch-black: unremittingly dark and frightening, as hell is imagined to be; of Styx: relating to the Styx, the river in Greek mythology that the souls of the dead were ferried across into Hades; binding: eternally binding, as were promises sworn on the banks of the river Styx in Greek mythology

she was falling, and falling fast. Cold air cut at her cheeks and stung her eyes as she descended into the chasm.

She's lost track of how much time had passed. She couldn't even scream for help anymore, because her throat was raw from previous attempts. Suddenly, she felt herself on ground again. Looking around, she was still surrounded by darkness.

Shifting her eyes back and forth, she took slow unsteady steps forward. She was sure she was still in the room and she didn't want to hit a wall. Step after cautious step, she continued in the darkness. It disturbed her slightly that she couldn't hear her footsteps. She was surprised by how big the room was. Apparently it was bigger than she first thought. The chill that she felt before was back and it felt like it was trying to freeze her to the bone. It felt like death himself was breathing down her neck. Turning quickly, she didn't know whether to be relieved or worried about what she saw. Nothing. Absolutely nothing but a deep, wide void. Turning her head quickly to the front, she strained her eyes. She thought she heard something in the darkness. She wasn't sure what it was, but she was sure she heard something there.

Her heart skipped.

There it was again. It reminded her of the heel of a shoe scrapping across the ground. She knew the sound well from the soft steps training Snake put her through to ensure that they wouldn't make a sound while walking. But, nobody was in here with her. Snake was outside, and he wouldn't lock her inside a room with someone. Granted she didn't know him that well, but she knew enough. He didn't get his kicks out of locking girls in a room with a male. If anything, he would kill any male that would attempt to force himself on a woman.

She stilled.

That wasn't a shoe scuff. Shoe scuffs weren't that drawn out. Shushing noise. Like one would give in a library. She stopped breathing as she tried to get a direction.

She gasped quietly as her eyes went wide.

It wasn't a shoe scuffle, or a shush. It was none of the normal things one would hear outside. It was a hiss. Her body was shaking like a leaf in a strong wind. Her palms were sweaty despite the cold that wracked her body. She's heard this hiss before.

Before her eyes, she spotted two glittering dots. They were the only things, besides the darkness, that she could see. As the feeling of dread began to fill her, she rushed forward, ignorant of the walls she was afraid of hitting, towards the two shinny objects. As she got closer, she stopped at, what she thought was ten feet away. The glitters weren't getting any bigger, as things normally get as you get closer to them. They remained the same size. Now that she thought about it, she didn't feel like she was gaining any ground. She knew her legs were moving, but she wasn't going anywhere. In front of her the two glitters stayed.

Looking closer she saw a thin line going down the middle of each one. They looked like four halves of a gold coin. Or maybe a crescent moon. As she heard the hiss again, the other options fled her mind as only one word came to her lips unopposed.

"Captain."

Although she knew she said it, and was aware of her lips moving, and even the breath that was required to form the word, she couldn't hear it.

"Heather."

His voice was soft and cold. Even though she couldn't see his face, she knew it was blank and devoid of any life that a normal person would express. The darkness that suffocated her seemed to caress his form lovingly. As if he was born in the darkness of this very room. It didn't sound at all outrageous. This room was not meant for humans, but for a reason beyond her, she knew he wasn't one. He was something else entirely. She was a scientist and a historian at heart. She spent a good portion of her time studying and researching. She knew what it was that separated humans from animals. It wasn't their opposable thumbs. It wasn't the notion that animals didn't have souls. Nor was it the theory that animals don't have emotions. What separated them was a conscience. The sense of right and wrong and the ability to discern what one should do and not do. He didn't have one. She didn't doubt that he knew right from wrong, but it wasn't what 'They' considered right or wrong. He seemed as if he followed a different set of rules. His reality was not theirs. His eyes were different as well. Not just because of the color or design, but the sheer depth of them was unfathomable. They were wise eyes, and yet cruel eyes. One who knew the absolute truth to the universe, but would still sooner slit your throat than accept any lip. She was curious of what would make someone so young seem ageless, but she also knew the saying 'Curiosity killed the cat'. That's what scared her. The sheer knowledge that seemed to radiate from his eyes was only eclipsed by what she knew to be blood lust.

"Heather."

He repeated her name just as softly as before.

"Yes Captain?" she was just noticing that he was asking, and not stating.

"Kill me."

The order was simple enough. Straight forward and to the point like always. But her body froze. His words echoed in her mind, but she wasn't sure if it was really all in her mind. He wanted her to kill him?

"Sir?" the hesitance in her voice was clearly heard, despite the fact that she couldn't hear it.

"Kill me."

He repeated it as calmly as one would order a glass of water.

"But sir-"

"Kill me, or you will never leave here. You will forever wander this realm."

That gave her pause. Looking into his golden eyes, she knew he was being serious.

"You would do that sir?" she asked. Granted, she's known him to kill people who step out of line, but she hasn't done anything to warrant such consequence. If anything, she has followed his orders to the letter.

"No." his answer was unexpected, but the rest made her breath catch in her throat. "You will."

She didn't understand.

"I don't understand."

"Kill me."

This time she felt a nauseating wave, similar to what happened three months ago, but stronger, hit her full force. Her blood froze in her veins. Her heart stopped beating. Her body was beyond shaking and was in a full seizer. Her eyes though, were wide and focused solely on his. The blood lust that she knew lurk within the honey eyes of her captain was finally letting its self be known.

She didn't want to kill him. He was a child, no older than eleven. She couldn't possibly kill him. Not to mention that he was extremely skilled for a child. She wouldn't be able to kill him even if she tried.

"I will not attempt to stop you. I won't defend myself. I want you to kill me Heather." He said as if he was reading her mind. And again, she didn't doubt that he could really be reading her mind. His eyes seemed to have seen a lot, why not thoughts as well? "Why are you hesitating?"

"I don't-"

"Kill me."

She could feel something wrapping itself around her neck tightly. He was too far away for it to be him. It was cold, scaly, and reminded her of a serpent.

"But-"

"Kill me."

The pressure increased.

"I-"

"Kill me. Now."

"I don't want to!"

The pressure ceased.

She screamed at him eyes closed. She was hyperventilating now and she was surprised at how forceful she was being. She gasped as she realized what she just did. Opening her eyes slowly, she peeked at his shadowed figure. His eyes narrowed slightly, but she knew a glare whenever she saw one on him. They gave off an ethereal glow that made him seem like a vengeful angel. From heaven or hell, she didn't know, nor did she care to find out.

"What did you say?"

Even though his voice was soft as it normally was, she could feel the razor meant to cut to the bone in the tone. It was a mixture between a threat and question. She flinched

"I—I don't want-t to kill y-you." She stuttered beyond her fear.

"You understand the consequences of disobeying me."

It wasn't a question he was posing. She's seen what he does to insubordinate ones.

"Yes sir." She was resigned to the fate. She would never harm an innocent child. But he wasn't innocent right? He's killed countless people, twenty of which she knew of. He wasn't innocent. He forced people to fight to the death. He wasn't innocent. He wasn't even human. He wasn't innocent.

Right?

Right?

As she closed her eyes to await her fate, the unsettling feeling vanished. Evaporated like the muggy air on a spring day. She took it as the calm before the storm. Bracing herself, she waited. And waited . . .

And waited . . .

XXX

"Open your eyes." Sera ordered as he watched her standing figure in the darkness. His eyes could see perfectly in a place like this. He decided to stay behind to see how she would react to the isolation. He wanted to see how she would react to being left alone to her own thoughts and devices without any outside stimuli. Watching her shiver, he knew the reason. He wanted to test the girl. See where she stood. Releasing a small amount of his intent, he watched as she looked all about herself to find where it was coming from. Her scream though was unexpected. He wasn't inside her mind, so he didn't know what she was seeing, because to him, she was still standing. As she began walking in circles, he found himself curious as to what she was doing. When she whispered his name, he quirked an eyebrow. She was thinking of him. Answering her call, he waited. The mind was a strange place to go. If one didn't know the ins and outs, they could become lost forever in their own mind. The darkness was another thing entirely. One was never sure as to what awaited them in the unknown reaches of the darkness. Anything and everything could reside within its comforting embrace. Humans prided themselves on what they knew. And what they know is limited to what they can experience with their five senses. Taking away any of them, one was left confused. He took away three. She couldn't see where she was going. She wasn't sure if what she was saying was really spoken or thought. She couldn't hear either without wondering if it was a thought or spoken. Her mind was confused. But, unlike most, he wasn't afraid of the unknown, because he knew what lurked beyond it. Within it. Inside it.

He knew the darkness. He embraced the darkness. He loved the darkness. In the darkness, it was all clear. The things that would be blinded by the light would 'come to light' in the absence of light. It was the truth. That's what waited in the bleak, dark, abyss. The truth. In the dark awaited nightmares. In the dark awaited the boogeyman. In the darkness awaited death. In the darkness, was him. It was always him. That was a constant that he's grown accustomed too. Where darkness waited, he resided. And wherever he resides, darkness awaits. One body, one mind, one soul. Forever it shall be, and be it shall.

XXX

Opening her eyes, she looked into his. She couldn't place what she saw in them. There seemed to be a mixture of pride and disappointment. And she wasn't sure, but she thought she saw loathing. But that didn't seem to be directed towards her.

"Sir?" she questioned softly. Her voice was tinged with uncertainty.

He reached out with a hand and palmed her cheek.

"Congratulations Heather." He praised monotone. She found the tone out of place with his words, but accepted that that was how he was. Although, the gesture was new, she didn't dwell on it. She only focused on his eyes. "You have passed your final test."

"Thank you sir."

As his eyes disappeared from view, she heard the sound of a door opening. Following, she walked out, and back into the dark hallway.

"Just because you can see it, doesn't make it real. And just because you can't see it, doesn't mean it doesn't exist." He said suddenly.

"Sir?"

"I mean, never believe simply what you are fed. If you do not like the food, then go and find another kitchen that will cater to your liking. And don't tell anyone about what happened inside. Each experience is different to the individual."

"Yes sir."

As they walked in silence, she found herself wondering just what went on in the dark room. Her legs were stiff, and her joints were tight. How long was she in there?

"Captain?"

"Yes?"

"How long was I in there?"

"Seven hours forty three minutes and twelve seconds."

"But it felt like I was in there for-"

"Don't." he ordered softly. "You will understand in time. At the moment, your mind is exhausted. Allow your mind to rest, and it will all become clear."

"Yes sir."

Coming to another room, she held the question that she was tempted to ask. She's been to this room before, but she wasn't hurt. As he opened the door, she followed closely.

"Rest." Was his only word as he stood at the head of the bed that was against the wall in the middle of the room.

Walking over, she sat down and pulled her legs onto the bed. Looking up at him, he stood looking down with a blank look.

"Sir, what room is this?" she asked softly as she felt an exhaustion over take her that she hasn't felt until now. Her body was more tired than she first thought. "I didn't ask the first time."

His words whispered into her mind as she looked into his eyes. For a reason she couldn't explain, she found it hard to keep her eyes open.

"My room."

Operation: Retainer

To retain is to hold back. To hold back is to restrain. To restrain is to limit. Everything needs a limit. If not, then total chaos.

Sera sighed to himself as he laid back on the bed. Over the last year, the missions were getting harder and he was getting injured more often. And the missions that he was given for his tithe were what some would consider suicide. His twelve and a half year old body wasn't really meant to sustain a bullet or thirty. Turning his head to the side, he looked quietly at Heather as she worked to get the ointment and medical bandages ready. Ever since he's finished their training, she became his favorite. And when he came back from a mission with a bullet in the arm and leg, she took it upon herself to help him. Originally, he turned her down, but soon after, Susan gave her the authority to heal him whenever he was injured. He didn't hate the idea of her healing him. She was always gentle with him. If he knew what a friend was, he would guess that she would be one.

"Captain," Heather sighed as she looked him over. "What do you do to end up in this condition? Do you just walk into the bullets as they come?"

And it would seem that over the year that she has been taking care of him, she's become more out spoken when it came to his health matters.

"No. I need to figure out a way to protect the entire body." He answered. "Perhaps full body armor."

"That would only inhibit your maneuverability and lower your efficiency." She stated. "The knights in the medieval era wore suits of armor, but were ultimately slow on the battle field when faced with an opponent that wore nothing as heavy."

"What about Kevlar?"

"That would further restrict your movements. Kevlar is heavy and not very flexible. It's only good as a vest, and even then, it's bulky. It can't even with stand more than three direct shots, let alone a hollow point. You would be killed before you finished the test run."

"Perhaps you're right." He conceded.

"I am right." She agreed. "Now, enough talk about that and let's fix you up."

Reaching over, she unzipped his vest and helped him out of it. Unbuckling his pants, she pulled them off as well. Looking down at his bloody body, she couldn't help the light flush that made it to her cheeks. Despite the fact that she has done this same act for almost a year, she could never fully get used to his body. It was hard and sculpted, not like the body of a normal pre-teen. He hadn't an ounce of body fat on him. Taking some cream from the side, she began to apply it to his stomach. She could feel each ab beneath his skin, which was a pale white. Almost pure, but not quite. Mixed with something, but she wasn't sure what. Her fingers further spread the cream between the dips in his abs and up his chest.

"What were you doing any way to get bruises like these?" she asked as she ran her hand over a large one that covered his chest. It was a dark, purple bruise that marred his pure skin. As she added pressure, she knew that anyone else would have flinched and or grimaced at the pain, but he seemed to be ignorant of it completely. Like the many other times she's had to heal him.

"Railing." He answered.

"Railing?"

"I was about to jump off the building onto an adjacent balcony, when I got shot in my leg. It made me lose balance and I fell an extra story and hit the railing with my chest."

She clicked her tongue disapprovingly.

"You shouldn't take risks like that. What would have happened if you had missed the railings all together?"

"I would be dead."

Every time she would bring about an alternate ending, he would always respond in the cold detached manner, with the same four words.

She sighed.

"Why do you always say that?"

"It's true."

"No, it's not. There is a possibility that you wouldn't die, but become paralyzed."

"I would ask for someone to pull the plug."

"Nobody would do that."

"I would order it then."

"They still wouldn't."

"I would ask you."

"You know I wouldn't do that."

"Then, I'll pull rank."

She didn't know what to say to that. He's never pulled rank before, because everyone listens to him.

"Don't."

"I would."

"Don't." she repeated. "Don't say things like that."

He didn't say another word. The silence that settled over them was beyond uncomfortable, but it was apparent that he didn't mind. Shifting from foot to foot, she began pulling out the bullets that rested in his right arm and left leg. She was careful not to go too deep. It wouldn't do for her to cause more problems than what were already present. Pulling out the first, in his arm, she looked at the bullet. She was grateful that it wasn't a hollow point round that went into his body, because she would be trying to seal up a gaping hole in his arm on top of finding the bullet. Dropping the bullet in a dish of ammonia, she moved down to his thigh. Fishing it out, she dropped it with a barely audible *tink*. Reaching over towards the medical tape, she began wrapping his leg and arm in gauze. She didn't bother with stitches. For a reason she couldn't explain or comprehend, he was able to heal wounds like these in only two nights rest. The only visible signs that there was a gunshot wound there was a slight redness and the new scar.

"Why shouldn't I say things like that?" he pondered aloud.

She was momentarily shocked that he would be asking a question like that. Looking into his eyes, she noticed a distant look. One she knew to be reminiscent.

"Because some people would be sad if you were to die." She spoke softly. She was surprised at her own response. She knew he was asking the question to himself, but she felt compelled to respond.

As his eyes turned to her, she was taken aback by the look she received. If he was anyone else, she would think it was childlike curiosity.

"Why?" the question seemed hollow, more so than his usual monotone. She shivered involuntarily.

"Because some people care for you." She answered again. Her mind was reeling. Never before has he ever posed questions like this to her before. Normally it was a short conversation comprised of nothing but work. This time, it seemed personal.

"Care is something I can live without." He said coldly, eyes hardening.

"Don't say that!" she chastised. As his eyes opened marginally wider, she was immediately regretful in her assertiveness. He was opening up to her and she yelled at him. He could close himself off and she would never be able to get the answers she sought. "I'm sorry Captain." She apologized quickly.

"Why shouldn't I say that?"

Looking at him, she saw a side of him that she's never seen before. The hardness in his eyes dissipated and they regained their usual shine. But his brows were set in a confused look.

"Everyone needs care and love." She decided to tell the truth. "No one can live without it."

He looked at her silently. Her heart was beating quickly in her chest as he gazed at her. Seeming to try and read her soul. He wasn't answering. His silence was deafening and she thought she would suffocate from the sheer weight of it.

"Cant they?" he asked quietly. "Can't they live regardless of if they have love or care? Does one really need to be loved in order to live? Does one need to care in order to survive?"

"Yes, they do." Despite him posing rhetorical questions, she answered them anyway. "To love is a wonderful thing. It's what makes life worth living. To find that special person in your life that completes you in every way."

"Have you found someone?" he asked in a whisper as his eye darted off to the side, avoiding hers. "Someone to love? To care for? To live for?"

She froze as her cheeks tinted a light pink. Has she found someone to love, care for, and live for?

"I-"

"Never mind." He relented with a shake of his head.

"Have you?" she found herself asking the question despite her better judgment. That was a personal question that was influenced by her own conscious and desires.

His head snapped back around to her and she recoiled at the speed. Slowly, he sat up in bed and threw his legs over the side. If he was anyone else, she would have told them to sit back down and rest, but he wasn't normal and he wasn't just anyone. Standing, he walked over towards the wall, away from her. He stood there silently staring at the stone before his eyes.

"Yes." He supposed.

She didn't think he would answer. He was still young, but he has experienced more in life than she has, and maybe more than the others put together.

"Can I ask who?" she ventured. The tone in his voice was filled with grief and she didn't want to ruin a relationship that took two years to build.

"Maya . . ." Was his answer as his voice overflowed with longing?

"Who was Maya?"

"My mother." He muttered. From behind, she thought she could see something red stemming from his tail bone. It was transparent, but she could still see it. It wrapped around his torso and she could see the tip coming over his left shoulder. Looking closer, she could see two small red triangles at the top of his head, but both were a little close to his head. Almost as if they were folded back. "She was killed."

"I'm sorry to hear that." And she truly was. No one should have to lose their parents at such an early age. "When?"

"Eight years."

She placed her palm over her mouth as she heard him. If her estimation was right, then he would have been only five at the time. He was so young. Is that why he was the way he was?

"When I was born, my parents were happy." He continued. He was obviously about to tell her something she's always wanted to know. "They both wanted a child, but for different reasons. My father wanted someone to carry on his name. My mother wanted someone to carry on the family traditions. But, my father's dream went out the window two minutes after he saw me."

"What happened?" she found herself immersed with his tale, and he was only beginning. Something happened to set forth the events that would make him into what he has become. As he turned around, she spotted his golden slit eyes glaring, only mirrored by a smaller set that seemed perched on his shoulder. She flinched as she caught sight of them, but knew they weren't directed at her.

"My eyes." He answered stonily.

"Your eyes?" she would admit, the first time she saw his eyes they frightened her. But, they also intrigued her as well. Something about them was different, and it wasn't just the color and design.

"The moment he saw my eyes, he called me a demon. A spawn of Lucifer. A serpent. He's hated me from that moment on." His eyes regained their original stare as he continued. "So, from then on, I spent every moment with my mother. She loved me regardless of my eyes and cherished me. That is, until I turned three."

"What happened then?"

His hand moved to his heart, right above the X.

"On the night of my birthday, my father stabbed me in the heart with an ice pick." He growled. She thought she saw his eyes flash, but they were still gold. "My mother heard my scream while she was on her way to read me a bedtime story and ran into the room. Finding me, she rushed me to the hospital. The doctors said that I was dead. My heart stopped. My body was ice cold. But my mother ordered them to help me. After three hours of trying, they finally gave up. As they removed the broken pick from my heart, it began beating again. I drew breath. I was alive, but I died that day. My mother was overjoyed that I was still alive. After that, I was never allowed to leave her side. For two years I was happy with simply being with her. Having her at my side. She was the one to protect me from the harsh words and glares that I got from the community. The cold shoulders I would receive from children my own age. But on my fifth birthday, my father gave me a present I would never forget."

"He killed her." She whispered morosely. She couldn't stop the tears that fell from her eyes as she listened to his tale. That was simply awful. To have your father attempt to kill you and then to have him turn around and kill your mother. And all of this on his birthdays.

"He was trying to kill me." He responded with a smile that made her tears come faster. "He was too much of a coward to kill me himself, so he sent someone else to do the dirty work for him. My mother didn't try and fight him off. I could see it all from a bush she wanted me to hide behind. He stabbed her and ran off. My mother, in her dying breaths, told me to go to my grandfather, and he would tell me the truth. Heeding her words, I went to him. He told me everything. About my last name. The true purpose of my eyes and what they meant. And why my mother had to die. As it turns out, it was my fault. Throwing myself into the family traditions and books, as she wanted me to do, I became what she wished of me."

"Can I ask what that was?"

He seemed to think about the answer as his eyes gained a considerate glint. The small reptile that rested on his shoulder seemed to whisper in his ear.

"Noir."

That one word sent her mind into frenzy. That name. That simple, one word name was a legend. She honestly thought it was nothing more than a myth. She's read about it before, but the only things she could gleam from the pages of history were a name: *Noir. Shadow. Darkness.* And even if a fraction of what was in the books were to be interpreted, then they were an influential part in the creation of the United States and countless other countries as well.

"Noir." She repeated the word on her lips. Never before did she think she would speak that name.

"When I finished my training, I went to visit my mothers' grave. I saw my father, for the first time in two years, in front of the very woman's grave that he murdered and had the nerve to mourn. I killed him in front of her grave."

This time, she was certain his eyes changed, as the red tinge seemed to make it self known behind him. It wagged, with what seemed like, delight. Reminded her of a dog that was happy. But his eyes dismissed the thought of a dog entirely. They were vermilion in color, and the slits seemed to have become slightly thinner. As one after another tail appeared behind him, she shuddered. This wasn't possible. It wasn't possible to have eyes that could change colors. It wasn't possible to have snakes appear and disappear randomly. It wasn't possible to have tails. But as she counted the tails, and stopped at nine, she felt ice settle in her stomach. There was only one subject she knew about that involved multiple tailed animals. She did a study on the myth for school. The Biju, or Tailed Beasts. They consisted of nine animals, each holding a different element. They were ranked from the weakest; who was Shukaku: the one tailed raccoon-dog. And the strongest. She swallowed. The strongest was the King of Biju and thought to be the king of Hell. That title belonged to Kyuubi no Kitsune, the nine tailed fox, and god of fire.

"Kyuubi." She whispered fearfully as she gazed at his figure. She couldn't turn her eyes away, in fear of angering him.

"And, one year ago, I killed my own grandfather with the weapon he gave me as a gift." He growled with a glint in his eyes. "He surprised me by attacking while I came for a visit about the family books. He didn't tell me why he was fighting me. The only thing I knew was that I wouldn't, couldn't die. As I severed his legs and arms, he told me of the Law. There could only be one Noir per generation. The stubborn old fool died telling me to continue the family tradition. He wasted his last breaths."

She was beyond stunned. Words didn't describe what it was that she was feeling at the moment. It was his fault that his mother died. He killed his father. He killed his grandfather. Who else did he have? He was alone in the world. Completely, utterly alone, and it hurt her. She wanted to know him better, but she wasn't prepared for something like this.

"Now do you understand why I should die?" he asked cockily. "Why I am not deserving of such things as Love and Care? They are both meaningless things only humans cling to in foolish faith."

Her body was moving without her mind. She couldn't comprehend why he would say that.

/Step/

No, she took that back. She knew why he thought that.

/Step/

He was blaming himself for killing his mother when he could do nothing about the situation.

/Step/

He killed his father for retribution. A man that even though he despised with all his being, was supposed to love and care for him regardless.

/Step/

And she knew that if he was honest with himself, he loved his father despite his hatred. Even if it was miniscule in comparison to the mother.

/Step/

And he killed his grandfather. The only person to take him in after his mothers' death and teach him what she would have. The only last living relative that accepted him as he was. The second person that betrayed him.

/Stop/

Looking down, she couldn't help the new tears that flowed freely from her eyes. He was a lost demon child. He didn't know where he belonged. Hated by his own, and despised and loathed by the rest.

"Such a lonely existence," She sobbed softly. Her hand went up to cup his cheek reflexively. "How could one live such a life?"

"I am not normal." He responded with trouble.

"Such sorrow shouldn't even exist." She caressed the skin beneath his eye as she shook her head slowly. "I'm so sorry."

"What are you doing?" he asked uneasily as his eyes shifted.

Not answering, she wrapped her arms around his chest and pulled him into hers. She wanted to comfort him. To shield him from further pain. To show him life.

"You are deserving of Love Kyuubi." She whispered as she buried her nose in his hair. Her use of the name was subconscious. "You deserve to be cared for."

"No," he muttered into her shirt as he shook his head. "I don't."

"You asked me if I loved anyone." She said softly as she pulled him from her chest. Looking down into his ruby eyes, she smiled lightly. "Asked me if I cared for anyone. The answer to both is you." As the words left her mouth, she knew she had an affect on him. His eyes grew wider, in what she knew to be shock and they deepened in color. The whites of his eyes were slowly beginning to become red.

"You love me?" he asked uncertainly.

She never thought she would see the day when he would be scared, but she didn't really care about it. Kneeling slightly, she brought her face to his. Looking deep into his eyes she kissed his lips lightly. She kept her eyes open, because she knew, that even in this distraught state he was in, he could still read her and be able to tell that the words she spoke and the actions were true. Breaking away, she smiled softly.

"I love you and I care for you Captain."

"Seraphim." He said as crimson streaks marked his face.

"Seraphim, I love you." She repeated as she wiped his tears. "You may not be human. You may be a demon. But either way, I will always love you and care for you." She hugged him close as he wept silently. Guiding him over towards the bed, she sat down with him straddling her lap. As his arms gripped her shirt tightly, she could feel the red tails wrapping around her.

"La vie est Enfer. Là mou est Enfer. Enfer est le Ciel. Permettez-moi de vous accompagner au paradis et vous soulager du purgatoire.[11]" He whispered.

"Oui, mon amour[12]." She whispered in French. "Life is Hell. Love is Hell. Hell is Heaven. You must go through it in order to live." She squeezed him slightly. "And as long as I am with you, I will make purgatory, paradise."

"Merci Lilith[13]." He replied drowsily.

As she looked down, she knew he was already asleep. Demon child or not, it mattered not.

"Good night Kyuubi. May you always remember that I will be there for you."

---

[11] Life is Hell. Love is Hell. Hell is Heaven. Allow me to be your escort to paradise and relieve you from this purgatory.

[12] Yes, my love.

[13] Thank you Lilith. Lilith being predecessor to Eve: in Hebrew Scripture, the first woman, believed to have been created before Eve but left because of a dispute between her position during intercourse with Adam.

Operation: Bloody Banquet AKA Masquerade Massacre

Sitting in his hotel room, Suen calmly looked at his weapons. His sword lay displayed before him, the black coating absorbing any and all light that came near it. Almost as if it were trying to darken the room further with its mere presence. The serrated edge of the blade seemed to sing as he reached forward to run his fingers across the edge, near the blade. As his fingers ran back, he could hear the teeth of the reverse side growl in anticipation. Or maybe it was him. He could never be sure. Smiling gently at her, he pets the blade on last time. Benehime always seemed to be ready for blood whenever he took her out. He remembered when the mistress smiled at him as he told her the name of his blade, but he found it fitting. Bloody princess, one who enjoyed and relished in the bloodshed. Turning his attention towards his custom Desert Eagles, he smirked. He was sure to ask for the most powerful automatic hand gun he could handle. One was jet black and had a fox on the barrel with its tail wrapped around the handle. He named it Noir, after his names sake. The second, a startling white, with a purple snake head near the barrel and its tail around the handle. Blanc. It was ironic that his favorite gun was snow white and yet covered in more blood than any one person has in their body. Looking back at his pillow he reached for his surgical gloves. Snapping the wrist of the gloves, he was reminded of how both his grandfather and Susan both had the idea of wiping down the shells of the bullets and loading them with surgical gloves to ensure the shells don't have fingerprints. It was always too much of a hassle to pick up the shells after a job.

After loading ten clips, he took off his gloves and took out his cell phone. Pressing his speed dial, he pressed the phone to his ear.

"Master." he greeted as he heard her pick up.

"Fox." she said over the line.

"I'm here and ready." he told her with a grin.

"Hold off on those orders." he heard her say on the other side. He growled in his throat.

"They are my sacrifices." he said threw gritted teeth. "They are mine now. Why are you telling me to hold off?"

"There is a news crew that's covering the dinner party. The targets are mingled with ordinary civilians. As it turns out, our information was a little off. We don't want to become public knowledge." he scoffed. A little off by over a hundred is like saying a car weighs more than a person.

"I'll call you back." he growled before hanging up. Standing, he walked out towards his door and into the hallway. Hitting the button for the down floor, he waited for the elevator. As the doors opened, he looked up towards a beautiful woman who wore a crimson dress. Her stunning blond hair was feathered and lightly touched her shoulder.

"Well, aren't you a cutie." she cooed as she bent down to his level. He smiled at her as he tilted his head. His gold eyes glittered as he regarded her beautiful visage. "And you have such beautiful eyes."

"Thank you." he said with a light blush. "You are pretty."

"Why thank you sweet heart." she said as she patted his cheek. Standing fully, "Which floor are you going to?" she asked.

"The party." he answered.

"I'm going there too." she said with a smile. "Can I get a dance from you?"

He nodded his head as the doors closed. As they opened, he walked out and into the lobby. Walking behind the woman, he walked into the brightly lit ballroom. He could see his targets dancing around and enjoying themselves. Taking a mental picture of the assembled masses, he counted over two hundred, with only about one hundred of them being the targets. Turning on his heel, he walked briskly back to his room. Walking towards his bed, he picked up his guns and placed them at the small of his back. Grabbing his sword, he sheathed it. Grabbing his spare clips, he shoved them into his deep pockets. Fixing his jacket, he made sure he covered his guns. Picking up his phone, he dialed home again.

"Fox?" she sounded confused as to why he would call.

"Master." he growled. "My guns are fully loaded. My sights are trained. My blade is screaming for blood. The only things that I await are your orders."

"Fox . . ."

"I await the order to kill, to eat, to feed." he sneered with a wicked smile. "I'm asking for you to tell me what to do. The orders have to come from your mouth. You are the one who has to sentence them to their fate. I can so easily destroy them, send them all to hells fire, and I will do it all just for you. I'm waiting, Susan 'Bloody Rose' Roth, *my* Master." he waited. And waited. And waited. To him, it felt like an eternity. His blood was literally boiling and he wanted to release his pent up stress. He could hear Benehime growling in impatience. She wanted to bite into flesh, to rend muscle from bone, to make humans scream in fear as death closes in on them.

"I have given you your orders Inari!" she shouted into the phone. He could feel his blood lust rise at her tone, her authority. "You are to kill everyone in sight. Leave no one alive!"

"Say it!" he growled in anticipation. "Say the words that I long to hear, the words that I love!"

"Release!"

He smiled wickedly as he laughed hysterically

"Yes! That's the Master I know!" he cackled. "You still know how to get my blood pumping Master. Your will shall be done." he finished as he hung up. Placing the phone in his pocket, he put on his cloak and hood and walked out of the room after grabbing a duffle bag.

Making it to the ballroom, he fixed his mask, to ensure it didn't fall off. Walking in, he placed his bag down near a far corner. Going back towards the door, he ensured that it was locked, before walking to the other doors and locking them as well. Turning back towards the party at hand, he spotted the woman dancing in the middle of the floor. He knew it was her, because even though she was wearing a mask, he knew her hair anywhere. Gliding towards her, he picked up on the slight gasps that were heard as he passed the tables of his targets. He smirked beneath his mask. *"You may have heard of me, but I promise you I am no ghost."* he thought evilly.

Reaching her, he pulled on her dress slightly to gain her attention.

Looking down, she smiled at him as he leaned on his cane.

"Well, are you here for me?" she asked kindly as she waved a man off.

"Yes." he answered.

As another song began, she placed her hands on his shoulders as he wrapped his around her waist. Swaying to and fro with her, they danced together. Her long red dress twirling as they waltzed.

"You dance better than the stiffs that are here." she commented idly.

"Thank you." he said as he looked up at her. "But, I'm afraid that our dance has to be cut short."

She stopped and looked down in disappointment.

"Awww," she pouted. "Does it have to?" she asked childishly.

He drew his blade from behind her back and thrust it up through her back, the tip of the blade bursting through the middle of her breasts. As she began choking on the blood, that he had no doubt been filling her lungs, he sneered at her shocked face.

"Yes, it does." he answered as he pulled the blade free. As she fell to the floor like a lifeless doll, he drowned out the screams as he looked at her. She was one of his biggest targets. He could hear the sounds of many feet rushing towards the doors and even the targets readying their weapons that were hidden on their person. He only pulled up his hood and awaited the impacts that were bound to come.

As the first bullet struck his side, he kneeled, head bowed, as the rest followed suit. He waited until the only sound he could hear was the screams and the clicks of empty clips. Slowly standing, he looked out amongst the rest and couldn't repress the evil grin that spread across his face. They were all standing, lining the walls with their persons, and cowering in fear. How he loved a cornered prey. Drawing his guns, he took aim at the targets first, deciding work before pleasure was the best course of action when he had so many play toys to choose from. Taking aim, he began firing into their non lethal targets. If he killed each one with a simple bullet to the head, he wouldn't be able to enjoy this. Reloading, he began again, slowly walking towards the frightened people as they dispersed along the walls, in an effort to evade him. *"Such silly creatures."* he thought amused. Reload after reload; he emptied his clips into their shoulders, knees and sides. After scanning the room for any targets he might have missed, he smiled happily that he didn't. Placing the guns back on his back, he drew his sword. As it was released from the sheath, he could have sworn that she squealed in excitement. *"Soon, my darling, you will be able to taste their flesh."* he promised. Dropping his cloak, he sprinted towards the nearest couple. They were huddled up next to each other, eyes closed in hopes that this was all a dream.

"Open your eyes." he said softly. "I want to see the fear." he finished as he cut them in half; the sharp blade cutting through bone and muscle like a hot knife through butter. Turning on the huddled masses he pounced on them like the fox he was.

He slaughtered them. Every single one was not left intact by the time he finished. Standing in the middle of it all, he relished in the carnage. The severed hands, legs, heads, limbs in general were strewn about in an animalistic fashion. He walked over towards the camera that filmed the entire thing on a tripod and pressed the stop button. Taking out the tape, he walked back over towards his bag. Placing it inside, he turned at the sound of a whimper. One person was left mostly intact, save for an arm.

Walking towards them slowly, he thought about what he was going to do with the survivor.

"S-stay away-y from m-me." the woman stuttered as she pushed herself against the wall, trying to hide herself beneath a bloody table cloth.

He smirked at her, behind his mask. Taking it off, his ruby eyes flashed with blood lust as he regarded her frantic expression. Stopping before her, he raised his blade and pointed it at her head.

"You, why would you do this?" she mumbled as she shook her head. "Why would the Spirits want to do something like this?"

So, she knows of the Spirits? Snake mused as he watched. He found it odd that she would know something about the organization, when she wasn't on the list. *How many others were subject to this information?* He asked himself as Fox lifted her chin with the tip of his blade.

"I am Inari." he said in a growl. "And they were my offerings. They betrayed the spirits and were simply at the wrong place at the wrong time."

"You Demon!" she shouted in hatred.

He chuckled at her accusation.

"I am." he conceded with a nod.

"How can you take so many lives and not care?" she asked mortified.

He looked around and allowed a content sigh to escape his lips. The gallons of blood that flooded the floor looked so beautiful with the light of the moon flitting through the windows. To him, it seemed to be a lake of black blood, the blood of the sinful. The countless body parts seemed to be the remains of a voyage that went awry. He could still hear their screams for mercy, like a distant lullaby meant to lull him to sleep. It was beautiful.

Turning back towards her, he tilted his head.

"I did nothing, but eat." he argued. "Do you question a mouse as to why it killed a bug? Why the snake eats the rat? Why the fox eats the snake? Why humans send their dogs to hunt the fox for its pelt? No, you do not." he answered his own questions with a shake of his head. "This is simply the natural order of things. The circle of life if you will. The strong shall live, and the weak shall die." he paused as he lowered his sword. "I was stronger, hence why I was the one to kill them."

"If what you say is right, then why am I still alive?" she asked aghast.

"For two reasons." he began nonchalantly. "The first being that you have the guts to stand up to me, and call me a demon; I found it amusing. And second of all, I want someone alive to tell anyone else and everyone else what will happen once you cross the spirits."

"I see." she said softly.

Kneeling down, he moved the table cloth from her person as he gripped her chin lightly, forcing her terrified eyes into his own.

"You will tell everyone of what has happened here." he ordered gently. "If you don't, then I will find you and sever the rest of your limbs." as he finished, he brought the butt of the sword to the back of her neck. He let her body fall to the ground.

Standing, he walked over toward his bag, he unclipped his mask. Taking off his face mask, he inhaled deeply. The scent of death was still so very strong in the ball room. After taking off his vest, he opened his bag and took out a spare set of clothes. Placing his soiled garments inside of the bag, he changed his clothes. Distantly, his ears picked up on the sound of police sirens. Rolling around on the floor, he was sure to get blood all over his clothes, before dabbing some on his face. Staring at his bloody hands, he growled in his throat. The blood was no longer warm. It felt so cold. He didn't like cold blood. It was unnatural. Not normal. Synthetic.

As the doors to the ballroom were forced open, and he could hear the SWAT teams calling over the radio that they found two alive, he suppressed a grin as they picked up his crying figure. He held his bag close to his body as they placed him in the back of an ambulance.

"Humans are so predictable."

After slipping out of the hospital they admitted him into, he called back home one last time.

"Master, the offerings have been accepted." he murmured.

"Seal." she said clearly.

"Mistress, what would you like me to do now?" he asked as he looked towards the sky.

"Come home."

Nodding his head, even though he knew she couldn't see it, he hung up the phone. Sighing, he continued looking out at the sky.

"One born in darkness can never see the light of day. For once they have gotten their first taste of the light, they are blinded and forever plunged back into the dark abyss." turning on his heel, he started his long walk back towards base. *And one, who has been born of bloodshed, must shed blood in order to live. Because since birth all they have known is how to bleed.*

Finally reaching home, he walked into the darkened base. Everyone else was either asleep or home, so he didn't have to worry about anyone simply popping out. Coming towards her door, he knocked once and waited for her to notice.

"Come in Suen." Susan ordered from the other side.

Opening the door, his eyes adjusted to the dim lighting quickly. Closing the door, he walked up to her chair. Standing before her, he waited for her to look up.

"So, mission accomplished?" she asked calmly.

He nodded his head.

"Yes. All targets have been silenced and the offerings have been accepted." He reported.

"Good." She approved.

"But," he paused as he reached into his bag. "I have something for you to look at." He finished, holding the tape.

She quirked an eyebrow, but nodded her head. Standing, she led him out of the room into the lounge down the hall. As he walked towards the TV and placed the tape inside of the VCR, she stood back.

Pressing rewind, he was mildly curious as to how she would react to what was filmed. He knew he went overboard on the victims, but they were his and he would be damned if anyone would tell him not to play with his food. As it stopped, he pressed play and returned to her side. As the tape played, he kept his eye on her out of his peripheral vision. He could see her flinch slightly as he stabbed the woman through her chest from behind. He assumed it was simply from surprise. After all, you couldn't see him draw his blade from behind her back. As the rest of the tape finished, he could see a slight smirk on her face.

"Mistress," he began, gaining her attention. "There was one survivor. She knew of the Spirits, but she wasn't on the list."

She nodded her head.

"I know." She answered. "The one hundred and three targets that were on the list were simply executives that were a part of the Dawn, Rooks, Royals, and some of the businesses here in Wind. None of them were of vital importance, but their absence will slow things down for them. The others that were there, fifty-seven of them to be exact, were moles from other organizations, including informants from the FBI, CIA, ATF, and DEA. They were trying to infiltrate the organizations. Normally, that wouldn't be such a big deal, because they weren't trying to get into here. But, if they were to gain entrance into one of our enemies, they would have access to information about us that would lead to questions. The other fifty were simply witnesses to something that they shouldn't have seen."

He nodded his head. He didn't really care about if they weren't on his list of targets or not. He didn't care if they were normal, loving parents, with families and friends. He only cared about completing his mission.

"Very good work Suen." She congratulated.

"There is something else." He began, while walking towards the VCR and pressing eject.

"And what might that be?" she asked with a raised eyebrow.

Walking back towards her, he held the tape out for her to take.

"This is a gift for our enemies." He answered with a smirk that only widened as he watched her make an identical expression.

"I love the way you think Sera." She appraised while taking the tape. "I'll have Twitch make copies of this and send it to them immediately." She reached a hand down and patted his head affectionately.

He smiled as he felt her fingers in his hair. This was the only other thing he cared about. Making her happy. It made him warm inside, like the many times his mother kissed his forehead.

"They will think twice before they mess with us wont they?" he asked, looking up into her eyes.

She nodded her head again with a smile.

"They will indeed Sera."

Chapter 12

Pandora's Box

Pandora opened the box Zeus gave her out of curiosity. All the sins, vices, diseases and troubles escaped into the world. As she closed the lid, the only thing remained was Hope. The one thing left to comfort man. I wonder what would happen if the lid was opened once more.

As Sera walked into his room and wasn't surprised to see Heather sitting next to his bed with a smile. He smiled lightly at her as he slowly walked towards his bed. She was the only person he could talk to about his problems. Of course, she was incredibly persistent in the fact that he communicates more. Normally, he wouldn't have accepted such talk from anyone and brushed them off, but she was persistent and he eventually gave in. Sitting down on the bed, he sighed.

"So, how was the mission?" she asked as she leaned closer.

"The new cloak was a success." He said as he looked at her. "They stopped every bullet that came my way."

"Well, that's expected. I told you the 'Dragon Skin' armor was the perfect bullet proof vest. It can withstand a grenade blast."

"True."

"But, you didn't tell me about the mission." She reminded with a small smirk. "Don't try and get out of telling me about it."

He smiled lightly.

"It was the most fun I have ever had thus far." He answered truthfully. "The blood, the screams, the bodies," His body shivered. "It was like a dream come true."

She smiled and nodded her head.

"Well, I'm happy that you had fun." She began while standing. "Now, let me get you out of these mission clothes so I can check you out."

Taking the cloak in her hands, she walked over towards his closet. Opening the door, she placed it on a hook that was present on the back of the door. As she was closing it, she spotted a small shadowy figure at the bottom on the floor. Kneeling down, she spotted a black box covered in a thin layer of dust. Her curiosity getting the better of her, she picked up the box and closed the door. She could see a tag tapped to the top with his name written on it. From the looks of it, it was written by a female.

"Sera?" she called as she began walking over towards him. "What's this?" as she caught his attention, his eyes instantly locked onto the box. His face was set in an odd expression that she couldn't immediately identify, but she thought it was a mixture of shock and fear.

"It's a box." He answered distantly.

"I know that." She wanted to know what's gotten into him to make him so focused on the box. Taking her previous seat, she placed the box in her lap. "But, what's in it?"

"I don't know."

"You don't want to tell me?" she asked as she tilted her head. Only getting silence as an answer, she nodded her head. "If you don't want to tell me, it's alright."

"I never opened it." He finally whispered.

"Never?"

She couldn't believe that he owned a box and was never curious to the contents. It was human nature to be curious. But, then again, it was him she was thinking about.

"No."

"Well then," she held the box out to him. "Open it."

"No." his voice held a faint tone of fear.

"Why not?" she asked as she held it out further. "It's obvious that the person who wrote the tag wanted you to open it."

"I can't." He whispered as he shook his head.

She's never seen him like this before, and it worried her. He's never been afraid of anything that she could remember. What was so frightening about a box? Pulling it back into her lap, she brushed away some of the dust. *Pandora*. So, that was the name of the box. Surely it couldn't be because of the myth. Taking the box from her lap, she placed it on the table. Standing, she sat next to him on the bed as he turned his head away from her. Whatever it is that's bothering him, it's serious. He's never avoided eye contact with anyone.

"What's wrong?" she asked softly. "You can tell me, remember?" slowly his head turned towards her, and she looked into his eyes. The gold rings seemed to be brighter now, and she was sure it wasn't because of the candle in the room. As his eyes flickered over towards the box, she caught the fear that flashed in them. "What's so special about the box?"

"My mother left it for me."

Receiving a gift from a dead mother, eight years after her death would be a little awkward, but she would still be curious to what it contains.

"You don't want to open it because it's hers?" she asked gently.

"I don't want to open it, because of what it might contain."

"How long have you kept it?"

"One year."

"And when was the last time you've seen it?"

"One year."

Reaching over, she grabbed the box and set it in his lap.

"I think you should open it." She suggested. He must be torn up inside to know what is in there. What his mother left him. He looked at her silently for several long moments. His eyes never blinked. Originally, she found it rather hard to keep his gaze. One who never blinked was rather intimidating. She asked him about it once, and he told her that his eyes had a thin, translucent layer of skin, and because of that, he didn't have to blink. He didn't even sleep. That originally gave her cause for alarm. Everyone needed sleep. It was the only way for the body and mind to rest. But, after countless tries at staying awake to see if he would, she found herself accepting the fact that he didn't sleep.

Slowly, he turned back towards the box that sat in his lap. Bit by bit his hands grasped the string that held the box closed. Pulling it, he allowed it to fall to the floor. Taking a deep breath, he opened the lid. Peering inside, he spotted a self addressed envelope and a small white book beneath it. Grabbing the letter first, he held it out towards Heather.

"Open it."

Nodding her head, she took the letter and opened it without question.

"It's from your mother addressed to you." She told him.

He nodded his head.

"Can you read it for me?"

Dear Seraphim,

Hello my little one. I'm so sorry that it had to come to this, but there was no other way. I saw this coming, and there was nothing I could do to stop it. I know that my death has hurt you deeply, but I want you to know that I am so, so sorry. I'm sorry for all the pain that I put you through. I truly wish there was something that could have prevented such events from happening, but there weren't. Inside this box is my diary. I leave this with you in the hopes that it will answer some of your questions. Take care, my darling little angel. I love you with all my heart and soul.

Love forever,
Maya Blanc

She watched silently as he absorbed the words. It was obvious that Maya loved him very much. She found the wording a little weird though. The way she was talking made it sound like she knew she was going to die, and that he was going to have some questions. As he picked up the book and handed it to her, she took it with care. This was something very important to him. She didn't want to damage it. Not waiting for the order to open it, she opened it to a random page.

October 11th,

I'm so happy. I have a son now. A son! The family name can finally be passed on. And what's even more unexpected is that he's the reincarnation of Valkyrie, one of our greatest. But, I must confess, I'm a little afraid. Marcus was enraged when he found out about little Sera's eyes. He called him all sorts of hurtful names, and it took all my will power to not strike him. How could he say that about his own son? Our son? But, not only does Marcus seems to not like him, the doctors called him a mutant, or rather his eyes a mutation. They don't seem to understand that his eyes are what make him special. It was no mistake that he was born with these eyes. I know it.

"Continue." He requested softly as he looked at her. "I need to know."

She didn't know what it was that he wanted the answer to, but she nodded her head. Flipping a few pages into the book, she stopped on one at random.

March 3rd,

Things are starting to become strained. I don't know what is wrong. Marcus won't even look at him. And once, when I was coming back from the restroom, I spotted him releasing killing intent at him! He won't even allow me to take him outside. I don't know what's going on with him, but I know it cannot be good. Whatever he is thinking, it's not good for little Sera.

She didn't stop. Turning the pages again, she stopped and resumed. She could tell that he wasn't exaggerating when he told her that his father hated him early on in life. From the moment he seen him, he didn't like him.

October 10th,

It's been one year since my little angel was brought into the world. Today, I spent the whole day chasing him around the house. He's a fast little thing! Like a snake he is. I was out of breath by the time I caught him. When he called me mamma, I wept with joy. And his cute smile only made him cuter. After

I put him to bed, I just had to write about it. I still can't believe it. He called me mamma! Yay!

She felt herself chuckle at that. It seemed that his mother was a loving woman who loved her son very much. Looking up at him, she found a small smile on his lips. It was obvious that he could remember the event. Flipping through the pages again, she stopped.

January 27th,

He can talk! He can say complete sentences! I was so proud of my little one I couldn't help but pick him up and twirl him around. He giggled and laughed as we fell onto the floor. I'm so happy. He's getting smarter. Although, it should be expected. He is after all, Valkyrie.

But as I walked outside with him to go to the grocery store, I heard whispers. I knew he could hear them too, but he couldn't understand them well. If his tilting of his head was any indication. It appears that someone has been spreading lies and I intend to get to the bottom of it. But, as I looked down at his face, I knew I couldn't stay mad.

She turned again, this time looking specifically for his birthday. It seemed that she became excited around that time.

October 9th,

I had a weird dream. I'm not sure why, but I dreamt about a conversation I had with my grandmother once before she died. I was only 5 at the time, but I can still remember, because it was so strange. She told me "he will be born on two strikes and be as pure as pure. Watch for god, for the third will come from his hand." I never had this dream before. It's a little unnerving, but I won't let it bother me. I have to get ready for my little ones third birthday and I won't let a dream stop me from celebrating it with him.

She turned the page.

October 10th,

I don't know what to do. Marcus tried to kill my baby boy! He tried to kill my Seraphim! How could he? I am going to kill him. He deserves to die for this. If my baby dies, he is going to die.

I can't lose him. I just can't. I don't have anything left in this world. I want him to live. He is going to live. He has too much to do in his life for him to die. Goddesses, if you can hear me, please answer my prayers. Please give me back my son. Don't allow him to be taken from his mother. Please give him the strength to endure the harshest of trials and to come back to me once more.

October 11th,

He woke up! I knew he would. The doctors told me he was dead, but he showed them! My baby boy is back. I thank the goddess that he's safe. I should have known that he wouldn't die. He can't die until the world is once again safe. When I went to meet him, he was franticly looking around for something, anything to hide under. His heart rate was racing and his eyes were wide with fright. It hurt me to see him like that. To be so afraid of everybody, because someone he was supposed to trust stabbed him in the heart. As his eyes landed on me, I could see them light up with joy, relief, and need. But, he seems different. He still acts the same, but his skin is paler, almost white. He clung to me for dear life as I held him, and I suppose it was to be expected. But I promise to never let anything happen to him again. And despite the physical changes, I don't care. He's still my Sera. And I will protect him with my life, even after I die.

April 7ᵗʰ,

How could Marcus say such things to people? And how could they believe him? He's spouting lies about an innocent child and they all believe him, simply because my son has special eyes. It doesn't matter though. Soon, they will realize how special he really is. And when they do, they will plead for forgiveness.

April 15ᵗʰ,

The children are so mean to him. It seems that they have taken after their parents in believing that he is a demon. A monster. He's none of those things. He is an angel. My little angel and in time the world will see. But looking at his crestfallen face brings tears to my eyes. He will never have friends if they all are like their parents. It seems that only time will tell if they will change. But I fear change is not forthcoming.

October 10ᵗʰ,

Marcus has taken to leaving on his birthday, which is just fine by me. It gave us time to create our own special Eden. He looked so happy while playing in the dirt, planting flowers that I almost thought of him as a nymph. He seems to love nature, just like Valkyrie did. He's so much like her. He seems to love it more than he loves other people, though I can not blame him. The children calling him names. The parents passing glares. It's too much for him. I fear that in time, if the people do not change, then he will be under tremendous strain. And I wonder about the path humanity is walking down.

At this point, she met nothing but blank pages. She was going to tell him that there was nothing left to read, but the last three pages had writing. Stopping at the first, she began to read.

October 9th,

It's that same dream I've been having for the last four months. But this time it's different. There's more. "He will be born on two strikes and be as pure as pure. Watch for god, for the third will come from his hand. After the third is made, the moon will be struck by a comet sent by god. The shadow will grow from out of the moons own and encompass the world in a shroud of darkness."

Normally, everyone passed what my grandmother said off as her old age, but before she was old, she was a seer. I've been thinking about this and I can only come to one conclusion. I am going to die soon. Seraphim was born on October 10th, 10, 10, X, X. two strikes. Priests are the disciples of god and Marcus stabbed him in the heart. Now he has an X shaped scar on his chest. "The third will come from his hand." I am to die by someone who is going to be sent by Marcus.

And it's because of this that I leave you these Seraphim. If I am going to die, then I will leave you, my little one, with my final thoughts.

I know you most likely thought that I only cared about you because of your eyes, but that's not true. I love you for you and you alone. I could care less what color your eyes are. You are still my little Sera and I love you with all my heart. Believe me, I wish there was another way around this, but there isn't. If you have learned anything, it's this: Just because you know the future, doesn't mean you can change it. Because what you choose to do, because of the information, may be what you were destined to do.

I only have two wishes Sera. Please, make something of yourself. Always want. Do not settle for second best. And last, give me grand kids. I want at least one. Please bring them to me when you have them. I would very much like to see them.

I love you with my heart and soul, and whoever gets you to open up, I want to thank you too. And please stay with him. He will need someone of your devotion and love to look after him. And hopefully you will give me some grand kids.

*With everlasting love,
Maya Blanc*

She couldn't help but smile near the last line. Even when she knew she was going to die, she still had a sense of humor. She couldn't hide the blush that tickled her cheeks as she read the final line. Looking up at his face, she saw a smile grace his features as crimson streaks marked his face. Next to him, on the bed, sat a red fox and a crimson snake, both seemed relaxed. It was the first time she's ever seen the fox. She's only ever seen his tails, but this time she could see his entire body, nine tails and all. Such an odd sight. At times, she wondered why she was able to see them, and others weren't, but eventually decided that it didn't matter. She accepted long ago that she was not normal. After all, she was sitting in a room with a cold blooded killer and she was comfortable. If that wasn't unusual, then nothing was.

Placing a hand on his, she squeezed it lightly.

"Are you okay?" she asked softly.

He chuckled lightly as he looked at her.

"Will you have my kids?" he asked suddenly.

She sputtered as the blush seemed to intensify tenfold and she could feel steam coming out of her ears.

"I—I—I-"

"You don't have to answer." He told her as he settled down. "But, it seems I have been worried over nothing."

She sighed as he changed the subject. The question caught her off guard and she was not ready for it. Although, she knew she didn't stutter because of her about to reject him. She wasn't sure about if she was ready to have kids.

"What were you worried about?"

"I thought my mother only loved me because of my eyes. It turns out I was wrong." He answered.

"Well, I love you because of your eyes," she wiped his tears away with the back of her hand. "Your face," she trailed his cheek. "Your fighting spirit." She leaned close. "And I love you because you are you. Nothing more. Nothing less." As he smiled at her, she leaned in and kissed him gently. As he deepened the kiss with a flick of his tongue, she moaned lightly into his mouth. Pulling apart, she panted lightly as she rested her forehead against his. "Bon anniversaire amour.[14]" She whispered.

He nodded his head gently against hers.

"The first one in eight years."

---

[14] Happy Birthday, love.

Chapter 13

Repent

Guilt brings about remorse. Remorse brings about regret. These events only lead to one logical outcome. Penance.

"Do you hate me Sera?" Susan whispered as she hugged him tighter, trying to keep warm from the cold.

"No." he answered swiftly. "I don't hate you . . ." his voice trailed off towards the end. "I *loathe* you." he whispered softly into the night's air. She never noticed when his eyes shifted, or the knife that made its way towards her.

She stiffened when she felt a blade point at her spine.

"I can't blame you for it." she said softly.

"I despise you with every fiber of my being for what you have done to me in the past. For the scars on my body, and my soul." he continued. Slowly, he let the blade tip trail up her spine to the base of her neck. "But," he paused as he trailed the blade back down her back. "I also love you more than anything in this mortal plane of existence. When my mother died, you were there to pick up where she left off. I loved my mother deeply. But, I find myself, loving you more. You brought me in, trained me, fed me, clothed me, and loved Me." he pulled her back and looked into her eyes. His eyes continued to flicker from red to gold. "I hate you, but I love you. An oxymoron if I have ever known one. And it's for that reason that I vowed myself to you my Mistress," his eyes stayed gold, before flickering back to red and stayed. He leaned in closer towards her lips. His breath ghosted off of hers. "My keeper," he whispered.

"Inari . . ." she whispered as she felt his lips graze hers. Tilting her head up, she caught him in a gentle kiss.

"She is strong, yet weak." Fox commented as his tail wagged to and fro behind him. *No.* Suen said as he stood next to Fox. *She is not weak. She is only ashamed for what she has done. "She should not doubt her decisions. They will only lead to unease amongst the other Spirits."* Suen turned towards him with a raised eyebrow. *I didn't think you could think so far ahead Fox. You are indeed a surprising individual.* He commented dryly as he faced forward again. *"Snake, you just don't know."* Oh, but I do know, which is why I am doing what I am doing now. *"Making out with a woman that is no doubt 20 years your senior?"* No. he answered simply. *That is not what I am doing. I am reestablishing her confidence in herself and her judgment. Mistress cannot be weak and indecisive. She must be strong, unshakable, and above all,"* he trailed off as he and Fox made eye contact. *"She must be a God."* Fox finished. *"Only the strongest can wield the mightiest of swords. After all, many have tried to claim Excalibur for their own, but only Arthur was able to draw it from the stone and prove that he was destined to be king."* a slight smirk played on Suen's face. *Somebody is mighty high of themselves. "I was referring to Us."* Fox stated. *I know Fox. I know.* Returning to consciousness, he broke the kiss and stared into her eyes. "My mother," he continued. "And My Savior."

"But, what have I saved you from Sera?" she questioned softly as tears pricked at her eyes. "If I would have left you alone, you would have been a normal child with a normal life."

He sighed as he looked towards the moon. So much time has passed since his mother's death, that he almost didn't think any of it was real. That it was all simply a strange dream brought about by another one of his mothers' stories at bed time. That she would be there waiting with a smile on her face, like always, waiting to listen to him tell her of his dream. But, he knew that wasn't the case. She was dead. Gone. And he was here. Now. With his new mother, who was obviously distraught, in his arms. He would have sneered at something like this normally, but he couldn't bring himself to do so. It was just too perfect of a chance, and he honestly didn't want to.

"Have I ever told you why I look at the moon so much?" he asked suddenly. He didn't wait for a response. "My mother's name was Maya. That name belongs to the Goddess of the Moon. When I was born, I was considered a mutant. But even worse than that, I was considered a demon spawn from the Devil by my own father. My eyes didn't just appear like they are over time. From the instant I was born, my eyes were golden slits. My mother loved me dearly and thought of me an angel sent from above, which is why she named me Seraphim, after the highest order of angel. When I was 3, I was playing with some children, when they saw my eyes. They screamed. They screamed and yelled that I was a monster. When their parents heard the screams, they called me a demon as they ushered their children off. I ran home to my mother and told her about it. She simply smiled softly at me as silent tears ran down her face. I finally know what she was crying about, because the next day, she handed me a pair of sunglasses. Apparently, my father has been spreading the belief that God has sent him a demon spawn in the form of a child, his child, to test him. He said, "His eyes are the golden slits of the snake. A descendant of the one who was the cause of Adam and Eve exile out of Eden. God has sent this Serpent to test, not only me, but you all as well. Are we to be as easily swayed as Eve," at this point, he turned his gaze upon my mother. "Or, are we going to resist temptation and the silent promises that the Serpent suggests?" She simply held me and sang a song. "Golden slumbers kiss your eyes. Smiles await you when you rise. Sleep, pretty baby, do not cry. And I'll sing you a lullaby. Care you know not, therefore sleep, while I o'er you watch do keep. Sleep pretty darling, do not cry and I will sing a lullaby." As the tears continued to fall. I find it ironic that my name means "the burning ones" or the "fiery serpents". When I was 5 I watched my mother as she was killed before my eyes. The only thing that kept me from running to her was her eyes. They seemed to plead with me to stay where I was. So, I did. When I finally made it to her, she was dying. I watched as the light faded from her eyes and I cursed the heavens. I swore to God that I would repay him for what he did. Taking away a woman that has done nothing wrong, only looking out for, and loving, her son. But, then again, I am a burning one, a fiery serpent. I guess it was my destiny to become the Demon my father always preached I was. A product of circumstance. I made sure that when I killed him, he knew it was his fault that I became what he so preached. I enjoyed watching him squirm beneath me as I plucked out his eyes and stomped on them. His screams were music to my ears after all of the pain he caused me. Then, you found me and gave me a new name, Suen, the God of the Moon. A Goddess for a mother and a God for a son. I took it as an omen. I went from an Angel to a God. When you locked me away in that cell, I could only think of killing you when I got out. I constantly prayed for my mother to help me get through it. I started hallucinating, but I swore I heard my mother answer me. She simply told me to live. That was all. That one word, live. So I did. When you let me out, you did what even my mother couldn't do. You made me listen where she didn't have to. As I fought with the wild dogs for my food, I was reminded of how much I hated you and planned on using whatever you taught me against you. When I finally completed my mission and you walked in, I was contemplating killing you then and there. But, I couldn't. I couldn't kill you, because you were my mother. And I would never hurt you, but a part of me will always wish for your death. As I stare at the moon, I am reminded, not only of my mother, but of you as well, for the name that you gave me and everything else that you have ever done. As time went on, the good times outweighed the bad and the urge to kill you was pushed further and further into the recesses of my mind." he finished.

"Sera." she whispered softly.

"You are my Mistress. I will follow your lead until I am dead. You are my keeper; I will forever be tied to you by the chain of fate that has been around my neck since the moment you released a part of me that was trying to break free. My savior from the light and watchful eyes of God. And above all else, my mother. For that reason alone, I will follow you until the ends of the Earth." Suen said as he kissed her forehead. "I am your blade to cut down your enemies. I am your shield to protect you from harm. I am Suen 'Seraphim Angelus' Roth, your son, and forever yours."

Slowly, she looked upon his face and became lost in his eyes. He looked back calmly as her face slowly drew closer towards his. As their lips met, he mentally smirked. *It seems the words of my grandfather have come to pass yet again. "It's about time too."* Fox commented with a grunt. *"I've been waiting patiently for her to become mine and I wasn't sure how much longer I would be able to hold on. Despite my hatred of the woman, she is Master, and a strong one at that."* Suen leaned away from the kiss and looked down into her soft eyes.

"You are drunk." he pointed out calmly.

She nodded her head.

"I am, but that doesn't mean that I don't know what I am doing." she said as she moved for another kiss.

He turned his head slightly as her lips grew near.

"I am your son, and I am also twenty years your junior." he said with restraint. Her willingness to cross the boundaries and into a sinful embrace was extremely alluring, but he wanted to make sure she was ready for such a move. If she wasn't, then it would severely hurt the relationship he had with her now. And as much as he loath to admit it, he has become rather attached to her in the years.

She shook her head as she placed her hands on his cheeks and forced him to look at her.

"Sera," she began teasingly. "You don't honestly think I have not noticed the way that you look at me? The way that you use to bathe me while you were younger. Your hands were increasingly gentle and roaming. I never knew such a young man could touch so many sensitive areas." she purred sensually. "Your eyes, no matter the color, no matter who is in control, continue to show your emotions. You are able to hide them from others, but I know what to look for where others don't. You are my son after all Sera. If I couldn't read you, then I would be a bad mother."

He chuckled lightly as he shook his head gently.

"I should have known." he murmured with amusement. "It seems its fate."

"And you should know that age means nothing to us." she continued. "In our line of work, you are lucky to live past your first year. That's what my father told me. And your physical age is one thing, your mentality is a whole different matter." she rested her head on his forehead. "You are by far the most intelligent person I have ever met, if not the most manipulative. You are surely much older than me in terms of mentality. I love you Seraphim."

He closed his eyes for a moment. So, she loved him. *I love her as well.* He resigned to himself. *"That wasn't so hard now was it?"* Fox asked as he placed a hand on his shoulder. *"Although, I could have told you that. I might have had some control over you at the time, but given the training good old grandpa gave us and the literature we have read in the past, you knew what you wanted, even if it was subconsciously. He was right after all. She is our fate."* opening his eyes, he smiled at her.

"I love you too Susan." he said truthfully. "Although, I find it rather odd that you knew of my affections for you and yet, you never stopped me from acting on them."

"I know of your love of strength Sera." she pointed out. "And I know of how you see me. I'm flattered that you believe me to be stronger than you. You have no idea how that makes me feel." she finished in a whisper. "I'm getting older and weaker."

"And you are afraid that when you get older my interest in you will fade." he summed up.

"It wouldn't be the first time that you have lost interest in a person." she grumbled sourly. "I have seen the countless girls you have courted and then left in the dust after they have served their purpose."

He shook his head slightly. She had to be the strongest woman, no, person that he knew, besides his grandfather. How could he ever simply ignore her because of her age? Age was just a number to him. He cared for the mind. *"And the body. That is always a good thing to have."* Fox added. *I love her body too.* Snake admitted with a nod. *But, she was the first woman to ever show genuine affection for me.* Leaning closer, he captured her lips in a gentle kiss.

"I care not for the age of the one who has captured my heart." he said with honesty. "And I would be a fool to simply discard you because of your looks." his hand cupped her cheek lightly as his thumb traced along under her eye. "To me, you will always be the young woman that took me in and gave me my first shower in years. That same beautiful woman who held me close when I had, and still have, nightmares. Nothing will ever change that."

"Sera?" she whispered as tears fell from her eyes.

He shook his head as he kissed her passionately. He didn't want her to be weak. He didn't want her to have any faults. Mostly, because he loved her, but also, because he knows that even though his words were true, even he couldn't predict the future. And if the master is no longer fit to order, then it is only right to find a different owner. *But I am not a dog.* Snake said defiantly. *I do not switch owners simply because they have something I want.* "No, but I am an animal. And when the source of food has dried up, I will look for a new one." Fox said, oddly wise. Snake turned towards him with a blank look. *I don't want that to happen.* He said evenly. *Not with her. I will do everything in my power to stop it from happening.* "Even though you know that it is inevitability?" Yes. "And when the time comes?" it seemed like an eternity before he answered. *I will do what needs to be done to keep my promise to mamma. Nothing will ever change that.* Coming back to reality, he stood up, taking her with him. Picking her up bridal style, he began walking back into the building, never breaking the kiss.

As he made it to his room, he placed her down on his bed. Breaking away, he looked down at her.

"Are you sure you want to do this?" he asked softly as he gazed into her glazed brown eyes.

She nodded her head as her hands went to cup his cheeks as she rubbed them affectionately.

"I'm sure Sera." she whispered softly.

Smiling gently at her, he brought his face closer and trailed kisses down her neck. He could feel her hands caressing his chest through his shirt. Reaching her collar, he opened it slowly, button by button, as he trailed kisses down her chest. Sitting up fully, he ripped the rest. Her startled gasp was deaf to him. Reaching forward, he unclasped her bra, mentally happy that she didn't wear one that clasped in the back. As he was greeted with her firm C cup breasts, he grasped them both in his hands. Kneading the soft flesh lovingly, he relished in her mewls of pleasure. At this moment, she was at his mercy, and it made him want to make her scream. Taking one of her dusky nipples in his mouth, he gently suckled. Her hands moved to his hair and gently pressed him further into her bosom, as if feeding her babe. He purred as he felt something warm enter his mouth. Her milk was delicious and he was set on getting a meal. When the first dried up, he moved to the other, while pinching and tweaking the other. Pulling away from the nipple with a pop, he licked his way from the valley between her breasts towards her neck. Kissing her gently on her jaw, he made his way to her lips.

"I didn't know you were still lactating." he stated with a grin as his eyes flashed once.

"You never asked." she responded quickly as she leaned up to kiss him.

Breaking away, he laid butterfly kisses down her neck to her chest, then down her stomach, slipping his tongue into her belly button. Her soft moans were driving him insane. Gripping her pants, he didn't bother with unbuttoning them as he pulled them down and off her body. Looking at her now, he could see dampness between her legs. *"My,"* Fox growled as he spied her moisture. *"Master seems to have truly wanted this."* It seems so. Snake agreed with a nod. *"I think she deserves a treat."*

Leaning forward, he opened her legs slightly and placed a kiss where he knew her clitoris to be. As she gasped and arched her back, he suckled through the cloth and was rewarded with a louder moan of his name. Placing his hands on either side, he pulled them down and off her legs. Taking her left leg into his hand, he gently kissed his way from her ankle to her knee, down her thighs and blew gently on her lips that were puffy and red from excitement, and back up her right. Placing both legs onto his shoulders, he closed in on the intoxicating scent of her flesh. Looking up into her lust covered eyes; he allowed his tongue to delve into her depths.

She gripped the sheets tightly as she felt him dive in. It felt so sinfully wonderful that she thought she would die at that moment. Looking down at him between her thighs, she could only see his golden eyes staring back at her, watching her, reading her. He was very good. She should have known as much from the countless women that call his work phone that he was talented. Taking her hands from the sheets, she threaded them into his hair, silently encouraging him due to her lack of speech.

Moving a hand from her thigh, he placed it at her entrance as he slowly inserted on finger. Moving it slowly, he leaned up and smiled at her.

"Do you like this Mother?" he asked huskily. His use of the title was purely because that was what she was to him, and they both knew it was the relationship that was being strengthened at the moment.

She felt a surge of something new to her when she heard him speak in such a way and addressing her like that.

"Yes." she hissed as she bucked once. "God yes."

Inserting a second finger, he sped up his pace. Her heavily breathing figure was tossing and turning in an attempt to figure out a way to escape the pleasure. Deciding to end his little game and get to the main event, he moved his mouth towards her button once more, and sealed his lips around the nub of flesh. Placing his tongue on the tip, he hummed as he sucked harshly. He was rewarded with her legs tightening around his head, her hands pulling him in closer, and his mouth being filled with a tangy substance. Swallowing, he finally lifted his head when her grip lessens.

Taking her momentary stunned state as the perfect time to undress himself, he did so. Climbing on top of her, he looked down into her eyes as she finally caught her breath. Allowing his hardness to rub against her slick folds he spoke lowly.

"You have no idea how much I want you at this moment, and the lengths I'm going through to not simply ravage you right now." he was speaking the truth. Her every muscle twitch, her soft mewls of delight, to her loud moans of his name were beginning to rile him up. She had no idea what she was doing to him, but he felt compelled to let her know.

As she looked into his eyes, she was stunned to see one honey colored halo looking at her intently and the other a lustful blood crimson ring.

"If you want it so bad, then take it." she replied, voice thick with anticipation.

Immediately, he shoved his full length into her warm channel. As he heard her yelp in slight pain, he paused and looked at her questioningly.

"It's my first time." she answered weakly.

"But you gave birth to Astarte." it didn't make much sense to him unless . . .

"I was artificially inseminated and had a C-section. No one was good enough for me when I was younger." she explained.

Nodding his head, he slowly set a pace. She was tight, wet, and warm, and it was torture for him to go so slow. As he heard her moans coming more and more frequently, he began picking up the pace. Her hands went to his chest and roamed over his body as he admired hers from below. The sweat glistening off her breasts and her tight stomach caught his eyes with every thrust. As he looked to her face, he saw tears falling from the corners. Leaning down, he kissed her gently on the lips.

"I'm sorry if I'm going too fast." he apologized. "I just can't help myself."

She shook her head.

"It's not that." she said in-between a moan and a sob. "How can you make love to me when I put so many scars on you?" she asked as she looked into his eyes.

Wrapping his arms around her back, he pulled her into his lap. Moving her back and forth, he interrupted her sobs with a loud groan.

"I accepted what you have done to Me." he said gently as he held her close to his body. Their bodies becoming slick with sweat. "You have to accept it as well Mother. In the end, we both got what we wanted. You got your weapon, and I got a mother."

She gripped his body tightly as she rested her head on his shoulder. He could feel her smiling into his skin.

"I guess you're right." she muttered.

"I am." he assured as he sped up. "Now, let me worship you like a son is suppose to." he gently ordered as he began nibbling on her neck. He could feel her tightening up and he was close already.

"It feels so good Sera." she groaned as she rocked back and forth in his lap. "I'm so close."

"I want you to feel good mother." he wished as he sucked on her neck.

"I'm gonna cum!" she screamed as she muffled her mouth by biting Suen on his shoulder.

"She marks us." Fox growled as he felt her teeth sink into his flesh. *"She is claiming us as her own."* it seems so. Snake agreed. *"Mark her back. Master will be ours."*

He could feel her walls spamming around him and he gritted his teeth in an attempt to hold off a little longer.

"Mother," he gasped. "If I mark you as my mate, will you accept?" he asked feeling his control slipping to her muscles.

"Of course." she whispered.

Pulling her down onto himself, he released himself into her depths. Latching his mouth on the junction between her neck and shoulder, he muffled her name as her blood entered his mouth. It was such an exotic taste. Reminded him of a fine wine. Sweet, but bitter. As he felt the last of himself shoot inside her, he held her lax form against his body tightly. Taking his mouth away from her skin, he lapped at the mark until the bleeding stopped and was mildly irritated that the bleeding had stopped. She was delicious and was tempted to bite her again so he could taste her once more. Turning around, he fell back into the bed, taking her along on his chest. His mind was still coming down from the fact that he claimed his mother as his mate that he never noticed her hands around his neck. He did, however, feel a weight taken off his neck. As he looked down at her, he could see, in her hand, was his collar. Looking down at her face that was using him as a pillow, he wondered what was going through her mind.

"You do realize that without the collar, I could kill you right now." he pointed out.

She nodded into his chest.

"I know." she answered softly. "And I would accept it, if it came from you."

His eyes flashed, although she couldn't see.

"You know I can't do that anyway." he stated. "But, why did you remove it?"

"I can't have my mate tied down like a dog." she said sleepily. "It's no longer needed to keep you in control. I've been meaning to take it off for a few months now, but I never got around to doing it."

He nodded his head and kissed her messy head of brown.

"Thank you." he said softly.

"You don't have to." she said lazily. Leaning up, she kissed his lips, before resigning herself to his shoulder, just in front of his mark. "I love you Sera." she whispered.

"I love you too Mother." his reply was soft, but he was sure she heard him. His eyes glowed vermilion and gold as he tightened his grip around her. *You do realize that this only complicates matters correct?* Snake said calmly. *"Who cares?"* Fox scoffed. *"Let's worry about that when the time comes and just enjoy her while we can. Because eventually she will be gone."* "I know." the words were not spoken, but mouthed, because even though he knew them to be true, he didn't want to voice them to the world.

Chapter 14

A plea from the past

Sera sat idly in his room, working his hand over his second blade. Zéro was his second favorite weapon next to Benehime. The jet black blade seemed to be a replicate of Benehime, but upon closer inspection, it was a single sided blade. On its flat edge, there was an engraving of words. *Sun becomes black, earth sinks, the stars vanish, steam rises, and flames touch the heavens. Ragnarök.* His mind was replaying the conversation he had with Susan two nights ago.

He was coming in from his training of Christine when she called him into her office. She told him it was something he might find important. Taking her word on it, he followed, curious as to what she might say.

She threw a file at his feet.

Stooping down to pick it up, he quirked an eyebrow at the name of the file. *To Noir.* This was a surprise. Opening it, he found that a family was requesting the help of Noir. To his knowledge no one outside of the family, political leaders and royalty was aware that Noir even existed. So, whoever wrote the letter was informed. Looking at the date of the letter, it was over three years ago. It seems that it took longer than they first though for word to reach him. Nodding his head, he turned and walked out. He had a mission to prepare for.

Sheathing his blade, he turned to check over his guns before placing them in his bag. He was going to be missing his junior year, but he didn't really mind. He already called Henrietta and told her about his mission.

She wished him luck after he shot down her attempt to go with him. Goddess, sometimes he thought Christine got her manners from her, but they never met.

Standing, he turned out of his room and walked down the hall towards the front door. As the light hit his eyes, he squinted, before he placed a pair of sunglasses on. He could spot Heather leaning against the car with an identical bag over her shoulder. He was allowed to go on the mission, but he had to bring his retainer. Since she took off his collar a year ago, he was essentially free of her, and could do whatever he wanted. That and the collar would have had no effect on him halfway around the world. Heather was a means to keep him under control.

"So, you ready for our long vacation?" Heather asked with a smile.

"It's not a vacation." He reminded. "It's a mission."

"Ah, but not one issued by Mistress." She countered as she placed her bag in the trunk. Taking his off his shoulders, she placed it with hers. "This is a personal mission."

He didn't say anything, because he knew she was right. He had to find out who knew about his family and how they came about the knowledge. Noir was a shroud. A shadow that casts a shadow over all. The chosen hands of God on earth to do his bidding and condemn their souls to eternity in hell for humanity. Despite his dislike of *humanity*, he had to abide by the oath he took long ago. Getting into the car, he closed his eyes only to open them once they arrived at the cargo plane landing strip. Susan arranged for a cargo plane to fly by the village that the letter originated from.

XXX

Un-strapping the parachute from his shoulders, he looked around his surroundings. Japan over the last century has changed quite a bit. It only proved that history repeats itself. Granted, the capital city, Tokyo, was still technologically advanced and decades ahead of American technology, the surrounding cities and towns seemed to have reverted back to the feudal era. Like the area he found himself and Heather in. The surrounding landscape was a vast field of green, stretching as far as the eye can see. The mountains in the distance were tiny mounds of green and white. The only thing that he could see that marred the greenery was a dirt road that seemed to wind its way through the small hills and prairies in both directions.

Turning towards Heather as she walked up beside him, he turned back towards the road.

"The village where the message originated from is west." He reported.

"So are we going to stand here all day enjoying the scenery, or are we going to get going?" she joked as she ran out a few yards ahead of him.

He shook his head as she turned to wave for him to hurry up. Sometimes he wondered just why she was his bride to be. Jogging up to her, they began a steady pace towards the village.

XXX

It was late in the evening when they finally made it. The village was what anyone would expect a village to be. The small houses with tile roofing. The stores and other various establishments with lanterns hanging in front of their doors. And many people walking around wearing kimonos.

Stepping into the village was only a small change to Sera. He didn't care what he looked like to them, because he rarely cared what anyone thought of him. But looking over towards Heather, he knew she was beginning to become a little self conscious of the way she looked. The many people were passing them strange glances. The glances he was used to.

"Lil, relax." He told her softly as he grabbed her hand. "They are only curious. It's nothing to be concerned about."

She nodded her head as she squeezed his hand lightly.

"I know, but it's just it makes me feel a little on edge, being in a new country and all Kyuu." She confided. "Not to mention that the first place we manage to find ourselves is Kobe. Do I have to remind you of what shrine is here?"

He shook his head. There was no need for that. He knew the myths and legends of human history like the back of his hand. The Hidden Alter of Gods is located in this region. Not that he cared.

"Just relax and everything will be okay." He reminded.

Walking through the village streets, he subtly looked for the address of the one who sent the message. Coming up to, what he concluded as, the village leaders house, if he was to go by the vast land that it occupied, he walked up to the walls of the estate.

"Excuse me, you can't enter without permission." A guard said as he stepped out. His hand was resting on his sword. "And without permission, I will have to ask you to leave."

Sera looked at him calmly from beneath his shades. This man was one of the many types of guards that roamed the outskirts of Tokyo. Because of the rising violence in the world over, Japan has decided that only their military and law enforcement were to have access to guns and ammunition. Everyone else was allowed to simply arm themselves with whatever they could for protection. Many went back to the way of the sword, bushido. He himself practiced bushido, and for that very reason he brought his sword. Tilting his head to the side, he regarded the man.

"Please tell your employer that I have answered his call three years post. He will know what I mean." Sera told the man levelly.

The guard looked at him for a moment, before calling a friend over to watch them as he ran the message inside. A few moments later he came back and bowed.

"He will see you now."

Sera nodded his head and led the way, Heather following close behind.

The inside of the place was more upscale than he first expected. The carpets were plush and the walls wore expensive paintings. There was the scent of flowers about the room that he couldn't put his finger on. Coming towards a door, he knocked once.

"Come in."

Opening the door, he spotted a man in his early fifties sitting behind an oak wood desk. His black hair was starting to gain gray areas in some places. He kept his fingers folded over in a bridge beneath his nose.

"So, you are the one known as Noir?" he asked as he watched Heather.

She shook her head.

"I'm sorry, but I'm not Noir. I'm"

"Blanc." Sera interrupted. "I am Noir."

He looked at him in mild irritation.

"Child, I am not amused by your games. This is a serious matter."

Sera quirked an eyebrow at the name child. This *human* thought he was nothing more than an infantile babe suckling at his mother's teat?

"Please, refrain from calling me a child." Sera began as he reached for his glasses. Taking them off, he leveled him with a blank stare. "I am Noir. Now, my question to you is how do you know about us?"

The man stared wide eyed at him for a few seconds, before coming back to his senses.

"I'm sorry Valkyrie. I didn't mean to offend." He apologized. Sera would have called him on knowing a name he shouldn't, but let it slide for the moment. "I just wasn't expecting a child to answer to my letter."

"You still haven't answered my question about how you came to know of us."

"Right, well, we knew the Noir before you. We helped her previously one hundred and fifty years ago when she was here. As a result, she told us that if we were ever in trouble, Noir would come."

"Very well," Sera nodded his head. That answered one question. "Now will you tell us what the favor is, so we may go?"

The man cleared his throat lightly as he motioned for them to take a seat. As both declined, he cleared his throat again.

"Three years ago, a yakuza boss threatened to destroy our village unless I handed over my daughter. I wasn't going to do it, but she insisted that she should be the one to sacrifice herself. She said that it wasn't right for everyone else to suffer because of one person's selfishness." He sighed. "So, she went with them. I wanted to search for her, but I couldn't. He told me that if I was to look for her, I would be killed after he made me watch."

"So, you are restricted to this village and not allowed to venture out in search of your daughter." Heather summed up.

"Yes."

"Do you know the name of the yakuza that took your daughter?"

"His name is Tsume. He's part of the Hidden Dragons."

Sera nodded his head. He knew of the Hidden dragons, but he didn't know where they were. Their name suited them perfectly. They were the biggest traffickers of illegal narcotics and underage sex in the east. He could feel a growl in the back of his mind at the thought. *Settle down*

Fox. All will be settled. He thought to himself. He was brought out of his thoughts as he felt Heather's hand on his shoulder. She could undoubtedly feel his irritation.

"We will find her." Heather told him. "What's her name?"

"Sakura."

Sera turned on his heel and began walking out.

"Come. We will be back once we found her and have her in our custody."

"Thank you."

"Don't thank us yet. You know information that you shouldn't. There is a chance that you will not live long after the reunion." Sera cautioned as he walked down the hall.

The man's face went pale as he looked back towards Heather.

"He's right Mr. Yakumi. The information you have is highly sensitive. Depending on how he feels after he finds your child will determine your fate."

"You are certain of him finding her?"

She turned and began heading towards the door. Stopping at the frame, she turned and looked back at him.

"Believe me. When a Valkyrie has chosen the ones they will take, nothing will stand in their way." She said seriously as she walked out the door, after his fading figure.

Finally catching up to him outside the house, she walked beside him.

"So where are we going?" she asked.

"We are going to go to Tokyo. The Hidden Dragons are a well known, but very well hidden organization. Everyone knows where they are, but they don't know their location." He answered as he continued walking out of the village.

"And how do you suppose we will get there? Are you going to sprout wings and fly us there?"

He glanced at her out the corner of his eyes.

"I've never tried to sprout wings, but I might be able to do so if I tried." He joked.

She didn't say anything to the joke. Mostly because she didn't know if he could or not. He wasn't normal. If there was ever anyone who could spontaneously sprout wings it would be him.

"But, in any case," he continued. "We are going to walk until we find someone who is willing to take us to Osaka. From there, we will catch the train to Tokyo."

"Excuse me." A male voice said from the side.

Turning slightly, he spotted a young man, most likely in his early to mid twenties, sitting behind the reins of a carriage.

"If you are heading towards Osaka, I'll be happy to give you two a ride."

"Well, thank you." Heather said with a smile as she headed over towards the cart.

"Hise."

"Thank you Hise." She smiled politely as they both got in the back. "So, why are you going to Osaka?"

"I have to pick up some rice."

"Oh?" Sera tuned out their conversation. It didn't concern him. Although, he didn't like the look in Hise's eyes when he looked at Heather. Deciding he would rather rest than talk, he lied back on the wooden bottom and looked at the clouds passing by as his basic functions slowed. He was distantly aware of Heather picking up his head and placing it in her lap.

XXX

It was night when he finally decided to get out of the back. Popping his back, he sighed as he released the pent up stress. Lying down on a wooden floor at an odd angle was not a good way to rest. Looking around, he spotted Heather and Hise next to a fire, that judging by the make of it, was made by her. His mind wouldn't let the scene of them together rest in his mind. It seemed to rub him the wrong way. Deciding that he didn't want to be with them, he got up and walked into the surrounding darkness. It was nights like these that made him feel safe. The everlasting darkness of night, which was frightening to humans, was comfortable and securing to him. He could see perfectly well, despite the light, which is one of the reasons he supposes that he likes the darkness so much. He can see others, but they can't see him. A part of him will always rather be unseen to others. His ears twitched as they caught the sound of a yelp. Turning towards the sound, he sprinted off into the distance.

Coming towards the fire, he spotted Heather standing over a groaning Hise. Slowly walking forward he stopped beside her.

"I take it that he tried something." Sera said calmly.

"After he realized you weren't around anymore, he tried to force himself on me." She stated. "I thought he was just flirty, but now I know he wanted something else."

Sera didn't say anything as he walked up to the man. Kneeling down, he looked him in the eyes. He took off his shades and placed them in his pocket so he could see him better.

"So, you tried to force yourself on her." He wasn't asking a question.

"I'm sorry." Hise groveled. His eyes began shedding tears as he trembled in what he knew was fear. "I'm sorry."

"No." Sera whispered as his eyes transitioned to vermilion. "You aren't sorry." He leaned in close towards his ear. "Not yet." He finished as he sunk his K-9's into his jugular. He could feel Hise trying to struggle, but the rapid blood loss was making him weak. The blood that rushed into his mouth was bitter. He didn't even allow it to satisfy him. Ripping his mouth away, he spit out a chunk of his skin and muscle. It was still twitching in a way that made him stare at it for a few seconds. "You tried to take what is mine you filthy pathetic creature. You are nothing but a disgusting human and aren't deserving of even touching her." He smirked as he watched the terrified light in his eyes dim as his spirit left him. "Disgusting little creature. I'm going to destroy them all." He muttered disdainfully.

"That was," Heather paused as she watched him turn his blood covered face towards her. She shivered at the look in his eyes. She knew he wouldn't kill her, but she wasn't sure about bodily harm. "New." She finished. "I've never seen you drink a person's blood before."

"Stick close and you might see a few things you've never seen before." He remarked with a growl.

She could see a tail flicking back and forth behind him. Apparently he was in a playful mood.

"And what might I see?" she found herself asking with a tremble.

As he stepped into her personal space, she looked up into his crimson eyes. At seventeen, he was seven inches taller than her, being only five foot five. He was covered in blood, and yet the smell didn't deter her. It lured her closer towards his person. His natural scent was one of ozone, fire, and ice. Mixed with blood, she couldn't control herself. Over the last six years, he's been around her and she's grown accustomed to his presence. His cold aura, his scorching touch, his calm gaze. But ever since he's started his projects, he hasn't been spending as much time as he would normally with her. The nights she would be alone in the room waiting for him to come back, he was out working with his projects. And most of the time during the day, she couldn't speak to him, because she had classes to teach. She would be lying to herself if she wasn't feeling neglected.

"I could show you anything you would like to see. The heavens, the moon, the world, or Hell." He whispered as he leaned close to her face.

She could feel the heat of his words on her cheek, and it made her shiver in expectation. But as he backed off, she found herself irked at his toying. He always did that. Tempt her, and then leave. For years he's done it, and she was getting tired of it. As he tossed the body onto the fire, she decided she would get some answers from him. Even if she had to force him.

"Seraphim?" she called as the light extinguished.

"Yes?" as he answered, she could see the gold halos watching her in the darkness.

"Can I ask you something?"

"Despite that being a question, of course."

She took a seat down on the ground. Pulling her knees up to her chest, she rested her chin on them.

"What's so special about your projects?" she asked softly.

"A war is coming. I wish to be best prepared." He answered.

"No," she shook her head. She knew she should have been straight forward. If you didn't ask the correct questions, then you weren't going to get your answer. "What I mean is, why do you spend so much time with them?"

"Their training is ongoing. They might be finished with their Hell Born training, but for them to be of use to me, they still have more to learn."

She sighed. She wasn't asking the right questions and she was starting to become sullen. She had no doubt that he knew what she was talking about, but he wanted to play, and she didn't.

"Never mind."

"What's wrong?" he asked softly. She could hear his footsteps coming closer. "Lil?" there was a faint sound of concern in his voice.

She sniffled. Just now, she was aware of herself crying.

"Why do you sleep with others?" she whispered after a sob. Hiding her face in her hands, she shook her head. "Why do you like to spend so much time with them and not me?" she flinched slightly as she felt hands grip hers. As he pulled them away, she turned and buried herself in his chest.

"Lil . . ."

She shook her head.

"I know you like to spend time with Sy. I do too, but what about me?" she asked, muffled by his shirt.

"I'm sorry I can not spend as much time with you as I would like, but things are moving." He explained as he wrapped both arms around her shivering form.

"And was sleeping with Mistress a part of your plans?" she asked spitefully. She was slightly surprised by her own venom. How she envied her. She controlled him, could do whatever she wanted with him, and he would let her because of his collar.

"That," he paused, which she knew was him searching for the right words. "Was not the plan. She started it, and I couldn't stop myself from granting her desire, because I wanted it too."

"So are you going to sleep with every project?" she asked fearfully. She wanted to know the answer to the question, but she was afraid of the answer she might get.

"Yes."

She hiccupped as she clenched her eyes shut in an attempt to stop the tears, but they came regardless.

"Why?" she managed to utter.

"Because, each of them are unique in their own way. I want them. All of them."

"So, does that mean you don't want me?" she asked softly. "The reason you spend all your time with them is because you found some younger girls that interest you more than me? Is that it? That's why you never attempted to sleep with me isn't it?" she was stunned when he pulled her away from his chest and forced her to look into his eyes. His brilliant golden rings were staring into her soul. By the light in them, she knew he was angry.

"Don't ever say that again." He ordered softly. "Don't you ever say that. I'm sorry that I've been spending more time with the others and not you, but they aren't finished with their training. And yes, they are interesting, but that doesn't mean you aren't. And just because they are younger doesn't mean that I find you any less appealing. You are beautiful Lilith. In comparison, you are by far above them in terms of beauty. But, it's not your beauty that makes me want you. I want you, because you accept me for what I am. Goddess knows that I do not deserve anyone. I was born a reincarnation of a woman who was an angel. I killed my mother, my father, my grandfather, and I'm more than likely going to be the death of you as well. That's why I've been trying to stay away from you Lilith. That's the truth. Everyone who has either loved me, or cared about me has died. I don't want the same thing to happen to you." His eyes softened. "Lilith, I can do many things. I can kill. I can heal. I can seduce. I can please women. I can take on armies without fear. I can do almost anything you can imagine, except two things. Die and love. I can not die, because I have to keep my promise to my mother. And I can not love, because I'm afraid. I don't want to lose anyone else that I care about. My mother told me to want, and I want to love. And I want to die as well." She couldn't believe what she was hearing. He was afraid of love? But then again, she could understand. He loved his mother; he even loved his father and grandfather. But in the end, he killed them all. He was alone, even while surrounded by others that didn't mind his uniqueness. His final line brought the experience five years ago back into her mind. While she was inside the room, she saw him and he was saying the same thing.

"I think I understand what happened in the room five years ago." She said suddenly.

She could see his eyes tilting slightly in question.

"What did you see?"

"I saw you. You were in front of me telling me to kill you. Telling me that I had to kill you."

"And what did you do?"

"I couldn't do it. You began choking me to force me to kill you, but I still couldn't do it. I didn't want to kill you. And now I know it was not just a coincidence."

"What do you mean?"

"The look in your eyes when you told me I passed. You looked at me in disappointment and resentment. Did you want me to kill you? Do you want me to kill you?"

He didn't answer her right away, and she felt herself dreading the answer that was to come.

"Yes."

When he finally spoke, there was a breeze that chilled her to the bone. It was colder than his usual aura. It was colder than the glares he's sent others way. It was the tone of a dead man awaiting the grim reaper to take his soul. Of one who was only a step away from diving into the river Styx. The tone of one who was tired of life. Tired of living. Tired of everything.

"No." she whispered as she shook her head. She reached out with her hands and cupped his face. "I will not kill you. I told you I love you. Why would I kill you?"

"Because you love me." He answered.

"No." she used a little more force in her voice as she tightened her grip on his face slightly. "You are not going to die."

"But I want to." He implored. "I want to see mother again. I want her to hold me like she use to. To tell me everything is going to be alright. To protect me. I want to."

"And she wants you to stay alive." She reminded. "Have you forgotten your own promise? You must stay alive and constantly want. You must live to protect the innocent. You are her incarnation. Your birth is proof that this world is in need of help." She leaned in close and rested her forehead against his. "And I need you. I don't want you to go." She whispered as she peered into his eyes.

"Lilith," he breathed. "I want to die, but I can't for the reasons you just named."

"But you can still love. It's not a human thing. Who's to say that demons can't love too? Doesn't the goddess Ishtar[15] and Astarte[16] consult

---

[15] Ishtar is a goddess of fertility, love, and war and sex. In the Babylonian pantheon, she "was the divine personification of the planet Venus" Ishtar was above all associated with sexuality: her cult involved sacred prostitution; her holy city Erech was called the "town of the sacred courtesans"; and she herself was the "courtesan of the gods"

[16] Astarte was connected with fertility, sexuality, and war. Her symbols were the lion, the horse, the sphinx, the dove, and a star within a circle indicating

love? Are you going to deny her teachings?" she realized that she has been rambling, but she didn't care. She wanted him to know that he was wanted, and needed. "Like your mother I love you for you; nothing else. Not as a weapon. Not as a brother. Not as a friend, but a lover. I love you. I don't even care if you don't love me back, but I want you to know that I do. I will always love you."

Sera looked at her in the darkness. The honesty in her words stirred something in him stronger than what he's ever felt for anything. *"Lilith. The first woman to ever step foot on this earth. The only pure human in existence. Pandora. Also the first, but also the one who released the sins and evils upon man."* Fox said softly behind his mask. *"I want to love her, but I'm not sure how."* Perhaps she would be willing to teach. Snake proposed. *It has been forever since it was unconditional. The last, being mother.*

"I never said that I do not love you." He began. "But, can you tell me what love is, so I may show you?"

Her heart stopped at his plea. He didn't know how to show love. He's never actually felt it before. The only thing close to unconditional was his mother, and now she was gone. Mistress only wanted him as a weapon. The projects only want him for their own reasons. But she was different, and she would show him. Leaning forward, she kissed him gently on his lips.

"I am not like the others." She said gently as she broke the kiss. "I love you for you. And I would be honored to show you how to love."

He didn't say anything as he leaned in and kissed her passionately. As she moaned into his mouth, he felt his restraints go. He's wanted to do this for so long. When he first saw her, she was cute trembling in fear. But the courage she showed while scared intrigued him. Her spirit to never quit caught his interest. Her complete and utter loyalty pleased him. And her body's submission to his touch provoked him. She was darkness. She was pure. And she embraced the darkness willingly. She had not an ounce of light about her and he loved it. But she wasn't to be like the others. She wasn't a project. She was a soul mate for him. She was his match. She was his Yin. She was his Blanc.

Placing his arms around her smaller figure, he led her onto the grass. Breaking away from the kiss, he looked down at her panting and flushed

---

the planet Venus. Pictorial representations often show her naked.

face. Even though he knew she couldn't see him, she was still looking only at him. Leaning down, he attacked her neck in a flurry of gentle kisses trailing down towards her shoulder. Her pleasant sighs told him she was enjoying herself. Sitting up, he slowly pulled her shirt up and laid kisses on her stomach and up her chest. Taking off her bra, he kissed each breast before working his way back up her neck to her lips.

"Goddess," she panted between kisses. Her body was on fire. His lips were scolding hot against her skin and it only seemed to make the heat in her core rise faster. "Please don't let this be another dream. I implore you." She didn't want this to be nothing but an illusion brought about like the room five years ago. She wanted it to be real. To be true.

"My mother wanted you to be my wife. It's obvious to me that she saw this coming." He whispered as he trailed kisses towards her ear. "Will you be my wife? Have my children?"

She was convinced this was a dream. He was asking her to marry him and have his children. This couldn't be real. She wanted it for so long now. She thought the same thing when she read the diary. It was obvious that his mother saw this coming and ever since then, she's dreamt of him saying those words to her.

"Of course my love." She whispered back into his ear. "I will be your wife. I will bear your children." She figured if it was a dream, then she would stay and hope to never awaken. As his hands slid down her sides towards her pants, she lifted her hips to help him remove them. Kicking them off, she was mildly surprised that she wasn't blushing. But then again, he's seen her naked before and if this was a dream, why should she be embarrassed about her husband looking at her.

XXX

Lying on her side, snuggled against his body, she let out a content sigh. He felt the same way about her that she felt about him. It was a relief to finally know for certain. Her body trembled lightly and he tightened his grip on her slightly. Just thinking about how gentle and caring he was while making love made her body tremble at the memory. She never told him that she's been looking into Ishtar and what she represents. Not even the fact that she converted to her side. As the necklace around her neck touched her chest, she was reminded of how strong their bond was. Looking into the night sky, she spotted one star that was off on the horizon, burning brightly against the dark canvas. She knew what it was. It was the morning star. Closing her eyes, she made a wish. She only had one wish. She wished for Seraphim to find peace in the living world. A reason to live beyond his promise.

If she would have kept her eyes open for a second longer, she would have caught the morning star twinkle brightly, before it regained its natural shine.

XXX

Waking up, she wasn't surprised to find Seraphim sitting up with her head in his lap. He was watching the clouds pass by. He always did that when he was thinking about anything. She supposed if one were to be awake for twelve years, they would have nothing but time to think. At first, she was concerned with his lack of communication, but realized that he was use to keeping his silence, only speaking when he deemed necessary.

"Morning, mon amour." She whispered as she leaned up and kissed his cheek. As he smiled back, she sat up. He was never one to greet in the morning. Standing, she walked over towards the carriage and took a seat in the drivers' side. She didn't have to look back to see that he was already in the back. Taking the reins, she gave them a snap, and the horses jolted down the dirt road, kicking up dust as they went.

XXX

Walking down the streets of Tokyo was something she never thought she would do. A part of her wished she could have brought little Sibyl[17] with them. She would have loved this place. Glancing out the side of her

---

[17] The word sibyl probably comes (via Latin) from the Greek word *sibylla*, meaning prophetess. The earliest oracular seeresses known as the sibyls of antiquity, "who admittedly are known only through legend" prophesied at certain holy sites, under the divine influence of a deity, originally—at Delphi

eyes, she spotted Sera wearing a blank look on his face. It was obvious that he was set on the mission at hand. She turned her attention back towards the surrounding stores. It was his mission. She was only here to insure he didn't go crazy in another country. So she had time to window shop.

"I wonder if they have that dress in my size." She wondered aloud.

"I'm sure they do." He said distractedly. "But, I wonder where the Hidden dragons are. I figured it would be easy to find them so I could give them what they asked for, but it appears that it isn't so easy."

She turned towards him with a raised eyebrow.

"What are you talking about?"

"Oh nothing." He brushed off as he turned his eyes towards the sky. "I just really hope that I can get rid of this thing before the police search me."

"Okay," she began. His talking was beginning to make no sense. Perhaps the three day ride was getting to him. "Well, what do you want to do now?"

"How about we go in there." He suggested.

As she followed his arm, she felt herself glare slightly at the establishment. She knows he was only kidding, but as he began walking over towards the door, she followed close behind.

"You are kidding right?" she pleaded. "Please tell me you don't intend on going into this dirty place."

He turned back towards her only to nod his head. She sighed under her breath. If there was one place she never wanted to go, it was inside a brothel. But, she supposed that if you were looking for an illegal human trafficking service, then it would be the best place to start the investigation. And considering Japan had various places like this spread all about Tokyo and other areas as well, it would be a while before they got back to their home.

As they stepped into the building, she scrunched her nose at the scent that assaulted her. This place was filled with perfume and incents. Taking a step forward, she noticed that he was still standing still. Turning towards him, she found his face set in a scowl. Walking back towards his side, she placed a hand on his shoulder.

---

and Pessinos—one of the chthonic earth-goddesses. Later in antiquity, sibyls wandered from place to place.

"What's wrong?" she asked.

"This place reeks of perfume, incents, male and female genitals, ejaculation and excrement. It's disgusting."

That was news to her. She didn't know he could smell such things. She blushed lightly as she was reminded of when they slept together. He could smell *that*?

"I didn't know you could smell things like that." She pointed out.

"I have sensitive senses." Was his only answer as he began walking forward. "Now, let's see if I can get us a lap dance."

Quickly walking beside him, she shook her head.

"Not us." She objected. "I am not letting a woman rub against me."

"Fine." He conceded. "How about just me then?"

"No."

He chuckled lightly shaking his head.

"We will see where this takes us." He said softly. "I would rather not be in here longer than needed. The scents are beginning to make me nauseous."

Walking over towards a back room, they were stopped by a big man wearing a tight shirt to show off his muscles and a pair of black pants. Across his arm was a red dragon wrapping around his wrist.

"I don't think you are old enough to be here kid." The man said looking at Sera. "I suggest you come back in a year or two. Now get out of here before I force you out." He turned his gaze towards Heather. "But your friend can stay. I'm sure we can find a way to entertain ourselves."

Heather frowned at the insinuation. Out of the corner of her eye she could see a crimson smile making its way onto Sera's face in the form of a twitch. That wasn't good. It seems that without the collar and the no rules makes him a little restless when confronted with hostility.

"You will do no such thing." His voice was still calm and soft, so she knew he was still in control. But for how long, depended on how this conversation went.

The man glared at him.

"Look kid, I'm letting you get off with only a warning. If the boss was here, he would kick your ass and break your legs, after he made you watch him fuck your girl. Now, get out of here before I kick your ass myself."

The crimson smirk turned into a full blown grin. Before she could stop him, he punched the man in the stomach. As he fell to his knees gasping for breath, Sera kicked him in the head, sending him sprawling onto his side.

"You couldn't kick my ass even if I was old and decrepit you foolish creature." Sera scoffed. "Now that we established that your boss is a hard ass, where is he?"

"Hey! You there! Stop that!" a high nasally voice screeched.

Sera only glanced out the corner of his eye as Heather turned to see an elderly woman rushing up.

"Stay out of this you fossil."

Yep. He was going to kill something in the next twenty minutes, and she knew it.

"Do you have any idea of who owns this place?" the old crone wailed. "He will kill you."

"I welcome the challenge." Sera said with confidence that she knew he acquired over twelve years of killing. It wasn't him being cocky. It was experience. "Now, tell me how many of these girls are here against their will illegally." He ordered.

"I don't know what you are talking about." The old one denied. "They all owe debts and are working them off. I have contracts with all of them. You can't arrest me."

He chuckled in a way that made her tremble in slight fear and arousal.

"Please you old coot. Do I look like law enforcement?" he asked. "No, and I will get my answers one way or another. So, you have two options. One, you can tell me what I want to know now, and there will be no use for violence. Or two, you can hold out. I will proceed to use methods that most would rather not know about and some don't even know exist in order to get the information I seek. It's your choice." He paused as his smirk became blood crazed. "But please, don't make it too easy for me." His eyes flashed once. "I like to work for my prize."

Heather watched, with hidden fascination, the look of utter disbelief as it gave way to undeniable fear. The old woman's eyes widened and began to shake in her skull. She was slightly curious to know if she was having a heart attack.

"Look," the old woman stuttered. "The owner is going to kill me if I tell you anything."

"I see you have chosen option two." He nodded his head. "A good choice. A lot more fun than you simply telling me what I want to know." He took a threatening step forward only to stop at the old wrinkly hand that shot up.

"Alright!" she screamed. "I'll tell you. But you realize that I might be killed for this."

He scoffed as Heather shook her head.

"I would have killed you if you had chosen option two. After, of course, I've gathered the information that I want."

"It's the Hidden dragons." She mumbled.

"Tch." Sera sucked his teeth. "It seems that we found who we were looking for on the first try Lil."

"It seems so." she agreed. It would seem that the goddess wanted them to finish this quickly.

"So, where is this place?" he asked.

"You tell him, and I will kill you myself." The man on the ground growled as he began to stand.

Turning quickly, Heather placed her knee to his skull, sending him back on the ground. She knew if she would have allowed him to stand for even a second, he would be dead. And at the moment, there needed to be no dead bodies.

"Be quiet stupid." She hissed. "You talk like that again, you will die."

"In any case, it doesn't matter." Sera said as he turned his attention towards the restrained man. "I have a message I want you to deliver to your leader. Tell him a fox is looking for a lost kit by the name of Sakura. She was taken by force three years ago. I want her back. Either, you can give her to me, and we can avoid the killing. Or, you can deny my request. If you do, then I will kill every single one of you that I come across until you are all extinct." Turning around, he waved a hand over his shoulder signaling for Heather.

Getting up, she jogged to catch up. Sometimes she could forget how tough and scary he could be when he was serious.

"Oh," he called over his shoulder. "I'll be in Tokyo for the remainder of this week. If I do not hear from you in the next twenty four hours, then I will assume that he has chosen option two. Clock's ticking."

She found herself swaying her hips like a pendulum while clicking her tongue *tick tock!*

"Do you think they will do as you instructed?" she asked.

"If they have heard of Fox, then I'm sure they will come. Either that or he will try to kill me. Either way, it doesn't matter. My death is not in the stars."

"So, where are we going to go now?" she asked as they walked down the street. They turned at the nearby corner and he stopped.

"I'm going to wait for them to contact me." He answered while walking into a building. "And while I wait, I'm going to get a drink." He turned towards her for a second before going back to the door. "Would you care to share a bottle of sake with me?"

She shook her head with a small smile as she walked with him into the bar.

"I have to watch over you until we get back to Wind." She answered calmly. "And I can't very well have you roaming around here drunk."

"Yes." He said softly as he opened the door. "A rampant fox will pester the fields."

She looked at him oddly, but passed it off as another one of his moments. If she didn't know him any better, she would have guessed that he was autistic. Following behind the door and into a back room where they both sat themselves on a pair of pillows, they awaited the sake.

XXX

"So, let me get this straight." A male voice said in the darkness of a room. His voice was rough and cold. "A child and a woman beat you, humiliated you, and then proceeded to tell you to pass a message onto me."

"Yes sir." The bald man from the brothel held his stomach as he nodded his head.

"Well, what was the message?"

"He said 'a fox is looking for a lost kit by the name of Sakura. She was taken by force three years ago. I want her back. Either, you can give her to me, and we can avoid the killing. Or, you can deny my request. If you do, then I will kill every single one of you that I come across until you are all extinct.'" He repeated.

The room was silent as the figure hummed in consideration.

"So, this kid thinks he can simply come into my territory and make demands?" the man asked rhetorically. "Bring me Sakura!" he ordered. Feet shuffled about to his call. A few moments later the sounds of chains rattling and bare feet slapping the ground assaulted the ears. She looked to be barely over the age of sixteen. Her black hair was neatly groomed, as was the kimono she wore. "It appears that someone has come for you Sakura." He told her. As she lifted her head, her eyebrows shot up in surprise, but her lids remained closed. "Send Ichi to pay our visitor a visit."

XXX

"You sure can hold your liquor." Heather pointed out as she poured another saucer of sake. She left to go shopping. Figuring that since she was in Tokyo, she might as well bring back something to remember the trip. After picking up a kimono, and wearing it out of the store, she picked up a few other trinkets for Sibyl when they got back. He didn't have time to tell her good bye and she would surely be worried and mad. He's been drinking since they came in, which was about seven hours ago, and he was still going. "How can you hold it all? Your liver must be in pretty bad shape. I don't think you should drink anymore."

He slowly lifted the saucer to his lips, "I told you many times that I am not normal Lilith." He held it there for a second before downing it and placing it back down for her to refill. "My body also works differently than that of a human. I can only become intoxicated if it is above 100 proof, and then, in mass quantities. My liver reacts to it in the way that yours would to water. It passes it through without having to do much of anything. And once I become intoxicated, it only lasts for a few minutes to an hour."

To her knowledge, the human body didn't work like that. She knew that his liver should be shot and his kidneys shutting down at about this time, and yet he still drank. She let the matter slide. It was just another one of the many things that made him unique and further distanced him from humanity.

"Well, I still think you should stop. You've been through over twenty bottles already."

"I am going to stop in about thirty-seven seconds." He said abruptly.

"What do you mean?" she asked as she refilled the saucer that was placed before her on reflex.

"I mean in the next twenty five seconds, I will have no further use to drink. I told you I was going to drink until they came, and they will be here in the next seventeen seconds." He answered as he downed his sake.

"How do you know that?"

"Drinking does a lot of things to my mind that I would normally have to focus in order to do." He replied cryptically.

She quirked an eyebrow at the explanation she got, but her attention was drawn towards the doors sliding open. Before them stood roughly seven guys, all wearing swords on their hips, with black kimonos on, and red dragon tattoos visible on random parts of their bodies.

"And I'm surprised it took you guys this long." Sera said as he placed his saucer down. She was on guard, with her hand on the handle of the gun she had hidden in her sleeve. "You only have seventeen hours left before I start genocide."

The man in the front of the group took a step forward with his hand on his sword.

"Listen you little punk!" he began, and she tensed her muscles. If he was going to throw down inside, she would put a bullet in his chest before he pulled his sword free. "Boss doesn't like it when people trespass on his territory. And he really doesn't like it when the one trespassing is making demands."

"Well," Sera began, slowly standing up to face them, eyes partially closed and focused on the floor. "I do apologize of the mix up. I see you haven't gotten the memo."

"What memo?"

"That this is no longer his territory."

"And whose territory is it?"

She already had a feeling of where this was going and where he was going with it. She could see his tail swishing back and forth lazily.

"How about we take this outside neh?" he suggested softly. "I would rather not waste good sake."

The men scoffed, but began backing out and into the street. The streets were vacant, save for the occasional person stumbling out of a bar. As she followed out behind him, she kept her finger on the trigger. If he was getting himself in over his head, she would step in and stop it.

"Oh," Sera said suddenly. "And to answer your question about whose territory this is. It's mine."

The surrounding men laughed loudly at his proclamation and she wanted to tell them to shut up. Not only were they digging their collective graves, but they were irritating her by underestimating him. They reminded her of the recruits that didn't make it. They would learn in time, just like the others.

"Fuck Ichi," one man, to the far left, said suddenly. "This kid is funny. I say after we kill him, we have our way with the girl. I'm sure she would like to have a real man."

"Ichi? As in Ichibi?" Heather asked softly. If it was true, then these men stood no chance. None of them did. And little Sakura was going to be going home in a few days.

"Yea." He answered as he puffed out his chest. "We are the demons of Japan. And I am Ichibi, also known as Shukaku."

She heard Sera chuckle and it wasn't one filled with humor. She knew very well what that meant, and she was sure that even he wasn't sure.

"So, you are a demon?" he said with a humorous tone. Even as he kept his eyes cast on the ground, she could see the red beginning to bleed into them, staining them an angry vermilion.

"Yeah punk." The man who yelled out first said as he pulled out his sword. "But, he won't have to dirty his hands with killing a kid." He charged forward, sword rose to cleave. "Cause I'll do it for him!"

She watched as the man grew closer, and she caught herself wondering what Sera was doing. He was still standing there, eyes on the ground, not moving. Her heart stopped in her chest. He said he wished to die. Was he going to allow this no body, this scum, this *human* to kill him? Well, if he was, then she would kill these guys and give him a long lecture about what they talked about. As her hand was in motion to bring out her gun, she stopped at the sound of metal on metal. She had to blink twice to ensure she was seeing things correctly. The man was in front of him, no more than three feet away, hand still raised, with sword still in hand. But as her mind began working, she found that the sword was not at full length. It was cut in half. To Sera's left was the tip of the blade sticking out of the ground. Turning back towards Sera, she found his black blade out of its sheath and in his hand. He was holding it in a relaxed grip, allowing the tip to just barely taste the dirt, being held only a hair line above the ground. He cut the blade in half, and unsheathed his blade all in less than a second? A second! She blinked and missed the whole thing. The human body couldn't move that quickly. Under no circumstances could the human body move that fast. The muscles would tear, ligaments would snap. But he seemed to show no signs of injury. Amazing.

"Wow." She caught herself saying as the events caught up to her.

"You will do no such thing." Sera said softly. As his eyes finally cast upwards towards the one who invaded his space, the entire area filled with a vile, sickening feeling that she knew could only emanate from him. This sickening bloodlust was something that, even if she weren't to admit it, only a demon could produce. Something that was not human. The wicked aura flowed over her, and she couldn't help the shiver that went up her spine. To her, it felt like he was trailing a finger up her back, and she involuntarily arched her back lightly as it made its way back down. But just looking into the eyes of the assembled, she could only guess what it was that they felt. They were in a position she hoped she would never find herself in. They were the prey. As he turned the blade over in his grip, she only caught a subtle twitch as her only indicator that he moved at all. "Because you were a dead man walking." She heard blood beginning to drip onto the floor and she looked for the source. Sera's blade, still in the same position it was in before, was now stained in blood on the tip. Looking up towards the guy, she caught the look of immeasurable pain fleet across his face, before he screamed to the sky above as his upper half slid off at an angle. The blood that gushed once into the air and onto him, made her lick her lips lightly. He kept his eyes on the other six and she could only guess as to what they saw. He was covered in blood from the head down, with crimson slit eyes that seemed to see into your very soul, and a small smile on his face that told all that he didn't mind the blood, or the gore one bit, but in fact enjoyed it. "Now, who will be next?" he questioned with a tilt of his head. "Because if no one will step forward, I will prevent you from stepping at all."

XXX

"So, you are the only one left?" the voice asked from the darkness. It held the distinct tone of irritation.

"Yes sir."

There was a growl that emanated from the voice, but it settled into nothingness. The silence stretched on into the darkness, only to be broken by the shifting of feet.

"Tell me what happened."

"Sir, he was like a demon. He moved so quick we didn't even see when he killed Yoshi. After that, he started taking us down like we weren't even there. None of us could land a single blow on him."

"And what of this girl?" the voice asked.

"She just stood there watching the entire thing. It was like it didn't even faze her." The man shuddered. "Sir, I don't think you should go against him. I think you should just give up the girl and forget about her. He was talking about genocide boss. Genocide!" the man continued to ramble. "He's going to kill us all if we don't hand over the girl in the next sixteen hours. We're all going to die. We're all going to die. We're all going to-" he was cut off as his head snapped back.

As the body toppled to the floor, others came to move it from sight.

"So, this 'Fox' seems to be good with a sword." The voice mused. "I wish to see what he could do against me. Bring Sakura to me at once. We are going to pay a little visit to her home town. Let them know who still runs things."

XXX

"Twelve hours thirteen minutes and twelve seconds." Sera reported aloud as he dried himself off. Heather watched his toned body as he dried the water from his person. She could think of a few ways to get the water off.

"So, what do you think they will do now?" she asked.

He didn't answer her until he put on the dark crimson kimono she picked out for him. It brought a smile to her face as he put it on. It fit him like a glove. The black trimming acted like the shadows as it outlined his body.

"They are more than likely stunned that I took care of the reception crew. They are going to take a few hours to come to grips with that. Afterwards, I don't know. They could either heed my demand, or waste the next twelve hours and seven minutes. Either way, I'm going to retrieve the girl."

She nodded her head. He's never failed a mission yet and she would be shocked if he did. He wasn't the type to quit until he died.

"Well, what do you want to do until then?" she didn't want to simply wait inside a room for half a day for them to come to their senses. There were a few places she wanted to go.

"What do you want to do?" he asked as he turned towards her. "You know I could simply wait until the time comes, but I know you don't really want to do that."

She smiled.

"I want to see more of Tokyo." Was her answer.

He nodded his head and began heading towards the door after placing his sword on his left hip. She got up and followed him out into the streets.

Even early morning, the streets of Tokyo were busy with people walking towards their destinations. School boys and girls were on their way to school wearing their uniforms. Although some of the school girls passed looks towards Sera's way as they walked. She wasn't ignorant of the looks she was receiving, but she didn't particularly like the looks of the girls.

"Stop glaring or else I will have to get you some shades."

She jumped slightly at his voice. She didn't even know she was glaring at them.

"I didn't know I was."

"You were." He responded. "Every girl that walked past."

"Well sorry if I don't like it when they check you out."

"I don't like the guys looking at you either, but I know I can't simply kill them or gouge out their eyes."

She smirked at him as she grabbed his hand, pulling him closer towards her.

"Aw, you're cute when you threaten innocent people." She cooed.

"Don't say that again." He requested levelly. "It creeps me out."

She giggled as she poked his cheek.

"Oh, so even the mighty fox can be creped out?" she asked mockingly. "I have to tell everyone about this." She laughed manically as she rubbed her hands together.

"You tell anyone, they will die."

"Fine, fine, I won't tell anyone." She conceded as she wrapped her arm around his again. She liked this. Away from everyone else, he played with her and even joked more often. This is what she wanted for him in life. To be able to be normal. But he could never be normal. This was all only temporary. Once they went back to Wind, he would only talk to her freely in the privacy of his room. "Do you forgive me?"

"I don't know." He said as he shrugged his shoulders. She pecked him on the cheek. "Fine." He relented.

"So how much longer until the deadline?"

"Only nine hours and five minutes remaining. Once time is out, I'm going to slaughter them all." He turned his head slightly in her direction. "You can join it too you know. I wouldn't mind sharing the kills with you. It could be fun."

"Only if you need my help." She told him. She didn't like killing like he did, but she didn't hate it either. She killed when needed, and nothing more. "But I doubt that."

"Don't be so sure about that Lil." He muttered to himself.

She would have asked what he said, but they spotted a man wearing a black kimono standing on a street corner. He was looking directly at them. He had to be one of the hidden dragons. He tossed his head to the left, behind a corner, and began walking off. Following after him, they came to an alley, with him standing before them.

"What do you want?" Sera asked as he sighed. "Please tell me that your boss isn't stupid."

"I have some news." The man began. "The boss has taken the girl back to her home town. He's going to kill everyone in town unless you come to fight. And only you can fight. If you win, then he will give the girl back. You lose, you die. You have until midnight." With that, the man began walking off.

Heather looked towards him and saw the crimson smile ghost his lips.

"So what are we going to do?" she asked, even though she had a fairly good idea as to what he was going to do. He was challenged.

"I'm going to answer their call. It's obvious to me that they haven't been paying attention to the subtle hints that I have been dropping. I wanted to get back home and do more missions, but now, it appears that I get to receive my tithe from a willing party." His lips moved to match the ethereal smile on his face. "There's nothing better than a willing sacrifice."

"How are we going to get there?" she asked. It took them three days to get here and they only had fourteen hours.

He didn't answer as he began walking out of the alley. She followed behind wondering what he was thinking. But as he pulled his gun, she could take a wild guess. A car was coming down the street. Aiming his gun at the driver, he ordered him to get out. The man scrambled out of the car pleading for him not to shoot, and judging by the sneer on Sera's face, he was tempted to shoot him. He told her once that he didn't like ones who groveled. Stepping up, she placed a hand on his shoulder and guided him towards the car. Best to avoid civilians in this matter. Climbing into the passenger seat, she didn't have time to strap on her seat belt as he shot down the street.

"In a hurry aren't we?" she asked rhetorically as she finally clicked the buckle.

"Not particularly, no." he answered, eyes still on the road. "I don't particularly care for the people of the village. But I do wish to see who I will be facing. And they are over two hundred miles away. I only wish to leave Tokyo fast. You can sleep while I drive. You must be tired after the long ride here and all."

She looked at him silently for a moment. There was something that she wanted to ask him for the longest time, and it was bugging her.

"Why do your eyes change?" she asked.

"How do you mean?"

"From gold to red." She elaborated. "Why do they do that?"

He found the question to be a little random, but he supposed it was her scientific nature showing again. Always wanting answers. Just like him.

"It only happens when I'm either angry or I see a threat."

"A threat?"

"Yes." He nodded his head. "A fool would think that they are untouchable. A child could kill a full grown man if the man let his guard down because he didn't think the child could do anything to him. Any outward hostility will be dealt with."

"Does your vision change when your eyes do?"

"How good are your reflexes?" he asked suddenly.

"Good why?"

"I mean how fast they are? How long does it take for you to react to stimulus?"

"Three tenths of a second."

"My natural reflex to a stimulus is three hundredths of a second. When my eyes change, it becomes faster, to the point of three thousandths of a second. At that point, I can predict what a person is going to do, almost a full second, before they do it. So to answer your question, yes my vision does change."

"You have the eyes of a serpent."

"I've noticed." He replied dryly.

"Do you see things like they do? I mean, in heat signatures and stuff?"

He glanced out the corner of his eye and regarded her expression. She was seriously asking this question.

"What would you do if I told you I could?" he asked.

"It wouldn't surprise me." She shrugged her shoulders. "But do you?"

He turned his attention back out towards the street as he made the turn out of the city.

"I can see perfectly fine Lil." He knew what he gave wasn't the answer she was looking for, but at the moment, he didn't really care. Some secrets are best kept to ones self. If someone knew everything about you, it could prove fatal. Granted, he didn't think that she would turn on him. She was after all his most loyal Hell Born. She followed his orders to the tee. Even without all the Serpents Charm or Fox's Seduction. But, two people already turned on him in the past, and he didn't want a repeat, otherwise she would be following them to hells fire. "Now, go to sleep. We won't be getting there until a few minutes before midnight. I might need you, so rest."

As she nodded her head, and closed her eyes, he brought his mind to the fight that was to come. If his hunch was correct, it would be fun. Perhaps, even more fun than that of the Bloody Banquet.

XXX

She awoke to a poke in her side. She was having a pleasant dream. It was her and Sera on a beach with Sibyl. They were just having a nice time. She wondered why they were at the beach, but it didn't matter. It was just the three of them. Father, mother, and child. Turning towards him, she noticed they arrived in Kobe.

"Come on. I want to see my opponent." He said as he got out the car.

She stretched slightly before getting out as well. As they walked the same street they walked down only a week before neither was surprised by the lack of people on them. Looking around the village, they both spotted a group of people in black kimonos standing in front of a building.

Stopping a few meters before them, she watched the surroundings. She could feel eyes on her back, and didn't doubt that they had more people hidden around this place.

"So, where is the girl?" Sera asked, finally breaking the tense silence.

"She's inside." A big man answered as he took a step forward. "I'm going to guess that you are the one who killed my men."

"That's correct." Sera nodded.

"I was expecting someone a bit bigger, so excuse me for being surprised that I find a child coming here."

"It's no harm." He waved his hand. "I don't particularly care how you viewed me."

"Well, I'm curious as to why you would come to me for this girl after three years. I can tell that, despite your fluency in our language, you aren't from around here. So I wish to know why you came all this way to die."

She quirked an eyebrow at the man who was the apparent leader. He honestly thought he could kill him. That was going to be his undoing.

"I didn't come here to die." Sera said softly. "I'm already dead. In fact, I do not exist."

"Well mister, I do not exist, what shall I call you? After all, I need to know the name of the one who thought he was good enough to take on the hidden dragons."

"You can call me Yoko."

"A spirit huh?" the man mused. "I suppose it's appropriate since you are going to die."

"And what is your name? I would like to know the name of the one who challenged me."

The man chuckled with a smile that showed white teeth.

"My name is Kyuubi. That's all you need to know." The man, known as Kyuubi answered. "But you are mistaken. I am your opponent, only if you can get past the others." He held his arms out, indicating the others that surrounded him. "Only then will you be able to fight me. And you must do it alone, or else I will kill the girl."

"That's no problem." Sera placed a hand on the hilt of his blade. Passing her a glance, she nodded her head and backed off a few steps. Things were going to go to hell in a hand basket real quick and she didn't want to get blood on her new kimono. "Now, let's do this."

She watched as a group of seven men stepped forward. Her own mind doing the calculations of how many there could be. As they surrounded him, she could still see him standing perfectly still. She would have been worried about him not having his sword drawn, but after she witnessed his display of swordsmanship earlier, she had faith in him. One man stepped forward from the circle and was moving his sword in a horizontal motion, trying to cleave him in two from his left. The resulting ring that sounded throughout the assembled told her that he blocked the strike. Another man must have thought that his cue to attack, because he came from behind with his blade raised for Sera's head. As the blade came within a foot of striking him, she caught a blur of movement, before the two bodies fell to the ground headless. Said heads were currently flying above their heads, landing in a wet thump. The other five seemed to take a step back from the gore, as the bodies fell.

"Please tell me that wasn't the best you lot had to offer." He was bored and she knew it. When he was bored, he tended to end things quickly. The men flinched at his tone. He sighed. "I guess it can't be helped." Before her eyes, she saw him make a swift movement from right to left.

The black blade was set parallel with his waist. As he brought the blade back to his right slowly, she saw the bodies fall over, sliced in half at the waist. He turned his attention towards the other group of men as they flinched slightly. "So, who are the next batches?"

"Impressive." Kyuubi appraised. "I must say when they told me of your talents, I was a little skeptical. I couldn't believe that a child would wield a blade like you. But I was wrong. But," he paused as she heard the sounds of hammers being pulled back. She clicked the safety off her own. "I came prepared."

XXX

Sera clicked his tongue in amusement. He could feel his receding bloodlust coming back full force. He smiled as he slowly took off his shades. Opening his eyes, he looked at the one who called himself Kyuubi.

"You know, I'm not surprised" he remarked, because he really wasn't. Any crime organization worth their grain in salt would be able to get their hands on some weapons. "But, it doesn't matter." As twelve of the men raised their guns, he tilted his head slightly. "Your bullets won't even hit me."

"You talk mighty tough child. And your contacts are good. But if you intend to intimidate us, you have another thing coming." Kyuubi scoffed. "It will take more than contacts."

"I can guarantee that before you are able to reload your weapons; my blade would have already tasted your blood."

"Surround him." He ordered. As the twelve created a half circle around him, he held his blade in a lax grip. This was going to be a little more challenging than dodging random bullets from in front of him, but he was comfortable enough to know that if anything, he wouldn't die from a shot to the head. They had revolvers. Only seventy two bullets. He would have to shift his body seventy two times in order to dodge each one, assuming they didn't shoot at the same time. But he didn't worry about that happening. The chances of them actually doing that were slim to nil. He calmed his breathing as he increased the beating of his heart. "Fire!"

Sera moved quickly. It was times like these that he valued the fact that he left his armor to Lilith. It would only slow him down and increase the chances of him getting shot. He could see the first bullet as it left the chamber. Turning slightly to his left, he immediately leaned back to avoid the second through tenth shot that came towards his chest. It appeared that they wanted to end it quickly. Jumping into the air, he dodged the shots aimed for his legs. Shifting his weight in mid air, he avoided the three bullets that would have claimed his left lung. Landing lightly, he parried two shells with his blade. Zero was not an ordinary blade. He had it custom made, just like Benehime. Within the titanium hybrid was his own blood. Something that even he didn't know the properties of. And yet for some reason he couldn't understand, it made it stronger. He assumed it was the iron in his blood. Because of that, he could easily block a bullet of almost any caliber without it breaking. Jumping from side to side, he dodged the last of the bullets, and looked upon them as they watched him with wide eyes.

"I told you that you wouldn't hit me." He said softly. Bringing his thumb towards the blade, he allowed it to slice into his flesh. He allowed it to slowly seep its way into the grooves of the blade, into the words, and pooled at the tip before a drop landed. "Now, it's time I held up my end of the bargain."

XXX

She didn't know what he was going to do with so many guns on him, but her worry soon proved to be not needed as he turned, leaned, tilted, jumped and spun around the bullets as if they were moving at a snail's pace. But then again, he told her that he could see, almost a second into the future, so it wasn't that hard to believe. As the final shot was fired, he was standing in roughly the same spot he started in. This was more than she expected of this mission. Him cutting his hand on his own blade didn't make sense to her, but he always had a reason for everything he did. No matter what it was, from brushing his teeth a certain way, to combing his hair, he had a reason.

As he slowly walked towards the closest one, she found herself smiling lightly at their trembling figures. They had no idea that the real demon fox was standing in front of them. And from the tail that wagged quickly back and forth, he was having a good time. As he reached the first one, his blade made a clean cut through his hand, dropping the gun with it. Turning quickly, he severed a mans leg off at the knee. Standing, he rushed another as he plunged his blade into two of them at once in the shoulders. Pulling his blade out, he cut another across his chest, while turning around to sever a mans arm off. She grimaced lightly as he stabbed a man in the left thigh. Three tried to rush him, only to become impaled on the sword. The final one was busy trying to stop his hands from shaking and to force the bullets into the chambers. She watched as Sera slowly walked up to him and placed his blade on the mans neck. She was surprised that all he did was knick it. As he backed away, he still had that smile on his face that said there's more to come.

"Now the real entertainment begins." He said in a growl. "There is a reason to why I didn't kill them out right. You see, my blade is special. He's called Zero. A titanium hybrid, specially designed for me by me. The grooves in the blade are to hold liquid. It can be anything from poison to simple water. In this case, it's my blood." The smile that made its way to his face seemed to become something of nightmares. Behind him, she could see tail after tail slowly emerging. "But my blood is special. It's highly toxic. You see, it's a veritable cocktail of various poisons and venoms from many places. Pure, and undiluted, is when it's the most potent. In truth, you only need three drops to cause severe pain. Five for death. In six seconds they will scream in agony."

That was news to her. She didn't know his blood was toxic. But how did it get that way in the first place? Another thing she would have to add to her list of things to ask. And true to his word, they began screaming in horrible agony. They reminded her of screaming souls on the river Styx. Their bodies writhed on the ground and twitched in pain, so horrible, that she couldn't possibly imagine.

"And twelve seconds after, they will die."

Again, true to his word, the bodies stopped moving.

"Now," Sera continued. "Will you be taking me seriously, or will I have to kill the lot of you before you do? Either way, I'm going to kill you all anyway. You seem to have forgotten the twenty-four hours I gave you to comply."

"Damn you!" Kyuubi yelled. "Torch em." He ordered in a sinister hiss. She would have wondered what he was talking about, but she felt the air behind her shift. Turning quickly, she spotted six men standing with flaming drinks in their hands. Molotov cocktails. Taking out her gun, she pulled the trigger. But she noticed too late as the bottles were already in flight towards his position.

"KYUU!" she screamed at the top of her lungs. He didn't seem to show any sign that he heard her or was even aware of the bottles heading towards his position. As the first one landed before him and the flames began to circle him, she was still hoping he would jump out of the way. The second, third, forth, and fifth also made it to his position, and she felt her heart stop. "Kyuu." She whispered as her bottom lip trembled. "Kyuu?" she whispered softly.

The cackling laughter of Kyuubi made her turn eyes towards him with a vicious glare.

"Ha! I knew he wasn't all that." He turned his eyes towards her and she snarled at him. "And you pretty girl are to be my trophy from this."

"You bastard!" she snarled, leveling her gun at him. "I'll kill you!"

"No, you won't."

She paused as she heard the voice. Turning towards the raging fire, she looked for any signs that he was in there, still alive, but she couldn't see anything save for the flames.

"Kyuu?" she breathed. It wasn't possible that he was still alive inside that inferno. It had to be over four hundred degrees inside there.

"Believe."

It was at that point that she realized that the voice wasn't coming from the flames, but inside her head. He couldn't be dead. He just couldn't be. He's taken a knife to the heart and still lived. He's taken countless wounds to his body and soul and yet he still lives. He still has a mission to complete. *I know you are still alive.* She said to herself with resolution.

"You can't kill me." Kyuubi said arrogantly as he smirked at her. "Take her way guys. I want to break this one in early."

She looked at the approaching men calmly as they began walking towards her. But as they stopped, her attention went to the fire. There was an overwhelming feeling of death coming from the flames and she had a feeling she knew who it was. The overwhelming bloodlust was back, but seemed multiplied by nine. As she kept her eyes on the flames, she spotted one after another tail appear, slowly swaying back and forth.

Then she heard his voice. It made her shiver in relief and fear. It was gruff and cold and sounded underused.

"You silly little human." He chortled. "You think you can burn me in my own element? You think you can kill me? Ningen[18], allow me to show you the true demon fox."

The flames around his person began to swirl around the center by an unseen wind. As they broke away, she spotted him standing in his same position as the bottles landed. His eyes were a brilliant vermilion and seemed to glow with lust. His grin seemed too big for his face, but she could see his lips set in a grin. On top of his head, two long triangles, red in color, were up and pointed in the direction of the hidden dragons. As she turned her attention towards his hands, she gasped lightly. There seemed to be claws instead of hands, ethereal red. And his feet looked to be the hind legs of a fox. And in his hand, was Zero. But it was different. The blade was still black, that much she could see. But around the blade, flames danced and licked the metal. She knew that if the liquor were to land on the blade, it wouldn't stay lit long after the liquid disappeared.

"Kyuubi." She said softly.

"What?!" the man screamed as he glared at them both.

"You are not the real Kyuubi." She raised a hand towards Sera. "I would like to introduce you to the true demon fox, also known as Fox God Inari, of the Spirits."

The look of recognition only lasted for a second before it shifted into unadulterated fear.

"H—Hold on a s-second." The man stuttered as he held out his arms. "Look. I'll give you the girl." He turned around. "Get her!" he screamed. The man he yelled at didn't waste any time in leaving. A few seconds later, he came back with a female that she took as Sakura. "Now, we can all go now."

"Send her over here." She ordered as she kept her gun trained on the escorts' person. As he dropped her off, the man ran back to where he came. "What is your name?" she asked as she looked at the young girls face.

"My name is Sakura."

---

[18] Ningen means Human

She looked at the girl who had her eyes closed and raised an eyebrow. "Blind?"

"Yes."

"Kyuu?" she turned her attention back towards Sera. It was time that he had the fun he's been waiting for. Apparently he was still awaiting orders to kill.

"Yes?"

"Enjoy." She said as she ushered Sakura off further down the street to avoid any backlash. He's told her that when he's in a blood lust, it doesn't matter who is in the way. If he doesn't know them, he will kill them and she didn't want that to happen to the girl.

XXX

Sera smirked as he heard her final words. It was time that he showed these humans what a true demon was capable of. As he held his sword in his hand tightly, he was curious as to two things. One, how was his blade able to stay aflame, and two, why wasn't he bothered by the fact that he was burned alive. But as he looked towards the terrified faces of his soon to be prey, he let the matter rest. He would have time to look into it with Heather later. She would undoubtedly have questions and he wanted answers as well.

"No." he hissed with a smile. "We can't *all* go. I told you, twenty four hours was the limit to heed my request. If you had of done so, we wouldn't be here now. But I do thank you for bringing me so many offerings. It's been a while since I've had a good feast. Please, scream and beg as much as you want. It will change nothing." Holding his right arm out, he slowly began walking towards them and was amused as some ran. "I will still have my fill!" he charged, slashing and hacking away at everything in sight.

The surrounding darkness swallowed every wail of pain, every scream of anguish, but seemed to reject the thunderous growling that persisted into the night. The surrounding people that hid in their houses, under beds, in closets, in their basements, in cellars, all shivered as they heard the animalistic sounds that penetrated their walls. They were reminded of the legend of which demon god's shrine was present in their village and told their children to never anger him. For he was a protector, but one who only gave a single strike to all, and once crossed, he devoured them, body and soul.

XXX

As morning came, Heather decided to go out and check on Sera. He's been gone for over three hours and the screams stopped over an hour ago. She didn't want him to be injured or anything. After all, he's been known to over do it at times.

She was the first one to step onto the streets after the event, and she wasn't surprised to see the streets covered in blood. He was truly an animal while fighting.

"Kyuu?" she called. She waited a few moments before repeating herself.

"Why are you yelling?"

She turned at the sound of his voice. If she was anyone else, she would have screamed and probably hit him out of shock, but she's been around him long enough to know that if he didn't want you to know he was coming, he wouldn't and if he did, he would. Taking in his appearance, he was drenched in blood, and his golden eyes seemed to have a glazed look to them. She knew he was riding out the high from the kills.

"Come on. Mr. Yakumi wants to thank us for retrieving his daughter." She turned and didn't have to look back to know that he was following behind.

Walking into the building where it all started, she spotted father and daughter in an embrace. She cleared her throat.

"Oh," Mr. Yakumi said as he broke apart from his daughter. "Let me introduce my daughter Sakura. Sakura, these are the people who rescued you."

Sakura bowed her head low.

"Thank you for everything. It was horrible in that place. I don't know how I could possibly repay you."

"That's not needed." Sera said with a shake of his head. "I've already had my fun."

"Please, can I see your face?" she asked as she fiddled with her fingers. "I would like to know the face of the one who saved my life."

Sera nodded his head as he stepped softly towards her. Grabbing her hands, he guided them towards his face.

"Sakura was the priestess of the shrine here in Kobe." Mr. Yakumi said as Sakura's fingers traced the outline of his face. "We have a legend around here that the one in charge of protection of the shrine is to be the purest of us. And as long as they are watching over the shrine, then the demon god that resides inside will be happy. Our priestesses live long lives, and the hidden dragons thought that if they kidnapped one, they would be able to get the secret of longevity out of her."

"I thank you Kyuubi no Kitsune." Sakura said softly as her fingers glided over his eyes.

"I told you already that you need not thank me." He repeated with a subtle shake of his head. She was curious to how Sakura came about knowing of his 'other' name, but she assumed it was because of her work with the shrine.

"No, I do." She insisted. "You were to be imprisoned and protected and cared for by me, and I instead left my post and you came to retrieve me. How can I ever repay you?"

"Be my betrothed." He said suddenly. Heathers eyebrows shot up in surprise, but settled off into her usual expression. He's already got six females, what's one more? Either way, she knew she had him, a special part of him, to herself.

"Very well." She agreed.

"That easy?"

"Yes. I may be blind, but I know a pure soul when I feel one. You may be a demon Kyuubi, but that doesn't mean that you do not feel. I know I will be happy with you in life, even though I know there will be some rough waters ahead."

"Fine." He said with a nod of his head. Standing, he walked back towards her, giving her a look that seemed to be asking her if she was okay with it. She nodded her head. "When I come back, I will be taking you as mine."

"I look forward to it." She said with a light blush.

"I believe it's now time for us to leave." He said as he began heading towards the door. "Come Lilith." She nodded her head as she began walking out the door. "Oh, and Sakura?"

"Yes?"

He turned and walked back over towards her. Kneeling down, he kissed her closed eyes with bloody lips. Standing, he walked towards the door again.

"In time you will be a beautiful woman. I look forward to taking you and showing you the world." He said as he walked down the hall.

Making it outside, she heard him sigh lightly. Turning towards him, she grabbed his hand.

"What's wrong?" she asked softly.

"There are more questions that I require the answers to Lilith." He answered softly.

"We'll get the answers. I promise." She swore as she squeezed his hand.

"Right." He agreed. "Now, let's get home so I can rest. All this killing has made me rather tired."

"I already called base and a helicopter should be here in the next ten minutes to take us to the airport."

XXX

As he lay back on the bed, she began administering the cream that he kept in his room. His body wasn't damaged, but his muscles were sore and tired. He almost fell out on the walk into the compound. He must have over exerted his self during all his fun. But now that they were back, she was glad. At the moment, he didn't have to deal with Sibyl and that was a blessing, because she knew that when he saw her, she would tackle him to the ground and drill him with questions about where he went.

"So, will you tell me about your blood?" she asked as she massaged his calf muscles.

"When I was a child, my father tried previously to kill me by poisoning my food. When I got sick, it only lasted for a few days before passing. After, my grandfather exposed me to many different types of poisons and toxins to ensure that I would be resilient to them. He told me that it was a part of the training that Noir's had to go through. I thought it odd, but I didn't question his teachings. But now, I know he was simply trying to kill me. One time, while I was training with the dogs," she scowled lightly as she was reminded of the treatment he received. "One of them bit me, hard enough to make me bleed. A few minutes later, it simply died. I became curious as to how it died. After I finished with my first mission, I gave my blood to another dog. It died in the same manner. After, I took it to the vet. They told me that his internal organs shut down and he died a horrible death. When I asked how his organs looked, she told me they were healthy. Looked to be almost like he was just born. It was then that I found out about two properties of my blood." He turned towards her. "The first, being it's toxic if ingested or injected directly into the blood stream. And second, it's a powerful healing agent. In fact, it's the main ingredient in the healing salve that you are putting on my skin and on you too."

She paused in the application of the cream as she looked towards him with slightly widened eyes.

"Don't worry." He assured. "My blood has to be ingested undiluted. By me giving you the salve for the last six years, you are immune to it, unless you got an ounce of my blood injected directly into your blood stream. If that were to happen, you would die a quick, but painful death."

"Well, I'm glad that we got that out of the way." She said with relief. "Is that why you kissed Sakura's eyes with your blood?"

"Yes. I want to know if doing so would be able to heal her eyes. Chances are that it wont, but either way, it doesn't matter." He said as he shook his head. "But what I would like to know is how Zéro was able to sustain flame."

"Well, I think it's obvious that your blood isn't just toxic." She suggested. "I mean, it's a poisonous cocktail. I'm sure there is something in your blood that makes it flammable as well." She didn't think it relevant that his other self was a representation of the God of Fire.

"I guess you're right."

"Sometimes, I wonder what's real anymore." She muttered as she placed her head down on his stomach. Things that she knew as fact were proven wrong. Things that shouldn't be possible were possible. She wasn't sure that aliens weren't real anymore. For all she knew, they could be out there on Mars, waiting to invade. "The things you can do. The things that you are capable of." She trailed off.

"What is reality?" he asked softly. "What is life? They say that your entire life flashes before your eyes before you die. If that true, then isn't it possible that what you are doing now has already happened and you're just reliving it before you die?" he posed a good question. "And when you get to the point in your life where you truly exist, it all repeats itself. What if all the people you know to be dead are stuck in a loop of their own life, repeating past actions over and over. If it's true, then what we are doing now has already been predetermined. What if in everyone else's lives, you cease to exist. But to you, you continue to exist in your own loop of existence."

"That would be unnerving." She confessed as she shook her head slightly into his skin. "To know that everything that you are doing has been done already and you are simply stuck in a loop. That would be bad."

"Reality is how the mind deciphers what the eyes perceive." She realized that he was going on one of his lectures again. And judging by the line of questioning, he's asked himself these same questions. After all, he's had twelve years to think. "But what about what the eyes can't see? The root word in reality is real. What can be considered really real? When you dream, does it not seem real? The food that you eat during the dream? The water? The feelings you experience? Or rather, is the reality of reality truly a dream? How would one be sure? A dream seems real, but it is only our perception of what 'we' consider real. What we consider real, is something we can experience ourselves with our five senses: Taste, Touch, Smell, Sight, and Hear. If we can not experience it with 2 out of 5 senses, then it doesn't exist. It isn't real. If a child creates an imaginary friend, it's considered okay and not completely out of the realm of possibility, but that doesn't make it real. "I think there for I am." Basically, it means because I can acknowledge my own existence, then I must be real. I must exist. To know ones existence is to know that they are alive. Imaginary friends tend to go away after a child has matured beyond the need for imaginary friends. But what if you didn't create them, but they came into being? What if they are able to think, act, and feel completely independent of the person to whom they inhabit? Does this mean that they are real, that they exist? If the theory of "I think there for I am" is true, then they must be real. Are you able to tell the difference between what's real and what's not? No matter what you decide, the outcome is already determined."

"Do you dream?" she asked. It was a good question. He didn't sleep, so she wanted to know if he dreamt while he lay awake in the darkness alone.

"I do not dream." He answered softly. "I can not dream. All I do is constantly see. The past. The present."

"The future." She added as she turned her head to look at him. The events in the bar coming back to her. He was able to predict when the thugs would come in and confront him.

He nodded his head.

"Even the future. Life is a series of events. It is the sheet music to which our actions are the notes. Sometimes you can get away with missing a few notes and nobody will notice. But when they are heard by the right ears, then you will be criticized. It's an ongoing solo which can span over a lifetime. And sometimes it can go beyond one person playing and be passed on to another to finish the tragic melody."

"I wonder what it would be like to see the future." She mumbled.

"It's neutral." He answered.

"How do you mean?"

"The future can be good, or bad. It depends on whose side you are on. Perspective. Sometimes knowing what will happen before it does, is a godsend. You could save lives. More importantly keep yourself alive. But what about the things that you saw coming, but could do nothing about? Knowing that someone you care about is going to die, and not being able to stop it."

"I wouldn't know what to do if I knew you were going to die but I couldn't stop it." She admitted. She never thought about it that way.

"I listen to the things some people in the world say about killing. And listening to them is by far one of the most annoying things imaginable. Talking about it being one of the greatest sins. And yet we train our solders to kill our enemies. When is it okay? To kill another human being is considered a sin in most major religions, and is to be punished by being sent to damnation. But what about unforeseen circumstances? Does the punishment change if you do it for the right reasons? But what would you do if your life was in danger? Would you be able to kill them in order to survive? And if so, then will you be able to live with being branded "Condemned" for the rest of your life, or would you have rather died instead? Self preservation is one of humanities most basic of instincts. It is only natural that they would want to live instead of die. The ends justify the means. It means that the methods used, no matter how unorthodox they maybe, if the action will serve the greater good, then is it still alright to kill?"

"I don't particularly care about killing." She admitted. "I don't think about it. If they need to die, then they die. If not, then I let them live."

"And what of being condemned?"

She turned over and kissed his stomach lightly before snuggling in further.

"From the moment I met you six years ago, I knew that I was going to be a part of your life until I die. And even now, after I've seen the killings, the deaths, the hate, and the evil, I still stand by you. I'm not concerned about what awaits me when I die. I'm comfortable with where I'm going."

He placed a hand on top of her head as he slowly combed his fingers through it.

"We both know where I'm going." He said softly. "And I know where you are going as well."

She would have asked what his last sentence was, but his door opened. She didn't have to turn around to know who would simply barge into his room unannounced.

"Papa!" the thirteen year old girl screamed as she ran into the room. The girl stopped at the side of the bed and fell onto his chest. "Why didn't you tell me you were going on a mission with mother? I could have gone too. You were gone for over a week. I thought something happened. I was worried. I thought-" she was cut off as he pressed his fingers to her lips.

Heather sat up with a smile on her face. She knew this would happen. And now, Sibyl, with her blond hair still tied in the long braid that he set it in four years ago, along with her golden slit contacts to look like him, and her face riddled with worry, was in his room doing exactly what she predicted.

"Little one, your mother and I are fine." Sera assured as he brushed the stray bangs that fell into her face.

"Well, if you say so." she said calmly. "So, did you get me anything?" she asked as she sat down on the other side.

He smirked at her.

"Quick to recover isn't she?" he joked.

"You said you both were fine, so you are fine." She pointed out. "Now what did you bring me?"

"I didn't bring you anything," he responded plainly. "But your mother has brought you a few things. And before you ask, you will get them in the morning. Until then, go to bed and sleep."

"Yes father." She said with a nod. Leaning over she kissed his cheek. "Good night father."

"Good night little one." He said to her as she walked out of the room.

"Now," he began as he moved over in his bed. "You may sleep here tonight. So, come on to bed. We need to christen the sheets."

She blushed at the rather crude statement, but complied nonetheless.

Chapter 15

Bloody Sand, Pure Water, Tainted Beach

Looking down at the operation that was taking place, Sibyl couldn't help but worry about the patient.

"It's not your fault Sibyl." Susan said beside her as she watched the procedure proceed. "He knew what he was doing."

Turning her head slightly, she looked blankly at her before turning back towards the doctors working diligently.

"He came halfway around the world to rescue me from being killed." she continued. "I didn't think he would do that though. The moment I was captured, I thought I would have to wait for the military to rescue Me." she made a non amused noise as she shook her head. "That would have been embarrassing enough. I'm supposed to be the leader of the Spirits, but I can't handle insurgents." she sighed. "I didn't know they would tell him though. If I did, then I would have told him to stay out of it and allow the military to handle it. If anything, it's my fault that he is in the predicament that he is in. I feel so bad about this." she finished softly as she turned around. "I'll visit him after he wakes up. Call me when he does."

Nodding her head in reply, she continued watching her father. She didn't pay any mind to the door closing behind her. Fisting her hands, she punched the nearest wall. As her knuckles bled, she made no sound. She didn't deserve to after what happened. *It's my entire fault.* She thought as she looked at her hand. The events of the previous week passed through her mind.

XXX

Sitting by his side, as she normally did while he was working in the security firm; she paid close attention to everything as usual. Today, they were to close a contract with a company over in Japan, which was good, because they had their sister organization to think about.

"I believe that we have to think about this some more." Mr. Kurama, the representative of the company said as he stood.

"Mr. Kurama, please give me a second." Sera said as he watched him rise with a calm gaze. "I would like to give you a demonstration as to what we can give you."

"Excuse me if I find it rather hard to believe that a child can run a company Mr. Angelus." Mr. Kurama began. "But I was under the impression that Ms. Roth was in charge of the company and its decisions."

"She is, but it is my job to do her job when she is not here." Sera answered easily. "Currently she is out of the country on business and couldn't be here."

During their back and forth, she was making sure to keep her attention on Kurama. He came to their agency to acquire guards to secure their offices and high personnel. What he wouldn't tell them was that he was coming to them, because the yakuza were starting to threaten their business.

"Mr. Kurama, please have a seat so we may continue our proposal." She said softly.

He looked to her with a slightly irritated look.

"And why is there a physically handicapped child sitting in on this meeting?"

"She is a bright individual and her age should have no relevance on her inquiry." Sera answered swiftly. "So, will you please have a seat so I may tell you of our deal?"

"I will only give you five minutes to convince me that your company can do more for us than the competition." he agreed, taking a seat.

"Thank you." Sera said with a small smile. He knew the man was only looking to get a bargain. Thinking that a company run by a 'child' would be easily intimidated. *Such a foolish way of thinking.* "Now-" he began, before being cut off by Rachel walking into the room. Turning his head slightly, he listened to her hurried whisper. *Not good*. Standing quickly, he turned towards Mr. Kurama and his guard. "I'm sorry, but something has come up. You will have to excuse me. We will contact you as soon as we can." he didn't wait for a reply as he began wheeling Sibyl out of the room with Rachel following closely.

Walking into the office, he spotted a man and a woman in black suits looking at photos on the desk. She was rather tall for a woman, about five eight, with short brown hair and a light tanned complexion. The man was of average build.

"You two look so cute together." the woman said as she placed the picture back in its previous position.

"Who are you?" Sera asked as he wheeled Sibyl to the middle of the room and approached the woman with Rachel at his side.

Turning to face him, he spotted her average face. Something in the back of his mind was telling him that he should know her from somewhere, but he couldn't put his finger on it.

"I'm Agent Harper from the FBI, and this," she pointed at the man. "Is Agent Gibbs from the CIA."

He quirked an eyebrow. They haven't done anything that would lead them back to HALO. But, what other reason could they be here?

"And what can I do for you both?" he asked as he leaned against the desk. "You two interrupted a rather important meeting with a foreign client."

"Aren't you a little young to have a gun?" Gibbs asked as he eyed the pistol on his hip.

"When you join the military, you are given an M-16 assault rifle at the early age of eighteen. Seeing as we have a contract with them and have a mutual relationship, we are given the same privileges as they are. You would have known that if you had studied before coming here Gibbs." Sera answered calmly as he tilted his head. Reaching out at an offered piece of paper from Rachel, he read it briefly, before placing it in his pocket. "Or, should I say Henry Gibbs, graduate from Harvard, and immediate recruit for the CIA. But you both haven't answered my question."

"I see the hype about the Puppeteer isn't just hype." Harper appraised as she smirked a little. "You are indeed impressive Seraphim. To have risen to such a position in a company in such a short amount of time after coming from a home like yours is rather impressive. And they eyes are a nice touch. Very intimidating."

"Well, it seems that one of you has studied. But, my eyes are real, and my past home life, as we both know, is not why you are here." he said impassively. "Now, answer my question."

"We don't work for you kid, so I suggest you watch it." Gibbs warned.

"No, but while you are here, you will listen to him." Rachel said simply as she eyed Gibbs. "Under the contract that we have with the military, we have rule over this property and any federal agents have to abide by our rules. Failure to do so is subject to ejection." reaching towards her own gun, she let her hand rest on the butt. "Forcefully, if needed."

He shook his head a little at her display. Always the one to jump in and protect him.

"Stand down Rachel." he said softly. "He didn't know. But in any case, you have still yet to answer my question and I must say it is getting rather irksome. So, either tell me of the reason why you are here, or vacate the premises."

Nodding her head, Harper turned towards Sibyl.

"Maybe it would be best if she was sent out." she suggested.

Quirking an eyebrow, Sibyl looked at her with a placid expression.

"She works here and is entitled to listen." Sera said as he crossed his arms.

"Right well," Harper said as she looked around the room. "Can I play something for you?" she asked as she spotted the TV and DVD player.

"As long as it's pertaining to why you are here."

Nodding her head, she pulled a disk out of her pocket and placed it in the player. Turing the TV on, she took a few steps back.

"We received this today." she began as the screen showed men in fatigues with masks on their faces. "It came from Iraq." she continued as the men on the screen stepped aside to show a person bound to a chair with a black bag over their head. They snatched the bag off of the persons head and revealed it was Susan, bruised, but otherwise okay. "They kidnapped her, because they say that she won't give them money. They are requesting that they be given twenty million dollars in ten days or they will kill her." as the screen went black, she looked at his stoic face.

"Is that all?" he asked as he walked over towards a window and looked out at the sky.

"What do you mean is that all?" Gibbs asked as he took a step forward. "That's your boss that they have over there. It almost sounds like you don't care what happens to her."

"Really?" he asked, still gazing out at the clouds.

"If I was to go by what I'm hearing, I would think that you are behind her kidnapping." he summed up.

"You are not here to question me about my loyalties to Susan or her involvement in the situation she finds herself in now. What you are here asking me is to hand over ten percent of our income to some insurgents. Here in HALO, we do not negotiate with terrorists."

"So, you aren't going to give up the money?" he asked.

"No."

"Well, that's good, because then we would think that you are in league with them for a pay out." Harper said as she walked over towards the door with Gibbs following. "You can keep the disk. We will try and get her back. In a week we will have either failed or accomplished our mission. We will give you a call when we have her." she finished walking out the door.

Turning slowly, he looked at Rachel.

"Get back to base and make sure you aren't followed. Tell Twitch to set up a drop over Iraq. Get cells one through thirteen ready and on standby for the next seventy-two hours. Anyone who complains put a bullet in their brain. We do not negotiate with terrorists. We obliterate."

Nodding her head in understanding, she walked quickly out of the office. Turning her head back towards Sera, Sibyl stood up and walked slowly towards him. The mistress being kidnapped was not part of his plans, and she knew how he felt when things didn't go according to plan. Touching his arm gently, she waited for him to lash out.

"Papa?" she asked gently as she looked at his face. His eyes were in a constant transition from gold to red, flickering back and forth, as if they were at war with each other. "Papa, what's wrong?" she was beginning to become slightly worried; because she has never seen his eyes shift so quickly. She was startled when his gaze focused on her. She suddenly felt the air leaving her lungs, and refilling them with air was incredibly hard. Her heart raced in her chest and her legs were starting to tremble. Never has she seen him this angry and it seemed for good reason, because she never wanted to feel this again. She's felt Snake's killing intent, which can transition from nonexistent, to heart stopping. And Fox's was simply horrifying and made you wish to kill yourself to escape the fear of such an animal killing you. He made her experience his intents during training and missions so she could get use to it, but this new one was something she couldn't handle. She felt like he was going to disembowel her and then rip out her throat. Shakily, she gripped his shirt and tugged. "Papa?" she whimpered in a little voice.

Like an illusion, it was gone as his ruby eyes stared at her trembling form next to him. Quickly wrapping her in his arms, he rubbed her back gently.

"Papa, what was that?" she asked shakily as she looked up at him.

"That was Snake furious kittling." he answered as he tucked her head beneath his chin. "I'm sorry if it scared you, but that was something even I wasn't aware of."

"What are we going to do about this?" she asked as she buried her face in his chest.

"We are going to destroy them darling." he whispered as he pulled her back and gripped her chin. Smirking at her, he kissed her gently before backing away. "Every single one of those *Human* scum."

"They dare attack the Spirits and expect an offering? They need to be punished." Sibyl agreed as she nodded her head with a slight smirk.

"And who better to punish them than the Angel of Death and the Demon of Life?" he asked as he pulled her closer towards him.

"No one." she whispered.

After the initial three days, Twitch scheduled a flight plan that would take them right over the position they knew Susan to be in five days, from her last cell phone position.

Looking out at the assembled teams, she waited with her blank white mask in place for her captain. Watching him come out, she could feel his aura from where she stood. It was calm and relaxed. That wasn't a good sign given what she felt a week ago. *The calm before the storm.* She thought idly to herself as she watched Rachel follow in after him.

"Listen up Hell Borns, today we will destroy the ones who dare to take our beloved Mistress, my mother, as a hostage. They plan on killing her tomorrow. Will we allow this to happen?" Snake asked as he watched everyone.

"No sir!" they all chorused.

"I will accept nothing more than excellence in regards to this mission. If any of you die, I will cross over the other side and bring your soul back so I may personally kill you for failing your Mistress. Is that understood?"

"Yes sir!"

"After this meeting, you all are to leave out in your teams to the airstrip that houses our company cargo plane. It will take us nine hours to reach our drop zone, at which point we will all drop and descend onto them like people possessed. Is that understood?"

"Yes sir!"

"Then, let's move out and introduce them to Hell's Children."

As all the teams filed out, he was left alone with Rachel and herself. They both stayed behind, because they knew he would wish to talk to them alone.

"Captain?" Sibyl said after a minute.

"We are to annihilate them all you two. I don't want anyone left alive except for one person to tell the tale of what happened and what will happen to any and all who think of crossing the Spirits."

"Yes Captain." they both saluted.

"Now, let's go and get Susan back."

During the plane ride over, Sibyl couldn't help but feel giddy at the opportunity to show her father how good she has gotten while he was busy. And since they were to kill everyone, she wouldn't have to hold back. Hearing the siren to drop, she stood and turned towards the opening bay door. Walking towards the edge, she allowed herself to fall and slowly drop towards the ground.

Landing, she allowed herself to look out at her surroundings. The waves and bumps of sand made it rather hard for positioning, but she wasn't worried about that. The heat of the sun though was making her sweat and they only just arrived. She was happy that they didn't have to wear the bullet proof cloaks, or else they would have passed out from the exertion. Reaching into her side pocket, she retrieved a pair of binoculars. Placing them in front of her eyes, she spotted a small island of buildings. That must be where they were stationed. Looking towards her right, she nodded her head towards Snake. Nodding in return, he signaled for everyone to spread out into flanking positions.

XXX

"You don't know who you are messing with." Susan said as she watched her captors' playing cards outside her cell. "Today is the last day."

"That's right you American bitch. They will either give us the money, or you will become the whore of this place. Either way, it's a win/win situation."

She chuckled lightly as she shook her head with a smile.

"You don't understand do you?" she asked rhetorically. "It's my last day here, but it's your last day alive. In a few hours you all will be wiped off the face of this planet with only one of you to tell the tale of what happened here."

"What are you talking about?" one man asked as he stood up and peered into her cell.

"I mean that the Gods are going to seek blood for their captured kin and retribution will be gained." she answered cryptically.

"What ev-" he was interrupted by an explosion that rocked the cave. Turning quickly, he could hear gun fire outside and lots of yelling. Running back towards the system of tunnels, he heard her haunting whisper.

"Pray that you entertain him."

XXX

Sibyl killed her fifteenth target and she couldn't have been happier. Their skills were average at best, with only a few of them actually posing a challenge. Turning her head, she spotted Snake carving his way through the opposition with twin Desert Eagles. He wasn't stopping for anyone or anything. He was so strong and powerful that she couldn't help but to stand and admire him as he worked. As he stopped and looked at her, she felt herself blush. He was watching her now, and it was her time to show him how much she has grown. She closed her eye as a red light crossed her vision. *Red light?* Turning her head, she froze at the sight of a sniper up on a nearby roof. She couldn't bring herself to move. She could hear her heart beating loudly in her ears. Blinking once, she felt tears invading her vision. She was going to die in this sandbox and in front of her father no less. She didn't want that. *I don't want to die.*

"Daddy!" she screamed as she closed her eyes. Hearing the shot fired, she braced herself. After a few moments she didn't feel anything.

"I will never allow anything to harm you little one." Snake whispered as he spied her. "You have grown into a truly deadly assassin and I couldn't be more proud of you, and you should feel proud of yourself for what you have done today. But," he paused as he turned around. "The rest of these humans need to die for attempting to kill my daughter and my mother." he growled as he reloaded both guns.

She shivered as she felt the same feeling that she felt in the office flow over her. She took a step forward because she felt herself drawn towards him. She didn't get a chance to touch him as he sprinted off, taking out every one in his and their path. She's never seen anyone take out so many people the way he did. Not even when she witnessed his other missions has he taken out so many people. This was more of Fox style than Snake's, but it was fiercer, deadlier, and calmer. It seemed that every second two people were already dead. Only one word fit what she was seeing. After all, it fit the stories she's read in the library.

"Valkyrie." she whispered as she watched him in the distance.

After he rushed off, the gunshots ceased, and she looked around. The only ones still standing were all wearing Hell Born gear. No one moved as they awaited the arrival of their captain with their Mistress in tow.

As both exited the building, Snake had a body on his shoulder. Dumping the body to the side, he turned and stood before Susan.

"Mother." he whispered, only loud enough for her to hear.

She nodded her head as she placed a hand on his masked cheek.

"You have done well Suen." she replied gently.

Kneeling before her, the rest followed his lead and paid respect to their missing leader. As they all stood on her command, Suen stayed down.

"I said you can stand Snake." she said as she watched his heavily breathing figure.

"I would if I could mistress," he replied softly as he fell on both knees. "But, I'm afraid that my body won't listen to me." he fell to his side as the words left his mouth.

Quickly rushing to his side, Rachel, Sibyl and Susan kneeled before him.

Rachel was surprised that he was injured. From what she saw, he was the one doing the most killing. She grit her teeth as she witnessed him hiss in pain as Susan removed his vest. It was her fault that he was hurt. She promised that she would always watch his back.

Susan has never seen him so injured in her life. During some of the more dangerous missions where he took on odds like this himself, he was bound to take a visit to the emergency room for a few stitches or X-rays before his upgrades, but nothing of this caliber.

Looking at her father's wound, made her choke back a sob. There was no other time that he could have been shot in the side other than the shot that was meant for her. Across his ribs were bits of shrapnel that had to have been pieces of the bullet and the metal plates in the vest. He was bleeding steadily and they couldn't close the wound, because the metal was still inside him and could kill him.

"We need to get him out of here. What's the ETA of the plane?" Susan asked as she looked at the assembled group that surrounded them.

"In fifteen minutes ma'am." one of them replied quickly.

"We need to get him back to base quickly and have the doctors look at him."

"Don't worry about me Mistress, I will be fine." Snake whispered as he shook his head, trying to stand, but failing.

"As my second in command, I cannot have you dying on me." she said with authority. "I am ordering you to stop trying to stand and allow us to help you. Now someone give me some ammonia so we can clean up this blood stain in the sand. And while we are at it, hit every bloody patch in the area. We don't need any evidence leading them back to us."

Nodding his head weakly, he made no moves to try and stand as he heard the others hurried footsteps, answering her call.

After they got back to Chicago, he was admitted into surgery immediately. She was brought out of her musings as the doctors announced that they were finished. Following them out of the room, she followed closely as they set him down in a sectioned off part of the hospital. Sitting down next to him, she grabbed his hand as she rested her head on it.

"It's my fault." she whispered to his prone form. "I should have been more aware of my surroundings. How could I have been so stupid? I should have died. If I did, then you wouldn't be in this mess father." sitting up, she reached for her braid that lay in her lap and pulled out her needle. Closing her eyes, she placed the tip to her neck. "I will pay for my negligence." she whispered as she readied to plunge the object into her jugular, only to stop as a hand gripped hers.

"Don't."

Opening her eyes, she looked at him helplessly.

"I thought you were going to be out for hours." she said with confusion. He just got out of surgery. He should still be knocked out from the anesthetic.

He smirked at her.

"You should know that even drugs can't keep me down for long." he replied with humor.

Looking down, she dropped the needle and collapsed onto his stomach.

"Why?" she sobbed into his clothed form. "Why won't you let me kill myself? I dishonored your teachings by getting distracted. I almost got you killed papa."

Sitting up, he looked down at her with soft eyes as he smiled at her gently while petting her hair.

"Because darling, I love you and I don't want anything to happen to you. I would give my life for any of my mates, because I care for you all." he said gently.

"But it was my fault." she argued.

"No, it was my fault. If you were anyone else, I would have let you die, but it was you my darling, my little one, that was in danger and I wanted to save you. And you calling out my name in battle was rather naughty. I never knew you wanted to do that on the job." he finished playfully.

She blushed at his claim and slapped his arm in reply, before looking at him with a small smile.

"You are such a pervert papa." she whispered.

"Well, if you ever want to do anything of the sort," he began as he trailed a finger up her spine. "Then all you have to do is ask."

She shivered beneath his touch and blushed as she saw something straining against the sheets.

"Father, you just got out of surgery." she whispered.

"That doesn't mean that I can't please my daughter, now does it?" he asked as he slid a hand beneath her shirt and traced her lower back. She arched at his touch. "Come now. It will be fun."

Her body was reacting to his touch again, and it took all her will power to sit up straight.

"No papa, you have to rest." she said after placing his hand in hers. "I'll be here when you wake up."

Nodding his head, he leaned back and allowed sleep to take him. It was taking everything he had to not scream while they were operating on him when he woke up half way through, and he was indeed tired, but seeing his only daughter about to kill herself was inexcusable and selfish on her part.

Watching his slumbering form, she smiled with soft eyes. He would always do anything to make her feel better. Leaning back, she allowed sleep to take her as well. She awoke to the sound of the door opening and her eyes trained on the figure of Henrietta.

"What are you doing here?" Etta asked as she spotted her sitting figure.

Sibyl looked at her blankly before closing her eyes again. Henrietta wasn't a human, but she was another person that was after her father's heart. That being the case, she would rather not talk to her, lest some unsavory words escape.

She was going to ask her what her problem was, but she spotted Sera lying in the bed. Walking towards his side, she laid a hand on his arm.

"What did you do to end up like this?" she whispered, watching his face. She turned as the door opened again to reveal Rachel. "What's up Rachel?" she greeted with a nod.

Nodding in return, she walked to her side and looked down at him.

"I've never seen him this way." she said softly, as her lavender eyes softened. "Sibyl, I'm here to tell you that we are on vacation until he is up and ready." she turned on her heel and walked briskly out of the room.

"She must be torn up." Etta said to herself. "To see your mentor in this condition. But, then again, I wish to kill the person responsible for this." she growled.

Turning at the sound of the door, yet again, Jessie walked in, before stopping to gasp. Running towards the bed, she half climbed on top of him as she looked at his face.

"Sera!" she gasped, placing a palm against his cheek. Turning her head at the sound of a cough, she spotted Etta standing with her arms crossed. "What happened?" she asked as she climbed down. "How did this happen to him? Who did this?"

Standing up, Sibyl looked at the others with a blank face. These were two of the women he has chosen to become his, and she would have to accept it, but it didn't mean she had to like it.

"You two are here, because I wanted to talk to you about something." Sibyl began as she unbuttoned her shirt. Pulling aside the collar, she displayed her mark.

Jessie gasped as she spotted his mark on her neck.

"Why do you have that?" she asked.

"I would like to know the same thing." Etta stated, taking a step forward.

"You two are chosen to become his Mates. At this moment there are only four, but he will gain more as time goes on."

"I thought he loved me." Jessie whispered as she placed her hand on her shoulder where her identical mark lay.

"I do." he said, finally opening his eyes. "But, that doesn't mean that I can't love others as well now does it?"

Shocked at an answer, she turned quickly towards him.

"But how can you love so many people?" she asked.

"It's a long story. One that I will tell you once you answer my question." he began. "I ended up this way, because I work for a secret organization that runs this city, as well as others, from the shadows. We kill those who threaten our territory and contribute to our communities. The mark that you bare is a symbol of your devotion to me. I would like for you to join me Jessie. I want you to be by my side as we rise to the top."

Listening to his story, she already made her decision. He was willing to kill so easily before, because he's done it already. And even then, she accepted that if he did, she wouldn't hate him for it. So what if he was killing others. He was only protecting their territory. Plus, he worked for a security agency anyway, so it was bound to happen once in his life. Besides, he loved her where no one else would. Smiling lightly, she nodded her head.

"I told you there was no one else I would rather spend the rest of my life with than you Sera." she said gently.

"That's good." he said finally. "Because if you would have said no, then my daughter would have had to kill you."

She tilted her head slightly.

"Straight to the point aren't you Sera?" she joked.

"You will get used to it." Etta commented off to the side. "Believe me, after dealing with it for four years, you have no choice."

"Ladies, I will be released in three days time. When that time comes, Jessie, I want you to come to HALO and ask for Henrietta. She will begin your training and in time, I will call on you to help me."

Nodding her head, she walked over towards him and kissed him lightly.

"I promise."

"Good." he said as he watched her leave. "As for you two, you can do what ever you wish. I need more sleep for the healing drugs to work."

Nodding their heads, they both left his room together. Walking down the hall, Etta stopped in front of Sibyl and leveled her with a blank look.

"I want him for myself, and I don't like to share." she stated.

Sibyl quirked an eyebrow.

"We both have known him for the same amount of time. And I feel the same way about him as you do. He is my heart and my soul. I would gladly die for him and face down the devil. His dreams are mine. But, know this," she paused as she walked past her only to stop at her shoulder. "If you get in his way," her golden eyes shot her a sideways glare. "I will kill you."

As Sibyl continued on down the hall, Etta smiled evilly to herself. "And I will do the same should you slip Sibyl." she hissed with a sneer. "He is mine."

Prologue 1

"A king that allows his pawns to fight for him dies by his own sword." Sera said gently to Sibyl as he held her close in the study. Between her legs sat a chess board. He decided to teach her strategy using chess two years ago. She was surprisingly good.

Tilting her head up, she looked at him questioningly.

"What does that mean father?" she asked.

Glancing down, he returned to the board.

"It means that a king, who only allows his soldiers to fight, allows his own skills to tarnish, and in time, when the soldiers have fallen, the king will die by his own hands for his neglect."

"But, in chess, does the king not sit idle as the rest move to protect him?" Sibyl asked as she moved her knight. "Check."

"Indeed, but when needed, he can switch places with his rook and take his revenge across the board one step at a time." Sera answered with a smile as he switched his king with his rook. "You are starting to speak in riddles and sayings my dear." he pointed out.

"The apple doesn't fall far from the tree." She moved her bishop down the board.

Kissing her head lightly, he shook his head.

"But, you still have a long way to go before you create your own set of codes." He said lightly as he moved his queen into position. "Check mate."

Chapter 16

Confrontation and Reacquainted

"Hello Mrs. Harper," Sera greeted as she walked into his office. "To what do I owe the pleasure?"

Walking up to his desk, she seated herself in a chair.

"Hello Mr. Angelus." she greeted in return with a nod. "I'm here to tell you of our success, or rather, the lack there of."

He quirked an eyebrow at her statement.

"Oh, you mean the retrieval operation."

"Yes." she agreed. "When we arrived to the camp, we found it in complete shambles. There were bodies that were tossed all over the landscape and enough shells that we thought we were at a beach. After we came back, and spent the next four days filling our reports, I thought I should come here to tell you that we couldn't find Susan."

"You don't need to worry about her." Sera said as he smiled gently at her. "She is back and safe and sound."

"How?" she asked.

"I hired some mercenaries to go and get her. I figured we could spend a small portion of our income on her retrieval."

"Well, there was something that was stricken from the record." Harper said as she leaned back in the chair. "We found only one survivor. When we found him, he was unconscious. Taking him back here, he finally regained consciousness. Coming too, he began screaming and babbling on about something I couldn't understand. Something about Inari, an offering, and yellow/red eyes."

He tilted his head again. If the information was stricken from the record, then there were no documents on what she knows. She's the only one who knows of what the man was saying. *This has to be handled delicately and with subtlety.* Snake thought to himself as he mulled over the information. *"She could become a problem Snake."* Fox commented idly. *"She knows from him the color of our eyes. From that information alone, she could arrest us with that information."* She could reveal this information to her superiors, but she hasn't. That alone tells us that she is holding out for something. Snake said as he shook his head slowly.

"Yellow and red eyes you say?" Sera questioned.

"Yes. I found it rather odd that he would be speaking about his eyes, but then I began thinking. There are only two people in the world that have eyes like the ones he described." she paused as she looked off to the side.

"Really? Who?"

"The only person with yellow eyes in the world is you Seraphim."

He nodded his head.

"I know. The doctors said that my eyes were a mutation on the genetic level." Sera said.

"And the only person in the world that has red eyes is an assassin/mercenary named Inari the Fox God. Or, Demon Fox. He works for an organization here in the mid west. But, what I don't understand is how their eyes could change repeatedly."

"I must admit, it sounds impossible to me." he agreed. "But, some things that seem impossible are in actuality a very likely possibility."

"True." she said as she turned back on him. "The only reason we even know of Fox, is because we have been looking into the multiple killings that have been happening since ten years ago. Every place this Fox character goes, he leaves carnage in his path. One of the largest ones was a dinner party a few years ago. Over two hundred people were killed. They were butchered, hacked up like live stock. Only one person was left alive. We haven't been able to finger print him or find any leads. He's an expert assassin and seems to be able to come and go like a ghost."

"Let me guess." Sera said with a small smile. "This too, is off the record." as she nodded her head, he continued. "But, what I would like to know is why you are telling me this. You and I both know that eye color can be changed by a pair of contacts, so there is no guarantee that they really have the color eyes that you think. Which by the way would be rather smart of them in the first place. The eyes are a very important part of an individual. They are as various as a fingerprint."

"Yes, well," she began as she stood. "I just came to tell you about our mission status."

"I thank you for your consideration Agent Harper." Sera said as he too stood and walked around the desk.

"I believe you know my first name correct?" she asked as she looked him in the eyes.

He stepped closer towards her and smiled.

"Indeed I do Janet, but I believe it is rather presumptuous to think that I should be on the first name basis with a person I just met. Wouldn't you agree?"

"I would." she said with a slight tremble.

"And I find myself wondering just why you would discuss, obviously, classified information with me. I know that we have a contract with the military, but that is no explanation to tell me about secrets of the government. So, tell me Jan, what was the purpose of your visit?" he asked as he traced a finger down her cheek towards her neck.

She shivered as she felt his finger ghost over her throat.

"Are you here to arrest me on an assumption?" he asked, slowly moving his finger across her throat. "Or are you here because you find yourself attracted to me?"

Turning her head, she hid her blush. Never before has she allowed a man to touch her in the way that he was. He was already invading her personal space.

"Don't be ridiculous Seraphim." she said softly.

"Is it being ridiculous to be attracted to someone of my background?" he asked as he leaned closer towards her ear. "To be attracted to a person who killed their father, because he killed his mother must make you sweat from the freight and aroused by the threat I pose."

Her body shuddered under his assault.

"Knowing that I am a person who has gotten away with murder and so close to you must make you crazy with fear and lust." gripping her chin, he turned her face towards him. Gazing into her slightly glazed over eyes, he mentally smiled. *"It was a risk, but a risk with benefits."* Fox approved with a nod of his head. *I was honestly taking a huge gamble on this.* Snake confided as he gazed into her clouding eyes. *If she would have denied my advance, then I would have to kill her in the near future so the information that she now has, won't fall into the wrong hands.* "Even though it would have been one wild ride to fight the FBI." Fox added. "Are you on fire?" he whispered seductively in her ear as he slid his knee against her. "Are you afraid?"

Her heart was racing in her chest. She was afraid of this man. Fifteen years ago, she was just a simple cop working the streets of Chicago. Having been born and raised here, she's heard of the local stories and gossip. She couldn't believe that a child was born with gold eyes existed. Let alone that same child was severely wounded by a stab to his chest. She was called in to investigate the attempted murder and found out it was her friend's son who was stabbed. She questioned her about it, but only got a general description of a man. Two years later, she tried out for the FBI and got accepted. She came back to tell Maya about her new job. Coming back, she found out her friend was murdered and the son was nowhere to be found. She assumed that he was taken as a hostage. Going to her funeral, she never expected to see little Seraphim walking in with an older man at his side. The speech he gave made her cringe. He was obviously a very bright child to be able to speak the way he did, but what he was saying was a bit too intelligent for a child of his age. It was also the first time she saw his eyes; the golden eyes of a snake, which would normally be out of place on a normal person, seemed oddly at home on his face. But, it wasn't the fact that his eyes were gold that gave her a chill. It was the lack of emotion within them. He gazed coldly out amongst them as if they were nothing more than cows in a line up, waiting to be slaughtered. After his prayer, he left with the older gentleman. After paying her respects, she went around the town looking for him. She was going to take him in after her death. After all, Maya and herself were close before she got married. But, in the end, she couldn't find him. She asked around, but the general opinion was that they were all glad that the Demon was gone and would stop terrorizing them and their children. Giving up, she went back to work, thinking of the child that loved his mother so much that he died with her in spirit.

Two years later, she heard of the husband dying in front of his wife's grave. He was decapitated and missing a hand when they found him. First, it was his mother, then his father. The child must be wrought with grief. After his burial, she asked around for any information anyone might have that could help her with finding the murderer. Everyone said that it was the Demon coming back from the dead to kill the only person that could stop him. Thinking that the child was dead, she went back to work, determined to find the killer when he struck again.

Five years later, she got wind of a child named Seraphim, going to a private high school in the area. She knew that the name was very unique and only a handful of people had the name in the world, if any, so she was sure that it was him. Finding the child was easy. As it turned out, he was a natural athlete and genius. But, the child didn't have the same eyes as the child she saw the day of the funeral. Thinking nothing of it, she headed back to finding the killer. She was convinced that he would show himself again in time. Two years later, she was called in to investigate, what the reporters called, 'The Bloody Banquet.', also known as 'Masquerade Massacre'. Walking into the crime scene, she vomited from the sights and the scents that assaulted her. Composing herself, she looked back towards the scene. Hundreds of pieces of human body parts were lying about the dining room floor. Not a single person was left intact; even the witness was missing an arm. Questioning her, she only found out that he was named Demon Fox, and worked for an organization known as the Spirits. She knew of the Spirits, but only passed it off as a simple local story, something cooked up to make the city more interesting. But, after hearing it from her mouth, she couldn't help but believe that it was true. And who ever this Fox was, was one person that, if she was honest with herself, she never wanted to meet, even if she had back up. After looking at all the shells that surrounded the one spot on the floor that didn't have blood, and all the used rounds that littered the spot as well, she was certain that this man was very good at killing. And judging by the fair amount of women lying around, he wasn't adverse to killing women either. But, the eyes are what caught her attention when asked to describe him. He had red slit eyes, as crimson as blood, and as cold as an arctic chill. If the eyes were gold, she would have thought it was the child from the funeral, but didn't dwell on it much.

After following his trail for three years, news of a new CEO of the Security Company back at her home town came to her. His name was Seraphim Angelus. Apparently, it was the same child that she saw four years ago. He's been working for them during his time in school, but they announced it after his eighteenth birthday. Looking at his picture, she thought her heart stopped. He was a very beautiful man, with short black hair that came to his neck and a body that she knew most men would kill for. But, it was his eyes that stopped her. He had the eyes of the child that she thought to be dead for the last ten years. She wanted to see how he was doing, but she still had one last case to finish. A warehouse was filled with fifty or so bodies, with one eye witness, who says that it was Inari the Fox God that did it. After that, she went back to her office to pack some things and see him in person.

When the owner of the company was kidnapped only a few days before she was leaving, she volunteered for the case. But, she found it weird that he would suddenly appear like he did. Looking into it, she found no previous records of anyone claiming him as their child. Further into his past, it showed that Seraphim died the day his mother did and was buried next to her. Visiting the cemetery first, she indeed found his tombstone next to her friends. But, she knew those eyes anywhere, despite the recent fad of the same design contacts. She wouldn't forget them for the rest of her life. The cold, calculating look he gave as he looked at everyone still haunted her dreams, along with the vision of crimson slit eyes that were filled with hunger and rage. Seeing him in person was something she was not ready for. He was breathtaking in person, and the two women, granted one was a child resigned to a chair for the rest of her life, were beautiful and it made her rather jealous of their position.

When the mission was over, the eyes that the man described to her were still fresh in her mind. She didn't tell her superiors about what she was doing with their resources, because she didn't want to lose her job. The man said that his eyes were slit, but the color transitioned from gold to red over and over. It didn't take her long to put two and two together. There was only one person in the world with slit pupils and golden eyes.

As the revelation dawned on her, she felt herself rather afraid of what he might do to her if he found out that she was tracking him, or rather Fox, and pieced together that he was, in fact Fox. He would obviously have no trouble with killing her and leaving no evidence, but that was what made her drawn to him in the first place. The simple knowledge that there was someone out there that could kill so easily and precisely and knowing that you are following right behind them gave her a thrill that she would have never guessed would surface when she began her search.

Feeling him rub his knee against her was making her lose her sight. The friction was delicious, but it was so wrong.

"Are you going to kill me now?" she asked shakily.

Reaching a hand behind himself, he pulled out his gun and placed it under her throat. He could hear her swallow hard.

"I should kill you." he admitted as he pulled the hammer back. "The walls are sound proof, and everyone here knows to stay away from here. No one would question why you came in and never came out." he pressed it harder.

She felt herself beginning to panic. If everything he said was true, then she would disappear and no one would find it suspicious. She was sure that if Gibbs were to question him about her coming here, he would simply lie, and any and all security footage would be wiped or edited. She was going to die. And yet, that wasn't the prevailing thought running through her mind. At the moment, the knee that was still rubbing against her was occupying a lot of her mind.

"But," he paused as he took the gun away and leaned in to whisper in her ear. "That wouldn't be very fun now would it?" he asked, licking her ear. He smirked as he felt her tremble beneath him.

"What will you do with me?" she asked softly, as her eyes were staring unfocused at the wall.

"What do you want me to do to you?" he asked seductively as he was sure to lightly blow in her ear. "Would you like for me to kill you?" he offered as he pressed his lips towards her ear. "To make love to you?" he moved his thigh between her legs. "Make you scream?" he kissed her ear, and she shivered. "Make you beg." trailing a hand up her side, he traced her left breast. She whimpered lightly. "Make you cry." squeezing her breast roughly, she yelped, before he attached his lips to hers. She moaned pitifully as he ravaged her mouth. Her tongue lay slack as his had full run over her. Pulling back, he tugged on her lip roughly, making it bleed slightly. Looking down at her glazed expression, bruised and puffy lips and heavily breathing face, he grinned. "Make you mine."

"Yes." she said pathetically as she looked into his orange rimmed eyes. Her body was in full revolt against her better judgment. Her body was screaming for him to do something, to put the fires out, but her mind was still telling her that this was wrong. To fraternize with a killer was close to treason. That having feelings for someone who was old enough to be her son was socially unacceptable, but she couldn't help herself.

"Yes?" he questioned as he took a slight step back, and was pleasantly amused when she shuffled closer towards him. "Yes to what?"

"You are going to kill me." she stated softly, while looking down. Looking back up, she placed both her hands on his chest as she looked at him pleadingly. "At least for my last wish, grant me what you promised."

"Why should I?" he asked. "What's in it for me?"

"Me." she answered quickly. "I've never known the touch of another. Never felt love." she continued downcast. "Take me Fox."

His eyes switched to vermilion red as he heard his name. Moving quickly, he gripped her neck tightly as he moved closer towards her face with a wicked grin.

"So, you know of me." he summed with amusement as he watched her wide frightened eyes. "That will make this more fun." he finished as he pushed her against his desk. Leaning down, he captured her lips roughly. She gasped, but otherwise made no objections. Gripping her shirt, he ripped away her buttons. Pulling back, he looked at her near topless form. He growled in his throat. "Take off your shirt." he ordered. Slowly, her head bowed, she did as she was told. Standing shirtless before him, she moved a arm to cover her chest. "For you to be thirty-nine, you have a great body." he admired as he watched her shiver. Her D cups were shivering beneath her bra, and it made his mouth water. Trailing lower, past her flat stomach, he focused on the area where he could sense her arousal. "You are so naughty for being turned on by this." he said with a grin. It widened as he saw her blush and turn away. "Take off your skirt."

Nodding her head slightly, she moved her hand towards her zipper and let it fall to the floor. Looking back at him, she couldn't help, but move a hand to try and cover herself. His eyes seemed to radiate lust and hunger. It felt like he was visualizing the countless things he was going to do to her body before killing her and she was trying to hide just how aroused she was getting from the knowledge. As he walked towards her, she turned her head the other way to avoid his piercing stare.

Gripping her bra, he snatched it away from her body and marveled at her bouncing chest. Leaning closer, he licked her from neck to ear.

"I'm a little thirsty." he whispered as his hand trailed her breast. "You better have some milk for me, or I will hurt you." he promised as he kissed down her neck and to the center of her chest. Moving towards his right, he took her left nipple into his mouth. Sucking softly, he rolled his tongue around her already hardened nub. She whined helplessly as she was assaulted by his roaming tongue. Sucking harder, he felt her putting her hands behind his head, forcing him into her chest. *"She thinks she has control?"* Fox mused with irritation. Pulling back, he squeezed her breast hard enough to force her to leak. "Keep you hands to yourself, unless I say otherwise. If you don't, then I will remove them for you." he threatened gruffly. Feeling the liquid roll over his hand, he looked down and smiled lightly. "And you are lucky that you do have milk."

"What would have happened if I didn't?" she asked in mild discomfort. She yelped as she felt him grip both her breasts roughly, before pulling them. She held her thighs together, trying to hold the overwhelming feelings that were dueling in her core.

"You don't ask questions." he ordered evenly as he twisted her nipples harshly. Looking at her squirming figure, he smirked. "What's wrong?" he asked as he slipped his foot between her legs and spread them. "Having a little problem are we?" he continued as he left her chest and moved behind her. Sliding a hand gently over her stomach, he slipped his hand beneath her panties and cupped her flooding flower. "What's wrong? Is the problem here?" he asked rubbing his palm against her clitoris. She thrust into his palm hard, before she clamped her legs closed.

"Please, let me use the restroom." she begged as she felt the urge to urinate increase with every brush of his hand against her.

"I'm not stopping you from going." he said as he continued to rub his palm against her. Slipping his middle finger within her, he was slightly surprised by how tightly she was squeezing it. Moving it in and out at a medium pace, he continued. "But you can't leave here."

She shook her head as she tried to keep it in, but the finger inside her felt so good, but it made her feel so dirty. As his finger brushed against something within her, she moaned woefully.

"No!" she wept as she felt herself let go against her will. As she felt the warm liquid flow down her thighs, legs and onto the floor in a puddle at her feet, she blushed in embarrassment. She felt further humiliation as she heard him sniff the air.

"You are disgusting." he commented. "You pissed yourself. And not only did you piss yourself on my floor, but on my hand as well." slipping his hand from her, he placed it at her lips. "Now, clean my hand, before I make you clean the floor as well."

As the strong pungent scent of her urine assaulted her nose, she scrunched up her nose and turned her head. This was unsanitary. It was disgusting. Yet, why was she feeling a thrill of excitement? When his hand forced its self into her mouth, she forced herself to do the job she was issued. As her tongue passed over his fingers, she tasted her salty waste. Her eyes stung as she felt tears rolling down her cheeks. *This is so humiliating!* She thought to herself, but she couldn't deny the feeling of excitement that eclipsed her humiliation.

"You like cleaning up your own mess don't you?" he asked as he placed his head next to hers as he slipped his fingers from her mouth and gripped her chin to turn it slightly towards himself.

"Yes." she mumbled with humility, feeling her face burn brightly.

"I couldn't hear you." he said as his other hand gripped her flower.

"Yes." she moaned as she ground against his hand. "I like to clean my own piss."

He chuckled in his throat as he kissed her neck gently.

"Good girl." he muttered against her skin. Moving back in front of her, he gently pushed her against his desk. Kneeling, he pulled her soiled underwear down and threw them on top of her clothes. Picking her up, he placed her on top of his desk. Opening her legs, he observed her wet folds. Taking a deep breath through his nose, he looked up at her crimson face. "I have to say, you smell delicious." moving his face closer, he allowed his lips to touch her clit. "Good enough to eat."

"No, don't!" she gasped as she got what he was going to do. "It's dirty there!" is what she would have said, if her other protests died on her tongue as she felt him lick her from bottom to top. As he suckled on her button, she moaned loudly, tossing her head back.

Despite the initial salty taste, he was rather enjoying her taste. She was extremely sweet with only a hint of sour. Reminded him of wine. He wanted more, and didn't have to wait, because she was constantly flowing. Slipping a finger inside her, he sealed his lips around her clit and hummed. Speeding up, he allowed her to yell to the ceiling as he felt her walls spasm around his finger.

She's never felt so incredible in her life. As her orgasm hit her hard, she tossed her head towards the ceiling and yelled.

"Did you enjoy that?" he asked as he spied her panting form lying back on his desk exhausted.

"Yes. God Fox yes." she whispered repeatedly as her eyes were clouded.

Standing, he began undressing himself.

As she heard his clothes coming off, she knew on some level that she should look. His chest was the first thing that she noticed. The snake head that came over his shoulder was the first thing that caught her attention. Moving down slightly, she spotted the X shaped scar over his heart, where he had to have stitches put in place after his surgery as a child. His stomach was riddled with so many scars; she couldn't fathom how he survived all of it. She knew her stuff and most of them were torture wounds. Moving past his stomach, she felt herself tremble in want and fear. He was huge. The head looked to be half as big as her fist. The rest was just as impressive. As she looked up at his face in fear and anticipation, she caught his smirk. A smirk that said he knew what she was thinking and would grant her wish until he humiliated her further.

"Do you want this?" he asked. She nodded her head. "I can't hear you."

"I want it." she whispered.

He looked at her silently for a moment.

"Call it the Weapon of the Gods." he demanded.

Closing her eyes, she turned her head.

"Please," she pleaded softly. She could feel her own arousal leaking onto the desk beneath her, further illustrating her wants and desires. "I want the Weapon of the Gods inside me. Please."

"You are such a naughty girl."

Walking over towards her, he held himself above her as he positioned himself. Looking into her eyes, he allowed them to soften.

"It's going to hurt." he said gently. She nodded her head. Slowly, he pushed the head into her heat. Feeling her give way to his head, he ground his teeth together. She was almost as tight as Sibyl. Pushing himself further into her, he came to her barrier. Pausing, he looked down into her eyes. Kissing her lips softly, he leaned over her ear. "Sorry." he whispered as he pushed past her hymen and sheathed himself completely inside her. He held himself still as he awaited her to become accustomed to his size.

The feeling of him entering her was intense. She could feel her walls giving way to allow him passage. As inch after inch entered her, she wondered when it was going to end. As she felt him press against her hymen, she was surprised he stopped. When he kissed her softly and apologized for what was to come, she felt herself become warm at his words. The pain of him tearing through her was lost as she focused on him finally being completely inside her. She was further surprised when he stopped and was waiting for her to signal the okay. Nodding her head, she felt him slowly pulling out until only the tip was still in. As he re-filled her, she groaned. It was slightly painful, but it was quickly becoming less and less painful and more enjoyable with every thrust.

"Please go faster Fox." she begged weakly.

He nodded his head as he picked up the pace. Grabbing her legs, he placed them on his shoulders to increase his depth and change his angle. Looking at her enraptured face, he sped up. He wanted to make her scream. He got his wish as he knew he hit that special place within all women.

"Fox!" she cried as her eyes went wide. As tears fell down her face, she looked at him with a small, sad smile. "Fox, Fox, Fox." she repeated as she wrapped her arms around his back and pulled him closer. She was in heaven. It really was the weapon of the gods. Her head was spinning and she couldn't tell what was up and what was down, but she didn't care to know either. All she knew was that a cold hearted killer was taking her and making her feel the best that she has ever felt in her entire life. The same one that she felt so depressed about, because she thought that he was dead and she failed her best friend, was making love to her. "I'm going to cum." she panted between breaths.

"Then cum." he told her as he thrusts harder into her. He was close as well. Her tight warmth that pulsed insanely around him was driving him crazy. She must have wanted this to happen more than he first anticipated.

She heeded his command as she has become accustomed to doing in the forty-five minutes of torture that he has subjected her to. Squeezing him tightly, she buried her head in his neck as she screamed her climax to the world.

"FOX!" she yelled.

"I'm going to cum Jan." he grunted as he felt himself reaching his end.

Wrapping her legs weakly around him, she shook her head.

"If I'm going to die, then I want it all." she said weakly.

Looking at her, he knew she was on her last legs. Nodding his head, she released himself within her. Her walls seemed to have become tighter as they seemed to have a mind of their own, trying to keep him inside her. Finally finishing, he looked down at her face.

"I'm ready." she whispered as she closed her eyes.

Slowly, he leaned closer towards her head. Kissing her lips lightly, he smiled into her stunned eyes.

"I never said that I would kill you." he whispered to her. "I said that I should kill you. Besides," he kissed her again. "You were the only person who didn't look at me with contempt as a child besides Grandfather and Mother."

She opened her mouth in silent question. He knew? But how long has he known? Closing her mouth, she turned her head slightly.

"You remember?" she asked uncertainly.

"Yes." he answered as he wiped her tears. "I never forget."

"How long have you known?" she questioned as she turned to face him.

"When you were in the middle of a mini orgasm," he smiled as she blushed. "I recognized your eyes. They are the same as they were then.

There was no hatred in them then, and even now, when you accepted a death that was never to be, you didn't hate me. You accepted it. Just like my mother." he added somberly. "Why were you so ready to die?"

"I wanted to take you in when I heard that Maya died, but I couldn't find you. When you came to her funeral, I was shocked. I tried looking for you after, but I couldn't find you and no one knew where you were. So I left. When I heard that there was a Seraphim at a private school I came back to find you, but I thought it was just a coincidence, because you didn't have the eyes of the child I saw at the funeral. So I left again. When I saw a picture of you in the news paper, with the eyes you were born with, I was stunned. And when I saw you in person, I felt so bad about not being there like I knew I should have, and leaving you to go through all of that alone. I figured it was the least I could do." she said with sorrow.

"I will not kill you, because you are my woman now." he said as he sat up. "And as such, you are to be with me. You can stay with me for tonight and in the morning, go back to work. As you most likely have guessed, everything that we have discussed today is to be kept between the two of us. If it gets out, I will kill you."

Nodding her head, she sat up slowly. She had no intentions of telling on him in the beginning or now that she knew he wasn't going to kill her.

"I promise that I won't tell anyone." she swore.

"Good." he nodded his head. "Now, are you ready for round two?" he asked as he got his second wind.

She trembled as she spotted his arousal at full mast. She knew this was going to be a long meeting.

Prologue 2

"When an animal gains human eyes, they are the most dangerous." Sera said to Sibyl as he watched the wild dogs in the exhibit. He decided to take her to the zoo today since he had the day off.

Turning her head, she looked at him questioningly.

"What do you mean?"

"Normally, the eyes of an animal are very expressive, as they should be on all beings, and as such, it makes them predictable. Animals are able to communicate with each other by their body language and eye contact. On a human, the eyes are the only thing that cannot lie. Tears are the most pure thing imaginable. If you are sad, you cry to express your sorrow. When you are angry, you cry to release your frustration. Crying is one of the only things that separate humans and higher mammals from the animals. But, when an animal acquires human eyes, especially dogs, they are unpredictable. The eyes of a human do not belong on a dog. You can no longer anticipate what they will do next, because the eyes will not express their emotions." Looking down at her, he leveled her with a serious stare. "I don't trust Dogs little one. Because they can turn on you at the drop of the hat for nothing more than a small reward. Never take your eyes off your dog, or else it will find a new owner to obey." He warned.

She nodded her head, because she knew what he was talking about. Riddles upon riddles were his way of conveying important information when in front of people or talking to the ones he trusted. She would do as he asked and keep her eyes open.

"Oh, and Sibyl?"

"Yes?"

"Here" he said as he handed her a manila envelope.

Taking it, she looked back at him.

"What is this?"

"If something happens to me in the future, I want you to open this." He answered. "Think of it as my will, and to be followed to the letter."

She gripped the envelope tight to her chest as she shook her head.

"Don't say things like that papa!" she chastised. "Nothing is going to happen to you, I promise."

He smiled lightly as he shook his head.

"What have I told you about making promises that you know you can't keep?" he asked. "Besides, this is just a formality. I have the Mistresses will should anything happen to her and now, you have mine. It's a very big responsibility to be the holder of a will. I trust you to look after it until it's time or I ask for it back."

Resolving herself, she nodded her head as she hugged him tightly.

"I promise papa to look after your will." She promised. "Even though I will do everything in my power to keep such an event from happening other than natural causes."

"Thank you." He said softly as he returned her embrace. "Tomorrow, I have to track down a traitor to the Spirits and question him on the information he's given out. The mission won't be long, but the missions I foresee after are going to be long and strenuous."

Nodding her head, she buried herself further into his chest.

"I guess it's time to create the pack." She muttered. "I will be sure to look after things while you are gone and to keep up my grades in school."

"That's my girl." He whispered as he kissed her head. "One, who knows not all the pieces, can never hope to win the game."

"And one who is ignorant to the game, can never hope to play."

To be continued in:
The Puppeteer:
Requiem